CW01663703

THE BEAR AND THE BASQUE

MAYHEM, MACARONS AND A SPRINKLING OF ROMANCE

MICHÈLE CALLARD

ABOUT THE AUTHOR

Michèle Callard grew up in France. A country girl at heart, she swapped her Paris flat for a cottage in rural Bedfordshire, where she lives with her Irish husband and son. She has written several as-yet-unpublished novels, each set in a different region of France bursting with local colour, flavours and history. You will soon be invited to discover them by hopping onto her characters' coat tails.

For Susana

"Menturatzen denak, hartza. Ez denak, ez eta bartza."

"Those who dare, will catch the bear. Those who don't, won't get a flea."

LIGHTNING STRIKE

The afternoon air inside the bedroom of our rented gîte was stifling. I pulled open the window set into the thick wall, but today, the ocean winds shunned the French Basque Country.

Cosmo ran a finger along the top of my corset. 'Will you do the Pavlova thing for me again, Pumpkin? You drive me crazy when you speak French.'

I knelt on the bed and stretched languorously, wondering for the hundredth time how I'd ended up in the French Pyrenees with my own version of Bertie Wooster.

I didn't love Cosmo, but we had fun together. Had it not been for him, when Pop died last month, I would have gone to pieces.

A deep sigh escaped me. Right now, Pop, not Pavlova was weighing on my mind.

'Start with the eggs, Chloe, I love it when you whisk the eggs.' Cosmo threw himself on his stomach and yelped with impatience. He was so happy, bless him, I didn't have the heart to say no.

I straddled his spindly legs. Beneath me, Cosmo fizzed with excitement.

'D'abord, battre les oeufs.' I lifted a hand and flicked my fingers over his skinny white bottom. Encouraged by his squeals, I soon found my rhythm, though a glance at my dishevelled reflection in the mirror made me wonder what the catering teachers back in Bletchley would have thought of my use of culinary French.

'Ajouter le vinaigre.' I could add any soupçon to the mix, Cosmo was not fussed, as long as the addition was in French and thoroughly *beaten* in. When he was good and ready, I flipped him over onto his back.

He gave a strangled gasp, sweaty and ecstatic. 'Gosh, Pumpkin, see what you've done to me?'

I raised an appreciative brow at my own handywork and slithered over him, whispering Gitane-infused promises. 'When the mixture is shiny and firm…' I lowered my voice, 'slip into a warm oven.' The sensuous *'glisser dans un four chaud'* drew out a long moan. Cosmo lay in total abandon.

I took my position and whisked him into a frenzy. Yelling out random names of French ingredients, I rode him to the finish and flopped back on the bed with the satisfaction of a job well done.

Cosmo was a foodie, I loved that about him. We'd met over a Pavlova I had baked for one of his mother's charity functions. He had grabbed my hand, drawn me to him and locked his slightly bulbous eyes to mine. 'Do tell. The divine raspberry coulis, is it a secret?'

My breasts level with his bald pate, I'd confessed in a murmur, 'I added a little cassis liqueur I bring back from France.'

For Cosmo it was, as the French call it, *le coup de foudre.* Love at first sight, or more accurately, love at first bite. Over the following months, he had introduced me to a world of flavours and promised me a job with 'someone he knew in London.' Yes, with Cosmo around, my future as a chef was assured.

'Was it fun for you too, Pumpkin?' He wrapped a sweaty arm around me.

I gave a small nod.

Cosmo noticed the change of mood, and ruffled my short hair. 'What's the name of the lake your grandfather chose as his final home?'

'Irrabia Lakua.' I rolled the double R. 'That's how they say it in Basque.'

He ran a finger down my corset, digging into my flesh after our exertions.

'. . . I am very partial to basques.'

I kissed his cheek, went to the sitting room and, leaning on the cool stone of the windowsill, glanced out at the mountains to stop the tears from welling up. What I had come to do could not be put off any longer. A strong breeze was now pushing clouds towards us.

'Cosmo? I think we'd better go. Storm clouds are coming in from the sea.'

After a quick shower, I wriggled out of my basque, pulled on a white T-shirt and was about to step into my shorts, when Cosmo joined me and fondled my bottom, squinting at the horizon. 'What storm? I can only see blue skies.'

I pushed his hand away with a nod to the Banania tin on the mantelpiece. 'You know I don't like us doing it in front of Pop.'

The Banania tin was the reason we were here. Bright yellow, it pictured a grinning Senegalese soldier and had once contained cacao powder. When my grandparents, Pop and Amatxi, had eloped from France to England in seventy-one, they had hidden their running away money in that tin, so when two weeks ago, the crematorium had returned Pop's ashes, it had seemed a fitting urn.

'Tell you what...' I threw Cosmo's red trousers over to him, 'let's drive over, sprinkle Pop over his lake and go on to Biarritz.' I rubbed my arms. 'This place gives me the creeps.'

'I find it perfectly charming.'

It was all very well for Cosmo. All he saw were Herriberri's terminally picturesque cobbled streets, whitewashed houses, blood red beams and garlands of drying chillies, but things had turned sour as soon as I had announced that I was Lazarro Etchegaray's granddaughter. Whispers and side glances followed us down the street. A chill fell over the *boulangerie* whenever we stepped in. Conversations stopped. The atmosphere may have escaped him, but it pervaded the town like a noxious vapour.

What on earth had Pop done to warrant such animosity?

'Chop chop, Chloe. Walking boots on.' Invigorated by our afternoon lovemaking, Cosmo jangled the keys to our rented car.

After a twenty-minute drive through densely forested slopes, we parked and followed a leafy path to the lake indicated by the GPS. Though it was only four o'clock, the sky had turned to ink.

Things had changed since the sixties. The idyllic refuge where Pop had courted Amatxi was barricaded by an eight-foot wire mesh dotted with signs like *'défense d'entrer'* and *'pièges à feu.'* Firetraps? What was all that about?

'I say, no trespassing, no fishing, no hunting, no swimming. They really don't want us in there.' A gust of wind flattened a wispy strand of hair over Cosmo's forehead. He picked up a stick and poked the base of the mesh. 'It's dug in.' He checked the top. 'Short of hurling the tin over the fence, Pumpkin –' he whirled his arm from the shoulder, cricket fashion. '– I'm not sure how we can do this.'

'Don't . . . even. . . think of it.' I placed a hand on his wrist. 'We are *not* hurling Pop over the fence. His remains will be scattered respectfully.'

Dark clouds from the west were galloping towards us, rattling branches. I pulled my cardigan tighter around me. We had to find a solution and fast.

'There must be wild boar here,' I said. 'I bet some have pushed their way through the fence to get to the water. Tell you what –' I pointed to the denser side of the forest. 'You go round that side, and I'll skirt the clearing along the other edge. We'll meet in the middle. I'm sure we'll find a breach.'

By now, the sky was jet black. A squall shook the canopy. Cosmo hesitated and headed for the forest.

To my left, a large field sloped down to the fence. A faint line of trodden grass ran down across it. Something had dug and nudged the chain link. I knelt down to see whether I could crawl through, but the netting ran deep into the soil. Holy Moly, what did they keep in there?

The air turned cold. I scrambled up, glanced across the clearing and froze as a solid wall of rain raced towards me, the drops so heavy, they bounced off the grass. Seconds later, I was drenched.

A flash tore through the forest, followed by an almighty crash. Christ, where had that come from? I rolled into a tight ball, hands over my ears, making myself as small as I could. A second crash exploded closer than the first.

I whimpered. *Pop? I know you're angry. I'm sorry your lake's fenced off, but I promised, didn't I? Hitza hitz. My word is a promise... though you've got to admit that it's not looking good.*

A third crash fell on the other side of the lake, right where I had left Cosmo. I pushed my hair from my face and squinted. The world had turned to water.

'Cosmo!' Huge drops pelting my face, I sprinted back through the slanting rain. Another flash of lightning hurled me to the ground, followed by silence. I slowly lifted my head and waited. The silence stretched.

'Cosmo, where are you?' I stumbled towards the dripping canopy and strained my ears. A solid swish of rain deadened faint echoes of thunder in the distance. 'Cosmo!' My voice wobbled. 'It's not funny, come out now. I'm soaked.'

I followed the fence, scanning the bushes. The rain swallowed my calls. Streams of bubbling water formed beneath my feet, rushing towards the lake. A scent of earth and moss rose from the soil, mixed with a feral smell. A growl inside the fence turned my marrow to ice.

I hid behind a large tree and called out in a thin voice, 'Cosmo?' I tried to swallow. My mouth was dry. I took a few more steps, Pop's tin clutched to my chest like a talisman.

A splash of red in the distance. I ran to it, the wet grass winding itself around my legs. I dropped the tin and fell to my knees. 'Oh my God, Cosmo, are you alright?'

He lay under a large beech, eyes closed, hair plastered to his deathly pale face.

'Cosmo, you daft bugger, what were you doing under a tree?'

His skin was cold to the touch. I checked his pulse. There was none.

I repressed a sob and, shivering, grappled for my phone, wiped the tears from my eyes and dialled 999. Damn! We were in France. Hell, France, yes, what was the emergency number again? Frantic, I dialled 18, then 15. Yes, that's what it was, 15!

There was no signal.

I sunk back on my heels and crumpled with a whimper. We were miles from anywhere. In this deluge no one would walk by here.

I bent over Cosmo. His lips were turning blue. I pinched his nostrils and blew into his mouth a few times. He didn't budge. I felt for his sternum with trembling fingers. Repeating the mantra I'd been taught during first aid classes, 'wrists, elbows, shoulders,' I placed one hand over the other and in a shaky voice, pumped his heart to the Bee-Gees rhythm, 'ha, ha, ha… staying alive…'

Crying, singing, I pressed, I blew, I sang and pressed again and cried and prayed and sang until hallelujah, Cosmo jerked back to life.

His eyes opened, filmy and confused. I collapsed onto his chest, laughing and sobbing at the same time.

He hugged me. 'Mummy?'

'Oh, thank God! Cosmo, it's me, Chloe. Welcome back, mate. You sure gave me a fright.'

'Mummy . . .' Cosmo's face relaxed into a beatific smile.

I huddled against him to keep him warm and listened to his heartbeat.

The rain stopped. A noise came up from the road. Ears strained, I lifted my head. An engine? Yes! Someone was driving up towards us. I ran out to the path and waved like a lunatic.

A man jumped out of a jeep marked with a leaf insignia. Late twenties, in khaki gear and boots, he looked like a ranger.

In garbled French, I told him what had happened. He called an ambulance from his car radio, followed me and knelt down underneath the large the beech where Cosmo lay.

'Qu'est ce qui s'est passé?'

What happened? Ah, that, I could tell him. I did know the French for lightning strike. It was the sentence they use for love at first sight.

'Un coup de foudre.'

He lifted an eyebrow and checked my ring finger.

'C'est votre fiancé?'

I hesitated and gave a small nod.

The ranger picked Cosmo as if he were a bag of coal and hoisted him over his shoulder, while I trudge behind him with a backward glance at the scene of chaos that had shaken my world.

The clouds had gone. Sunshine spilled over the forest, gilding the edges of damp leaves. Replete, the earth was lapping up the last of the rivulets. Around us, birds were singing and behind the tall mesh, a veil of pink vapour rose from the lake.

Oh, Pop. I hugged the tin. *I don't know what sorcery this was, but I promise you will reach your lake, if it's the last thing I do.*

CHLOE TURNS DOWN A LUCRATIVE POSITION AS A NANNY

'*Votre nom... Mademoiselle...?'*

'Etchegaray.' I took in a breath, ready for the tedious spelling of my name and remained mouth open.

The nurse had already scribbled it down.

That had never happened before! I checked her badge. Maria Etcheverri. It figured. We were in the Basque Country after all.

'Relation avec le patient?'

I glanced at Cosmo's hairy legs sticking out of a too short blue gown, his face pale as the hospital sheets, and searched my inner lexicon for 'friends with benefits.'

'Euh, son amie?'

I was his friend, though cook, confidante, therapist and mistress would have covered it. Poor posh boy. We were going to have such fun here in the Basque Country, just the two of us, his last fling before he bowed to his mother's will and his father's nineteenth century values, and proposed to Lady Araminta.

Realising I was biting my nails, I pushed my hands deep into the pockets of my long cardigan and waited in the corridor for the porters to transfer Cosmo to a bed. I blamed myself for the accident. From the moment we had arrived in the Pyrenees, I had felt the bad vibes. No wonder Pop left. This place was jinxed, though it had not worried Cosmo who was fascinated by the paranormal. Ironic really. He would have been thrilled to know he had fallen victim to witchcraft.

I repressed a sob at the memory of Cosmo and Pop getting drunk on whisky at the pub, exchanging ghost stories, only three months ago... so far away now, it could have been in another life. Funny how they had got on. Cosmo knew many things, not all learned at the expensive boarding school where his mother had disposed of him at the tender age of seven. He'd picked up some kinky habits there too. They all had, poor motherless mites.

'Your grandfather tells me the Basque Country is full of dark forces,' Cosmo had said to me one night, 'sorcery, that sort of thing.' His eyes shone in the candlelight. 'The myth that witches fly on broomsticks originates from the Basque Country; did you know that, Pumpkin?' He had cleared his throat and switched on his professor's voice. 'In an attempt to quickly reach an altered state, women would anoint their mucous membranes with unguents and potions from the end of a stick. Hence the myth of witches riding broomsticks.'

He had then anointed himself with tingle gel and asked me to ride him.

Such easy fun we had. Why did it have to come to this?

The nurses left. I wiped my eyes with the end of a sleeve and tiptoed into his room. In the bed next to his, a shape was curled up; alive or dead, I was not sure.

Cosmo was resting on pillows, pallid and lifeless. Why him? Surely the lightening had been aimed at me. Or was it the misguided result of Pop's fury at finding his lake fenced off?

I could pinpoint the moment the bad stuff had begun to

happen. It had started in the café overlooking the *fronton,* the pink wall where locals played *pelote,* a Basque version of squash, a rattan scoop tied to their wrist. I was sipping a Kir on the terrace, Cosmo was on his second Pernod, when soft sounds reached us like muted jungle drums from the bar.

'She's says she's Lazarro Etchegaray's granddaughter... '*Lazarro biloba da... Lazarro biloba da...*'

Cosmo stirred and let out a whimper. I held his hand. Poor love, would anyone ever ride his broomstick again?

In the bed next to his, the shape unfurled, mumbled something and pointed to teeth in a glass on the bedside table.

I stepped out, called a nurse and leaned against the cool corridor wall. An ache grew around my heart, squeezing it like a vice. I missed Pop desperately. My parents were no help. They had flown in from Australia for the funeral and gone home after two weeks. I was alone, orphaned and abandoned.

In my twenty-three years of life, Pop had always been a phone call away, full of wisdom and guidance. My parents were busy and... well, they were parents.

'Don't worry, *Chacha,*' Pop would say to me in times of trouble, 'this is what we'll do...' I thought he would live forever, but he wasn't here anymore and I was lost. I slid onto a chair, my stomach hollowed out by a raw pang of grief.

A commotion disturbed my ruminations. A bassoon-like voice bellowed at the end of the corridor. Cosmo's mother.

Her Ladyship in full sail, XL linen dress flapping down the corridor was an impressive sight.

I jerked up in panic and searched for the emergency exit. Basque witches were one thing, but if her ladyship got it into her head that I had harmed her only son and heir, I was done for. 'That little gold-digger,' she called me.

I flattened myself behind a potted palm and inched towards a door marked 'Dr Bolivar'.

'Nurse!' bassooned the Baroness. 'I am the mother of Cosmo Molyneux-Fitzwalter.'

She spotted me, narrowed her eyes, clenched her fists and charged with a low growl.

Docteur Bolivar stepped out of his office, halted and went to turn back, but it was too late.

The Baroness towered over him. 'Where is my son?'

The slim man adjusted his glasses and opened his mouth to speak.

'Why is he in this – *clinique*?' She looked down her nose at him. 'You have not given him penicillin, have you? He is severely allergic.'

'Madame, heuh, Molyneux-Fifi– je– je–'

She glared at him. 'Surely, you speak English.'

'We are doing our best.' The young man ushered her into Cosmo's room, took a long, ragged breath and admitted it was bad news. I crept to the door to hear the rest of his diagnosis

'Your son's – hum – brain has remained without oxygen for a – a long time. I am very sorry, Madame, but Monsieur Mo–Molyneux will remain at a mental age of two. I am so sorry.'

My legs went from under me and I slid against the wall.

'Nonsense!' the Baroness bellowed. 'We will call upon the best –'

Cosmo whimpered, 'Mummy!'

'Darling,' she clucked. 'Mummy will take you home to be properly looked after.'

The corridor echoed with the clatter of heels. Someone else was coming. Jeepers, news travelled fast.

Docteur Bolivar's door was half-open. I gathered myself and crept into his office.

Lady Araminta, Cosmo's triple-barrelled fiancée in-waiting cantered past me, quietly sobbing into a lace handkerchief. A typical English rose, Minty was long and thin, as if she'd spent too long in a flower-press. She must have rushed straight from her stables, still in jodhpurs and pink polo shirt with the collar turned up.

There was nothing left for me to do but relinquish Cosmo to his dreadful family. A weight on my chest, I left the Emergency Department, walked out onto the lawn at the front of the *clinique* and collapsed on a bench, where I cried for a long time, wondering why Fate strove so hard to destroy all the people I loved.

The sun was setting when a great paw on my shoulder made me jump. A smell of whisky and tobacco pervaded the air.

'Ah here you are, dear girl!'

Dear Girl? Whatever happened to the gold-digger?

'I hear you saved the boy's life. Good show.' Loud and rubicund, Molyneux *Père* had served in the cavalry with Colonel Parker-Bowles. He sat next to me, ran a hand though his crew cut, and gave me a paternal look, just stopping short of fondling my thigh. The hand strayed up to his shirt pocket and crinkled the few notes he always kept there.

'I say, jolly good of you to stick by the boy.'

'Huh?' I stared at him wide-eyed.

'Wife tells me you're so fond of Cosmo that you can't part with him. Very broad spirited of you, I must say.'

I leapt away from the bench and found myself surrounded by the whole dynasty. Cosmo's sister, Portia, gently took both my hands. Portia was an *'it'* girl, her life lived in instalments in *Chatter* and *Tattle* magazines.

'Dear, dear Chloe,' Portia said in a tremulous voice, 'we don't know how to thank you for saving Cosmo's life.'

'Wha – what do you mean?' I'd expected them to accuse

me of killing him and here they all were, grinning at me like a pack of hyenas.

Alarm bells began to ring.

'We are so grateful.' The baroness uncovered large teeth in what passed for a smile. 'You have been such a rock.'

'I don't – I didn't –'

'It's a grand gesture, dear girl.' Old Molyneux placed an arm around my shoulder. His whisky breath made me gag. I shook my head, hoping the nightmare would pass. This did not make sense.

Further down the road, something caught my eye. Araminta was scurrying away in a taxi. Talk of standing by your man.

'We know how much you meant to Cosmo, how close you two were.'

'Well –'

'Of course, we had other plans for our son, but circumstances have changed. We have met with the chief consultant,' his mother said. 'Cosmo will never get better.' The woman struggled with her emotions, but years of stiff upper lip got her through. She swallowed hard. 'We would be delighted to have you amongst us.'

'I don't – understand.' Actually, I was beginning to see where this was going. They wanted me as a nanny. 'I'm sorry, Mrs Moly – I mean Your Ladyship, but I came to France on a mission and I can't just –'

'We'll make it worth your while.' The old man crinkled the notes again.

Mrs Molyneux's bassoon voice dripped over me, all sweet and sugary.

'We'll give you and Cosmo the pad over the stables. Or the dowager cottage if you prefer.'

The old man balked at the mention of the dowager cottage.

'Hold on there, dear girl –' He lifted a hand in protest but thought better of it.

Now something else was going on. Why was Portia scanning the car park with such interest? Araminta had gone. Who was she expecting?

Quivering under the voltage of their aristocratic glares, I saw my future fade to nothingness. My prospects of a career as a chef, the apprenticeship in a London restaurant, the promise I'd made to Pop, the three months I had left on my Bletchley lease tumbled and clattered like pebbles inside my mind.

I yanked out Pop's final resting tin from my bag and held it aloft.

'Thank you for your generous offer. I would love to look after Cosmo, but I came to the Basque Country to honour my grandfather's wish to –' I faltered, took a shaky breath and tried to remember the assertiveness course I'd taken last year '– to spread his ashes over Lake Irrabia. I promised to do it, and I won't go anywhere until I have. Perhaps when this is done, I will –'

I was interrupted by a screeching of brakes. Men in jeans and white sneakers jumped out of a van and ran towards us. A microphone wrapped in a dead rat was shoved in my face. Cameras flashed, questions were machine-gunned at me.

'Chloe – it is Chloe, isn't it ? Is it true that your fiancé was struck by lightning right on the day he asked you for your hand in marriage?'

'Huh?'

'You must have loved Cosmo Molyneux-Fitzwalter very much to accept his offer, even though he will never again be the man he was.'

'Pardon?' What tale had Portia spun to these French paparazzi?

'You have agreed to marry him?'

'No!' I turned to Portia. 'You can't do this. You can't bulldoze people into doing what you want.'

I knew then that if I let the Molyneux-Fitzwalters get their clutches into me, I would forever be at their mercy. I backed away.

Banania tin clutched to my chest, I ran towards Dr Bolivar's office for safety, muttering, *Oh Pop, what have you done? What hornet's nest have we disturbed by coming back?*

A PITYING OF DOVES

'*Only pick the mushrooms that are open, Chacha.'* Pop's voice echoed inside my head. *'Leave the tiny ones. You can never be sure of what they are. They might be venomous.'* Even after half a century, Pop's English still carried the rocks of his native mountains, and toadstools remained 'venomous mushrooms.'

I gazed down at the valley where my grandfather had yearned to rest for eternity. Lush, washed a deep green by rain from the Atlantic, the slope ahead was already in darkness. Below, nestled inside the beech forest, Lake Irrabia twinkled. Edged with an impassable fence, the blue Cyclops eye stared up at me, portent with a message I couldn't decipher. I had tried to reach it and Cosmo had paid the price. Guilt burned inside me. What on earth did they keep down there that was so dangerous?

A movement caught my attention. I squinted and peered down. A large creature was rustling the undergrowth at the edge of the lake. Eyes screwed, I berated myself for being suggestible. Was it the Basajaun? The mythical yeti-like king of the forest?

Cosmo's accident had been so bizarre, so pre-ordained somehow, that I was now reading supernatural signs in everything I saw. It was as if the lightning strike had released all the superstition and mythology trapped inside my Basque genes.

According to Pop Basques were a special genetic 'hap-logroup.' Their mysterious language – which had no known origin – the way they venerated women and bulls, and their passion for cooperatives and high kicks had confounded anthropologists from time immemorial. Belonging to this tribe was a privilege given to very few.

I didn't feel very Basque. My mother was Australian. She'd met Dad at the Glastonbury music festival, and married him after a whirlwind romance. She had done her best to anglicise me but had found it a struggle. In cosmopolitan Bletchley, English was not the dominant language.

My grandparents were Amatxi and Pop. 'Amatxi' was pronounced Amatchi, the Basque word for grandma. Her first name was Paloma, which meant Dove. She was plump and soft and told me tales of Basajaun and pixies.

My childhood had been a battlefield between Kaz the Kangaroo and the Basque yeti. Inside my young head, the Basajaun had simply morphed with the Cookie Monster, the laminak pixies with the Smurfettes, and we had all lived happily in a multicultural version of Sesame Street.

Basket in hand, I faced the valley, acres of Iraty forest behind me. I closed my eyes, shook off my espadrilles, planted my feet in the cool grass and, with a long in-breath of compost-scented air, imagined roots sprouting down from my toes, reaching deep into the earth, entwined with those of the beeches around me. An image took shape. The hirsute Basa-jaun– the link between our world and the underworld Pop was still struggling to reach– lumbered towards me, sat on its haunches and tried to deliver a message I couldn't understand. I shivered. Above me, dry leaves rustled in the autumn wind. A jay screeched. I shook myself, slipped my damp feet back into my *espadrinak*, picked up my basket, headed for a fairy ring twinkling at the foot of a tree, and selected several plump mushrooms, carefully layering them on top of each other.

A sign nailed to a trunk attracted my attention. I shaded my eyes from the low sun and read, '*Chasse aux palombes, sifflez.*'

I studied it for a while. '*Sifflez*' meant whistle, of that, I was sure. 'Please whistle?' Weird. I put my lips together and blew. No sound came out.

A flock of doves on their way south flew up from the valley, searching for a place to roost. They flapped about, settled on tall branches, scattering leaves and twigs, and began to coo. Their sad song took me back to Paloma, my grandmother, and to Cosmo, who had so loved to impress me with words. 'A pitying of doves, Pumpkin, not a flock.'

Poor Cosmo back in his nursery, sentenced to eternal 'teas' of sausages and semolina. He'd been so looking forward to my wild mushroom stroganoff. He had even selected a 'fantasmabulous Bordeaux' that would have cost me the equivalent of a week's wages.

A shot shattered the peace. The 'pitying of doves' flapped in panic and I understood why I had to whistle. Of course! '*Chasse aux palombes*' meant 'dove shooting.' I hunkered down in the grass, hands over my head and waited for the moment to pass.

Silence. I lifted my face. Tantalising, another fairy ring caught my eye, shiny and white poking through a mat of dead leaves. I scurried towards it. More shots rang out. I froze, wondering what to do next, remembered the sign '*sifflez,*' put my lips together and tried again. It was no good. I couldn't whistle to save my life.

A dove dropped at my feet, its grey plumage splattered with blood. My heart went out to the poor bird, but the cook inside me already imagined thin slices of breast seared with garlic and chopped parsley on a bed of mushrooms.

A retriever burst from the undergrowth. I pounced, snatched the bird from its fangs, stuffed it in my basket and, ducking to avoid stray shots, raced back to the car where, heart pounding, I collapsed in the driver's seat.

The Pyrenees were a dangerous place. However mythical and wonderful they had been painted by my nostalgic grandparents, they had not welcomed me like a prodigal daughter, the local gods obviously still debating whether Lazarro Etchegaray did deserve a place with his peers in the Basque Underworld.

What heinous sin had Pop committed to be cast out in the wilderness, back in the sixties? Why had he eloped with Amatxi? I leaned on the headrest and thought back to the mild old man I had loved, toddling off to St Mary's church in his Sunday garb of thick cotton shirt and woollen jacket topped with a beret. Pop was a good man. He wasn't tall but straight as a rod, both in body and character. That he should have perpetrated a crime was inconceivable.

I glanced down at my hoard of mushrooms. They looked innocuous enough, but you could never be too sure.

'In France, once you have picked your wild mushrooms,' our French teacher, Madame Hart, had explained to the puzzled catering class back at Bletchley College, 'you take them to the *pharmacie.* The *pharmacien* will tell you whether they are *vénéneux* –poisonous – or good to eat – *comestibles.*' Madame Hart, like Cosmo, was a mine of information. She knew for instance, that Dame Nelly Melba had once been the toast of Melbourne as an opera singer, and that '*chicken*

Marengo' had nothing to do with meringue but was named after one of Napoleon's victories. She had been a great help to me when preparing for this trip.

I parked in the centre of town and, basket on my arm, hesitated in front of the *farmazia*, feeling like a complete idiot. Relieved to see a poster in the window inviting wild food lovers to have their crop checked, I mumbled *'bonjour'* and joined a small queue.

All eyes turned to me. Self-conscious, I hid behind the bulky frame of a local housewife. The glance she gave me could have fried a cockroach. Perhaps not knowing one's fungi was a sin in these parts, and made you stand out as a foreigner – or worse – a Parisian. I pushed my basket under a display of corn plasters and concentrated on the instructions.

The *pharmacienne*'s scrawny pink neck protruded from her white coat. Her beaked nose, short bristly hair and darting avian eyes reminded me of those *cous-nus,* the naked-neck chickens common in the region. She was uttering knowledgeable tuts, nonchalantly studying the blotchy arm of a middle-aged belle, running a finger over the bubbling skin, offering diagnoses and pulling creams and potions from a long flat drawer.

An atmosphere was growing inside the shop. I unzipped my jacket and fanned myself with a verruca leaflet. New customers piled in, took one look at me and exchanged knowing glances.

'It's her.' A thin woman nudged her husband, berating him with a kick when he gawped at me. Urgent whispers reached me from the back of the queue, spoken by someone I couldn't see. *'It's her, I tell you.' 'Bera da.'*

I checked my sweatshirt for traces of blood, brushed away a feather, lifted my shoes and squinted at myself in the mirror of the makeup display. My round cheeks were flushed, my dark bob unkempt, but it was nothing worse than usual.

The rumour swished around, over and over again, in Basque now, as if I couldn't guess.

'Bera da. Bera da.'

The queue shuffled forward, gripping me tighter in its coils.

Squashed against a pile of incontinence pads, I grew hotter, inwardly urging the blotchy blonde to buy her cream and get out. Heck, whatever happened to 'consult your GP?' My eyes strayed to the chemist's nametag *'Arrantxa Arroztegui.'*

Arrantxa was pronounced Arrantcha. I knew that. Amatxi had taught me a few rudiments. The Basque *tx* is nothing to worry about, just a *tch* with a touch of *'couleur locale'*. To pass the time, I amused myself by making up words, substituting the *tx* for the English tch. Tetchy would be tetxi for instance and patchy patxi. Detecting movement, I lifted my eyes. Heads snapped away. I shrugged it off as small-town nosiness and uttered a loud sigh, cursing Blotxi and Bitxi at the front, still discussing skin creams.

When at last my turn came, naked-neck Bitxi glowered at me, grabbed my basket of mushrooms and disappeared at the back. Whispers grew louder. I even heard my name. Was I imagining it? Moments later the *pharmacienne* returned the basket with a squawk. *'Comestible.'*

I left the chemist's, eyes burning a hole in my back.

Glad to be out of the *farmazia,* I headed for the *superette* to buy the ingredients for tonight's dinner. Herriberri was beautiful in the warm autumn dusk. Sturdy housewives carried their shopping home. Berets drawn over one eye, men in checked shirts polished their boules on the town square. The last rays of the sun gilded slanting roofs, catching the red of the timbering, and flaming geraniums in window boxes. Bunting of chillies on pristine white walls gave the place a festive air, as if Herriberri was planning a party to which I wasn't invited.

And still, eyes lingered. Whispers followed me. I studied my reflection in a shop window and saw a healthy girl, a neat dark bob framing a round face. My blue waterproof jacket was clean and since I wore trousers, no skirt was caught in my knickers. So, what was it about me that fuelled such interest?

I focused on my recipe. With the addition of bacon and a dash of Cosmo's fantasmabulous wine, I would call my windfall *coeur de palombe aux champignons sauvages*. 'Pigeon heart with wild mushrooms.' My eyes misted up. Cosmo would have loved it. Poor darling. Had I done the right thing in refusing to go home with him?

Riddled with guilt, I halted outside the window of a pâtisserie selling *gateaux basques* and in my mind, went over the previous day's scene. If his parents had asked nicely, I would have agreed to look after Cosmo until they could find a suitable replacement – I was no nursemaid – but balked at the way they had tried to bulldoze me into it. I wouldn't have been much help. Cosmo had no idea who I was any more, Old Moly was a soak, and as for the two harpies, once I was trapped at Fawcett Hall, they would have made mincemeat out of me.

Nah, it wouldn't have worked. I trudged towards the supermarket.

The doors to the *superette* slid open. I stepped into the coolness, went to grab a basket near the newspaper stand and froze. My throat closed up. The horror hit me with full force. My own face stared back at me from the front page of *Sud Ouest* under the title, '**ELLE ABANDONNE SON FIANCÉ.**'

CHLOE FALLS PREY TO A DASTARDLY PLOT

Buying a paper with my face plastered on the front page was the most humiliating moment of my life, even worse than being caught having sex with Jason – my ex – in his dad's car in the garage.

The article was pitiless, an exquisite revenge for Portia – that professional manipulator of media – to punish me for having the gall to turn down a life of luxury with her brother at Fawcett Hall.

I hurried through the shop and, back in the rented car, seethed at the trash she had fabricated. *'Chloe Etchegaray, a kitchen scullion* – a scullion! I was a qualified chef – *was holidaying in Herriberri with Monsieur Molyneux, a gentleman of means...* My eyes popped out of their sockets when I read what followed. *'Monsieur Molyneux had just proposed to Mademoiselle Etchegaray with a diamond ring, an antique family heirloom. She had accepted, only to renege later after he was struck by lightning, claiming that he had lost his faculties.'*

Lies, it was all lies! I bunched up the paper with a growl, threw it into the passenger footwell, collapsed over the steering wheel and howled.

Later, as I blew my nose, a thought struck me. Back home, Portia would not be spinning those yarns to *Chatter* Magazine. She wouldn't risk damaging her precious reputation. Portia Molyneux-Fitzwalter's brother engaged to a kitchen scullion? Really?

I would bet anything she would use Cosmo's demise to consolidate her place in the limelight.

I drove back to the gîte and opened Cosmo's expensive bottle of wine, hoping it would drown my shame.

It only made me sadder.

There was no sense in staying here. Cosmo was gone. The lake was fenced off. I was hated.

'I'm so sorry, Pop.' I stood by the tall mantelpiece and rested my forehead against his Banania tin. 'You'll have to wait till I come up with plan B.'

I called the landlady, a lovely woman called Christiane, and told her I would be leaving early the next day. She agreed to collect the key in the morning.

Once this was arranged, I drank a second glass of Cosmo's divine nectar, shook my crop of fungi into the sink and turned on the tap, reassured that the chemist had pronounced them *comestibles*.

I pulled the pigeon onto the chopping board, sliced it open and simply tore out the breasts, not bothering with the fiddly task of plucking.

While the mushrooms softened in butter, I switched on the television, glad to catch *Plus Belle la Vie*, a long running soap set in Marseille. '*A more beautiful life,*' the name gave it away. The French love happy soaps and happy was just what I needed. An episode of East Enders would have finished me off.

It was 'impotence week' on French television. The theme popped up everywhere. Sipping my wine, I watched men –

young and old, impotence could strike at any age – shout at their frustrated wives, *'Je ne suis pas une machine!'*

The sentence had tickled Cosmo who would shout he wasn't a machine at the oddest moment, making me shriek with laughter. Crikey – impotence had been the least of Cosmo's worries. Lack of sex drive was never a problem for the Molyneux men, quite the opposite.

Elbows on the counter, I sank my chin into my hands, wondering for the umpteenth time whether I should have moved into Fawcett Hall and married Cosmo.

I knew from my stints of working at the Hall, that Old Molyneux was known to grope the serving girls. The old fornicator even had a mistress, though who the woman was, I wasn't sure. Who would want him? He was beyond ancient.

Like father like daughter. If *Chatter* Magazine was to be believed, Portia was alphabetically bonking her way down Burke's Peerage, struggling to find a peer whose name began with Q. It was ironic because Q was the way the French pronounced *'cul,'* the colloquial word for butt, and by extension, sex. Appropriate that she should have *des problemes de Q.*

I dragged myself out of my torpor and tasted a mushroom. Hmm, a little more salt perhaps. My stomach twisted at all I had lost. Cosmo had such faith in me, believed I had a gift, and was about to introduce me to 'some people he knew,' a famous chef I hoped, who would take me on for an apprenticeship.

Another rush of guilt knocked me for six. Here I was, feeling sorry for myself, while in the great snakes-and-ladders game of life, Cosmo had – because of me, tumbled right back down to square one.

Sniffing loudly, I seared the meat, added parsley – fresh coriander would have been better, but hey, this was France – wiped my tears and tasted the sauce. Hmm, it was scrumptious.

Plus Belle la Vie was over. I plated up, turned off the television, offered a toast to Cosmo, Pop, and L'ami Y'abon, his kindly face forever grinning on his Banania tin, and tucked into my *coeur de palombe aux champignons sauvages*. It was delicious, though it would have tasted even better shared.

I soaked up the sauce with a chunk of bread as Pop had taught me, finished the last of Cosmo's Bordeaux, washed up and went to bed feeling rather woozy.

I woke up at first light drenched with sweat, tried to get up and gripped the bedstead. The room pitched slightly. I rubbed my eyes, waited until it had righted itself and went to make a cup of tea. Unsteady, nauseous, I banged into the doorframe. Christ, I'd had some hangovers in my time with Leah, but this one was a killer.

From the Banania tin, the Senegalese sharp shooter rolled his eyes and called out, 'Thinking of leaving today, girl? Giving up?'

L'ami Ya'bon had a point. I staggered about in a half-dream, opening and closing cupboards, looking for the teabags. I turned to the tin and muttered, 'I don't have much choice, do I? I've only been in Herriberri five days and they've made it clear that I'm not welcome. Whatever Pop did is still alive in their clo - their collec - their eclectic memory.' I narrowed my eyes, lifted a finger and slurred, 'They're watching us, you know.'

'Does it have anything to do with the lake?' L'ami Ya'bon asked sensibly.

'Hmm. I wondered about that.' I burped. 'I understand why my grandparents might have eloped, but why did Pop never go home, huh? You were there at the time, you tell me.' I waited. There was no answer.

Bumping into worktop and chairs, I eventually found the tea on the deep windowsill, took out a tea bag and steadied myself against the sink. Something was very wrong. Inside the stone recess, the window frame was buckling and warping like melted cheese.

'Come on, L'ami Ya'bon – Tell her.' A second lilting voice called out from the other end of the mantelpiece.

'Huh?' I whipped around. How did that tin get there?

'You know what Lazzaro did, and why he had to leave.'

'*Non*!' L'ami Ya'bon cried out. 'He didn't do it. He was tricked. I should know.'

My head snapped towards the first tin. My heart rate doubled. Staying in this house was a bad idea. I should have left last night. This gîte was jinxed. I'd been hexed from the moment I had arrived. Not only had the curse nearly killed Cosmo, now the whole house was turning against me.

I had to leave, and I had to leave now. A touch to the forehead confirmed that I was running a fever. I didn't want to spend a moment longer in this place. I ran to the bathroom and was stuffing toothpaste and creams into my toiletry bag, when I caught sight of someone in the mirror. I screamed. The 'naked-neck' *pharmacienne* was staring back at me.

'Go away, witch,' I whimpered. 'Leave me alone. What have I ever done to you?'

'You're Lazarro Etchegaray's granddaughter,' the vulture in the mirror squawked.

I gripped the toiletry bag and aimed it at the mirror. There was a knock at the front door. My stomach lurched. They were here. They were coming for me. I searched for an escape. The window! My spirits sank. It was too high, too deep.

'Coucou!' A French voice called out. *'Mademoiselle Etchegaray?'* The sound of steps came nearer. The witch had a key. She was in the house. *'Mademoiselle Chloe? C'est moi, Christiane Arroztegui.'*

Arroztegui? I froze. How could the witch be both inside

the mirror and outside the bathroom? Heart in my throat, I flattened myself behind the door.

'Mademoiselle Chloe?' She knocked.

The knock went right through me. I muffled a scream. A bout of nausea propelled me to the toilet. I was sick. Hair plastered to my face, I pushed myself up, ran a hand over my mouth, yanked the door open and lurched forward.

Christiane put her hand in her pocket. I tried to block her way.

She took out her phone and edged towards the mantelpiece.

I growled. 'You're one of them, I know. I don't know what you all want with Pop, but you won't get him, you coven of witches.' I lunged towards the tin and tripped on the rug. Christiane screamed. My forehead hit the stone mantelpiece. The world went dark.

CHLOE IS BACK AT THE CLINIQUE

I woke up at the *clinique* where Cosmo had been taken after his accident, wondering how I'd got there.

I lifted a hand to my head. It was bandaged. There was a bump on my forehead and my belly felt as if it was about to explode.

At the foot of the bed, Docteur Bolivar was studying my notes, and a dour grey-haired nurse was setting out medicines on a tray. She had a black eye. I wondered how she got it. They see all sorts in that job.

A young copper-skinned nurse pulled up my sheet and beamed at me. 'The doctor saved your life, you know.'

The two women crossed their hands on their chest and turned to the physician, their faces aglow with awe.

The doctor basked for a moment in the amniotic warmth of their combined veneration, adjusted his glasses, cleared his throat and launched into a diagnosis that totally bypassed my befuddled brain.

I caught the words overdose, fungus, venomous, comestible and common error, but, lulled by his voice, all I could do was smile beatifically. Behind the rimless glasses, his eyes were so kind, so brown, so liquid, so like those of Doctor Zhivago – an old film I'd watched with Amatxi one Christmas – that I was smitten. Crikey, was he dishy! If only I could stop burping. It was embarrassing. My insides churned horribly and I still had no idea how I had got here.

'Now, Mademoiselle Etchegaray,' the doctor said, 'I suggest you apologise to the nurse for hitting her this morning.'

'Pardon?'

The older nurse grumbled, 'I was helping you out of the ambulance and this is what you did by way of thanks.'

'L'ambulance?'

'Yes,' the doctor repeated in a conciliatory tone. 'You owe Nurse Arroztegui an apology.'

I jolted at the name, clutched my covers and scrambled away from the woman.

'Where's my Banania Tin? What have you done with it?'

The doctor placed a cool hand on my forehead and enveloped me in his liquid gaze.

'Calmez-vous, Chloe, calmez-vous.'

I let out a volcanic belch, 'S'cuse me.' I squeezed my eyes shut to stop the walls from warping.

'What did I tell you?' Docteur Bolivar aimed a modest grin at the nurses.

'Hallucinations, flatulence –' He opened his hands and delivered his verdict. '*Fungus foedissimus*.' He turned to me. 'Chloe, have you eaten mushrooms in the last twenty-four hours?'

'Yes but –'

'Did you pick them yourself?'

'Yes, I –'

'You drank wine?'

I nodded. Ouch. Nodding wasn't a good idea.

Toadstool poisoning? There had to be some mistake. I tried to sort out the events of the previous day. No. It couldn't be the mushrooms.

I was the victim of black magic, so much was obvious, but I didn't really want to tell him, not in the presence of that old nurse anyway. I didn't trust her.

The doctor turned to the two women with a self-satisfied smile and recapped, '*Hallucinations dix ou quatorze heures après ingestion, champignons vénéneux.*' His whole body language spelled out 'Q.E.D.'

'*En anglais s'il vous plait?*' The knock on my head had flushed out all the French from my brain.

'At first, I had assumed that you had taken an overdose of drugs, but the combination of hallucinations and wind indicates that you have ingested a small quantity of the very dangerous *fungus foedissimus.*'

'Oooh!' cooed the nurses awestruck by his polyglottic display.

The doctor delicately pushed down my blanket and pressed my ballooning tummy.

'We will give you some charcoal. It will make you feel much better.'

Charcoal? Really? What was going on here?

The West Indian nurse shook some black granules onto a plastic spoon and told me to open my mouth. I was about to refuse – eating coal could not possibly be the antidote to black magic – but, hypnotised by the doctor's brown eyes, my lips parted and I swallowed the granules, surprised at how sweetly they dissolved on my tongue.

'Activated charcoal will absorb the poisonous toxins and gases.'

Doctor Bolivar's voice alone was activating several nerve centres, increasing the turmoil inside my gut.

The nurses plumped up my pillows. I wished they would

stop faffing. The tiniest movement played havoc with my insides.

'I can't have.' I searched out the doctor's eyes.

He halted. 'Pardon?'

'I can't have eaten toadstools. I took my mushrooms to the pharmacy to be checked. If it really is toadstool poisoning, then someone slipped them into my basket when I was there.'

'This is a very serious accusation.' The young physician supported one elbow in a hand and cupped his chin in his elegant fingers, obviously convinced I was still delirious. He lifted an eyebrow. 'And which pharmacy did you go to?'

I was about to answer when a thunderous fart, a fart of nuclear proportions detonated, propelled me above the mattress with ballistic force, shaking the metallic hospital bed.

'Yes!' Docteur Bolivar jumped up, triumphant. 'Ha! Only *fungus foedissimus* can do that.' Jubilation lit his handsome features. 'My diagnosis is correct. Flatus eliminates all doubt!'

He leapt out of the room before the toxic cloud could reach him, and hurried away to save other lives while the nurses rushed to open the windows.

I collapsed with a defeated sigh. No, I had not imagined it. Someone in Herriberri really was out to get me, but who and why?

CHLOE GOES HOME TO ENGLAND

'Jeepers! There's someone in my house!' Cold fingers of fear clamped around my throat. I glanced at the taxi and lifted a hand, willing it to come back, but it was too late. Its taillights were disappearing into the English night. Alone on the damp pavement, suitcase at my feet, heart in my throat, I hesitated outside my little terraced house.

A chink of light was seeping through my lounge curtains. Squatters? Surely not, I'd only been gone a week. Burglars? The hairs bristled on the back of my neck. Had the curse of the Arroztegui witches followed me all the way back to Bletchley?

I raised my eyes to the row of slate roofs and searched for broomsticks, but all I could see were grey wisps of smoke blown downwards by the rain.

I shivered. No one knew I was back. Had Portia in her fury sent her henchmen to trash my place?

I wiped away the tears shed on the bus from Luton airport, dug my mobile out of my pocket, pressed nine three times but didn't send the call. A thumb over the call button, I unlocked my front door, stepped in cautiously, put down my case as quietly as I could and crept into the lounge, phone tightly clutched in my left hand, key sticking out between the fingers of my right hand as a weapon.

Good grief, what was going on in here? The place was a mess. It didn't make sense, instead of taking things, the burglars had added to them. My furnished house was hardly larger than a hobbit-hole. It didn't take much to clutter it. A knitted blanket was bunched on the sofa, old cane chairs crowded around my modern pine table, and on top of the chest was a dust-covered suitcase.

A noise made me jump. My fingers tightened over the phone. Someone was moving overhead. They were in my bedroom. I stood, paralysed.

My parents! A chink of hope lit up the gloom. After clearing Pop's rooms, they must have spent longer than planned with their Yorkshire cousin, and returned here to wait for me! Of course, these were Pop's things and the blanket was Amatxi's. A weight fell from my shoulders. I wouldn't have to cope with all that grief alone.

'Mum? Papa?' I rushed up the stairs and rapped on my bedroom door. 'It's me, Chloe. Are you in there?'

My bed squeaked. The door opened a fraction. A tousled mop of blonde hair appeared.

'Leah?'

Leah brushed her hair from her face and stared at me with panda eyes. 'Chloe?' She gulped, as startled as I was. 'What are you doing here?'

'I live here, remember?'

It all came back to me. In a fit of generosity, I'd given Leah a key and told her she could use my place. Leah lived with her parents, and her boyfriend with his. Finding a private place was difficult. Who the boyfriend was, I wasn't sure. She'd been unusually circumspect about him, simply calling him 'this bloke I'm seeing.'

A vanilla smell reached my nostrils. The cheek of it! She'd been burning my scented candle. What else had she helped herself to?

Leah cast a furtive glance back into the room, muttered something to whoever was in my bed, shut the door, followed me downstairs and stood barefoot, rocking on the balls of her feet.

'Sorry, Chlo, I could have sworn you'd said –'

'I had to come home early. Something happened. I couldn't call you, my phone didn't work from France.' I tilted my chin towards the bedroom. 'Is *he* up there?'

Leah nodded. 'He's getting dressed. Wow –' She ran her fingers through her tangled hair. 'This is a bit of a shock.'

She perched on the arm of the sofa. Her breasts wriggled inside the T-shirt and her long legs shimmered with fake tan. Leah was dead sexy. I caught myself thinking that the boyfriend, whoever he was, was a lucky fellow.

She grinned. 'What happened then?' Did you give Mr Posh the push?'

'No.' I lowered myself onto one of the cane chairs and rubbed the tips of my fingers together. My voice wobbled. 'Cosmo had an accident while we were in the mountains. He had to be flown home to England.'

'Oh, how awful.' Leah reached out and touched my arm. 'Are you alright?'

I gave a half-hearted nod.

She took a sharp breath and lifted a finger. 'Wait a minute. I think I read about that. Wasn't he the brother of – that posh girl named after a car?'

'Portia.'

'Porsche, that's it. There was something in the Express

about her. In fact, I kept it for you. Hold on, I'll just get it.' She sprinted back to the bedroom.

Moments later, my door squeaked and heavy steps trod down the stairs. Sheepish, a hand tucked into the pocket of his jeans, a leather blouson thrown over a shoulder, 'the boyfriend' appeared, trying very hard to look casual.

'Hi,' he said with a self-conscious grin.

'Jason?' My eyes popped out. Mouth open, I stood and watched him saunter out into the street.

'Here it is. The Express.' Leah bustled back holding a folded newspaper.

'But – but – that was –' I stammered. 'That was Jason.' I thumped my chest. 'My ex!'

'Yeah.' Leah shrugged and pursed her lips. 'Sorry.'

'How could you?' I gave her a withering stare. Christ, how could she?

'Ah come on.' Leah brushed off the offence. 'You'd finished with him over three months ago.'

'Yes, and you cheered. "Well done, Chloe, for getting rid of that loser," you said.'

'Did I?' Leah took a step back, the newspaper folded against her chest.

I glared at her. 'You said the only way he could improve was by dying and coming back as a turnip.' I took a step forward. 'Didn't you?'

She shrugged again. 'Yeah well, from what I remember, you agreed with me at the time.' She took another step back. 'So, I've changed my mind. He's not that bad when you get to know him. It's no big deal.'

I got closer and stopped. Yuk, I could smell the sex on her.

She sidestepped away from me. Her foot caught a bag pushed under the sofa.

'Urgh.'

The bag – a glossy carrier from Harrods – spilled some of its contents over the rug.

'Aw, what have you got in there?' With a grimace, Leah shook the mess of ashes and clinker from her foot.

'Oy, leave that alone!' I knelt down and scooped up the ashes with my hands. 'Careful, that's my grandad.'

'What?' Leah screamed and ran into the kitchen.

I sat back on my heels and explained over my shoulder. 'The funeral director said I'd get five pounds of ashes back. Pop asked me to scatter them in France, but what with the weight restrictions on the plane, I couldn't take more than two pounds with me, so I put what I could in a chocolate tin and left the rest here.' I brushed my hands over the carrier bag. 'I was going to spread them in Woburn near a badger sett we used to watch.'

With a deep sigh, I pushed myself up and went to fetch a dustpan from the kitchen.

Leah looked at me strangely and spread the paper on the countertop. 'The article talks about a climbing accident,' she said, trying to redeem herself. 'It's in here somewhere.'

'Huh?' I turned on the tap and washed my hands. 'What climbing accident?'

'You said you were in the mountains. Ah, here it is. Listen to this.' She smoothed down the paper and put on a newsreader's voice. *'Socialite Portia Molyneux-Fitzwalter, formerly linked to the Earl of Quimble –'* She lifted her panda eyes to me. 'The Earl of Quimble no less. He was on the Antiques Roadshow the other day.'

'I'm not surprised, he's ancient.'

'No, not him, he brought in a vase. You'll never guess how much it fetched.'

'What else does it say?' I didn't share Leah's fascination with reality programmes.

'The socialite had to cancel her holiday in Mustique with her

new fiancé, Viscount Rutherthorpe – eighteenth in line to the throne – to fly over to France.' Leah lifted a hand to emphasize the next sentence. *'Her baronet brother Cosmo is fighting for his life after a climbing accident in the Pyrenees.'* She opened her hands and turned to me, plucked eyebrows raised in question.

A climbing accident? I was confused. I joined her and briefly scanned the article for any mention of a kitchen scullion, relieved to find none.

'Cosmo could never have a climbing accident. Poor chap was so terrified of heights, he couldn't even stand on a chair.' I faced her squarely. 'He was struck by lightning, Leah. I had to resuscitate him.' I added woefully, 'Those first aid classes we took in our first year really came in handy.'

'Wow,' Leah said, impressed. 'But if you resuscitated him, why does it say in here that he's fighting for his life?'

'I didn't reach him soon enough.' My eyes welled up. 'He's brain damaged. He's got the faculties of a two-year old and he'll never get better. I feel so awful about it. It was horrid. And then, when his parents realised he'd never be normal again, they put pressure on me to marry him.'

'Really? How did they do that?'

'By holding their double-barrelled name to my head!' I tore a sheet from a kitchen roll and dabbed my eyes. 'They offered me their *dowager cottage* –'

'Wow,' Leah said dreamily, 'must be worth a fortune.' She giggled. 'Is the job still going?'

'It's not funny. Cosmo might have the mind of a two-year old, but he's still a man. It'd be *'who's been a naughty boy then?'* and spanking morning, noon and night.' I blew my nose. 'Nah, if what I'd wanted from life was spanking brain-dead men, I'd put in a discreet ad in a Conservative club. Being a nanny isn't what I'm about, Leah.'

'I know. You want to win Top Chef.'

I didn't, but let it go.

Pensive, I leaned against the worktop, chin in hands, wondering if back in France, Portia would have been capable of paying someone to drop a deadly toadstool in my basket. But how? I let my eyes drift around the kitchen and noticed the light flashing on my answerphone.

I pressed the button. My boss's smoky voice filled the room.

'Hiya, it's Carmela. I couldn't reach you on your mobile. I'm sorry, pet, but while you were away, I had to make adjustments to the staff rota. Ring me when you get back so we can discuss it. Tada!'

'Who was that?' Relaxed now, Leah had put the kettle on and, completely at home, was taking fresh milk out of my fridge.

I wondered how often she'd been here with Jason while I was away.

'That was my boss. I can guess why she called –' My stomach churned. Adjustments to the staff rota? I was her only chef.

'She'll want you straight back to work I expect.' Leah took out two mugs, dropped teabags into them and poured boiling water.

'Fire me more like.'

'Why do you say that?' She stopped pouring.

I paced the kitchen. 'Because Cosmo's mother will have warned Carmela she'd take her custom elsewhere unless I'm fired from Posh-Nosh. That's why.'

Without Lady M. F's furious appetite for vol-au-vents, cucumber sandwiches and petit fours, Posh-Nosh would struggle to survive.

'But – but you always said that Carmela couldn't cope without you. You run the show, I know you do,' Leah protested, remarkably loyal for someone who had so light-heartedly filched an ex, still warm from my bed.

I suddenly felt very tired and though Leah had been a little hasty in the way she had recycled Jason, I was jolly glad she was here tonight. There was no telling how wretched I would have felt on my own. My anger melted away. Leah was a good friend. I was going through a rough patch, but she would see me through. She was always there for me.

We carried our mugs to the lounge. I slumped on the sofa. Leah leaned against the doorway, eyeing the Harrod's bag distrustfully.

I lifted my face to her and chuckled, casual-like. 'Any jobs going spare at your pub? I've still got to pay the rent for this dump.'

Leah chopped onions in a gastro pub – the gastro part, she joked gloomily – came from gastroenteritis.

She shuffled uncomfortably. 'Actually, now that you ask, mine might be, at the King's Arms. I – I mean, we – Jason and me, we've applied for jobs.'

'Applied for jobs?' What was she talking about? 'Huh? Where?'

'Ahem – on a cruise ship.' Her voice was so low, I hardly heard her when she said, 'We're leaving in three weeks' time.'

The bottom dropped out of my world.

'Christ, Leah. How long for?'

She bit her bottom lip and stared at her toes. 'Two years?'

CHLOE REACHES A CROSSROAD

"There are only two days in the year that nothing can be done about. One is called Yesterday and the other is called Tomorrow."

I leaned against the worktop, sipping my lukewarm tea and stared at the fridge magnet, pondering about the wisdom of the Dalai Lama.

He was usually right about most things. Yesterday *was* best forgotten. It had been rubbish. Tomorrow however I *could* do something about.

I stood at a crossroad, orphaned, friendless, my job hanging in the balance, but I did have choices.

Option One was to keep to the road-well-travelled, work for temperamental chefs in average restaurants and save every penny, until I'd gathered enough funds to start my own catering business. Working for Carmela at Posh-Nosh was full on, but the autonomy it afforded was rare. Running my own business was my dream.

A lump formed in my throat at the realisation that I was about to lose that job. I had hoped to keep it for another couple of years, or at least until Cosmo had found an apprenticeship to help me up the ladder. I was after a job in a real restaurant, one with Michelin stars.

Option Two pointed to Warrnambool Beach, to Oz, down the yellow brick road. Joining my parents in Australia would solve everything. My mother was Australian by birth. It gave me dual nationality, which meant no hoops to jump through, no need for sponsors, no point system. The door to Oz stood wide open.

Mum and Dad had moved to Melbourne four years ago. It had been all rather sudden. Hardly had Amatxi passed away and Pop been shoehorned into his sheltered accommodation, that mid-life crisis struck both my parents like a second adolescence. My father, Matteo, a bland civil servant, grew what was left of his hair into a ponytail and took up diving. He practiced in the local pool, gained all his certificates and morphed into Merman. Only weeks after retrieving his first shopping trolley from the local Blue Lagoon, he declared himself fit for the Great Barrier Reef.

My mother gave up her job as a school assistant, spent her savings on a sequined frock and a new pair of breasts and became Jayne Morton, the karaoke queen. (Reluctant to inflict the unpronounceable Etchegaray on her Australian relatives, Mum had kept her maiden name.) The two of them flew to Melbourne to live out their middle years on Warrnambool Beach, leaving Pop and me to look after each other.

I didn't mind beach life. It had a certain appeal, especially on a grey day such as this, but I'd somehow pictured myself in Cannes, not Cairns. The nutritional qualities of barbecued kangaroo were undisputed, but my career, as it were, was at stake.

I had some unfinished business with France and Option Three, the one pointing to that culinary nirvana, definitely offered the most promising alternative.

Dining out with Cosmo down in the Basque Country had given me a tantalising glimpse of what I could aim for. I dreamt of being immortalised for delights such as *'Côtelettes Chloe,'* remembered for my divine raspberry *'Chloe coulis,'* my name etched in glossaries amidst crêpes Suzette, Melba toast and Jesus sausages.

Yes, as long as Pop was still inside that Banania tin, his ashes waiting to be cast over Lake Irrabia, France would always beckon.

After all, was *'Hitza hitz'* 'a promise is a promise' not our family motto? I could not let Pop down.

I emptied my cold tea into the sink and yawned. Galled by Leah's treachery, aching with grief and nostalgia, I double-locked the front door, turned off the lights and trudged up to the bedroom. The rank odour of sex and messed up sheets sent me back to the lounge, where shivering, I turned on the gas fire and shook out Amatxi's knitted blanket. Something fell with a clang.

Pop's walking stick.

'Back in *Euskal Herria,* every man has a stick,' Pop would boast. Carved out of medlar, the handle hid a dangerous stiletto, the purpose of which certainly was not to dislodge stones from horses' hooves. It was a real weapon.

I wrapped myself in the blanket, turned on a side lamp and studied the stick. The round black horn handle felt comfortable. I ran a finger over the motto engraved on a wide silver ring. *'Hitzemana zor.'* It was a more powerful way of saying *Hitza hitz*. 'A promise is an obligation.'

I scrunched up my face and repeated the phrase like a counter spell, as Pop had taught me to pronounce it, the z a soft hiss. *'Hizemana zor... Hizemana zor...'*

With its susurrations, unusual vowel combinations and rolling Rs, Basque could have been Elvish. I regretted blocking my ears when Amatxi had tried to teach me, desperate as I was to conform with my school friends, Donatella Baldassare and Jamila Patel. Poor Amatxi, it had made her so sad.

French however, I'd always found easy. Hearing my dad, Matteo, speaking to his parents had dug grooves into my brain and had picked up quite a bit of colloquial French on the Biarritz beaches.

I clutched the makila stick, glanced over at the old suitcase on the other side of the room and closed my eyes.

I conjured up a young Lazarro about to leave for exile, wondering for the millionth time what had made him leave his village. No, that was not quite right, tales of his elopement with Amatxi – Paloma Loyola as she was then called – were legendary. But why did he never go back?

I imagined him as a young man, a little younger than I was now, preparing to leave home, stealthily packing a suitcase.

Lazarro glances up at the crucifix on the whitewashed wall of his bedroom and fervently crosses himself. In my mind's eye, he clicks the catches of the case, grabs his makila stick, hesitates and pulls out the sharp stiletto. His eyes narrow, he runs a finger over the blade and pushes it back into its sheath with a defeated sigh. The weapon might be deadly in close combat, but it won't save him from the dark forces at work against him. Exile is the only way out. He reaches under his mattress and pulls out a bundle of large Franc notes, the sum total of his savings. If things had turned out differently, he would have stayed at home, Paloma by his side. He has no choice. The clock is ticking. He rolls up the notes, pushes them into a yellow Banania tin together with his identity card, throws the tin into a canvass rucksack, slings it over a shoulder and grabs the cardboard suitcase.

He is outside now. A sliver of moonlight bounces over the cobbles leading to the main square. The soft rope soles of his espadrilles make no sound. Lazarro's heart tightens by the *fronton,* rising pallid in the moonlight. Tomorrow, the *pelote* match will take place without him. He is the star player. Herriberri will lose. His right hand clenches inside the curled rattan of an imagined *chistera.* He doesn't belong here anymore. He might never play *pelote* again.

A dog barks. He must hurry. He can just see the roof of the Loyola's house. No mud hut as the word *lohi-ola* would suggest, but a substantial farm. The Loyolas are rich. Paloma's farm is one of the largest in Herriberri. If everything had gone according to plan, they could have had a good life. If only –

Lazarro veers towards the church. Paloma said she would wait for him in the churchyard. If they are caught, they don't know whose wrath will be worse, her father's, his brother's or –

I opened my eyes. Who was the enemy? Was he or she still there, lurking in wait? Whenever Pop hinted at the story, after he'd had a few, Amatxi always hushed him with a glance. What on earth could Pop have done, so unforgivable that it reached out beyond the grave, threatened my own life and had ruined Cosmo's?

It just didn't make sense. Pop was a kind man, a nature lover. A man who rose at dawn to watch kingfishers along the Grand Union Canal, a man who tracked badgers in the Woburn woods, a gentle soul.

I closed my eyes again.

. . .

I'm ten. I'm crying. Donatella has moved back to Naples. Mum tells me to stop whinging, I'll get over it, but Pop understands about losing friends. He says he will show me something very special.

It is dusk now and we are alone in the woods. I am sitting near him on a fallen tree trunk. My plaits hang at the front of my anorak. Pop's canvass jacket smells of tobacco and earth. His makila stick rests across our laps. The trunk is hard. A knot of wood digs into my thigh. I shuffle to find a more comfortable position and raise my eyes to him.

'What's written here, Pop?' I run a finger over the silver ring. '*Hitz-ema-na-zor.* What does it mean?'

Pop repeats the phrase. 'It means that once you have promised something –' His gaze darkens, his voice is hard as flint, '– it is binding.' Under the bushy brow, his old eyes stare out into the darkening forest. 'A promise is an obligation.'

'It's bad to break a promise. I know that.' Donatella had sworn she'd never leave Bletchley. 'But what if someone can't keep it, you know, what if –'

'Shh. Watch. Here he comes.' Pop points thirty feet away to a large gap in the soft clay twice the size of a rabbit hole. 'Look.'

The snout of a badger emerges from the sett. Plump and wet, it sniffs the evening air.

I huddle up to Pop. The rough canvas of his jacket grazes my cheek.

The badger crawls out, heads for a depression in the earth and squats over it. I repress a giggle.

Moments later, a smaller badger crawls out of another hole. The power emanating from the animals is astonishing. They are so much bigger than I had imagined. Pop puts an arm around me and whispers that the two badgers are about to go for their nightly forage.

The smaller one heads away, nose to the ground. Without warning, the large badger charges and knocks the young one over. I muffle a cry. Claws out, the two animals lock together and roll, soft fawn underbellies exposed, teeth bared. This is no play fighting.

I raise imploring eyes to Pop, who responds with a sad shrug. There is nothing we can do. The fight intensifies with bites, barks and snarls. Blood trickles from the mouth of the young badger. He stands his ground for as long as he can, then abruptly turns and scurries away across the field, head lowered in defeat.

The sigh Pop exhales is so long, so sad, that I reach for his hand and look up, startled to see his eyes glisten in the dim light.

'Remember what you've just seen, Chacha. Young one's just been banished from his home.' Pop falls silent. A deep shiver runs through him. He pronounces in a sepulchral voice, 'he will never be able to go back now. He knows that if he does, he will be killed.'

Night has fallen over the woods. We can hardly see the path. Pop pushes himself up with his makila stick.

'Come on.' He brushes leaves from his cord trousers. 'Let's go home.'

'Why did the big one chase him away, Pop?' My fluty voice pierces the thick silence.

'Because Big Brother over there –' He straightens his legs with a grimace, '– wants the place for himself.' He spits. 'Same story the world over.'

I slip my hand inside his rough fingers. We walk back to the car.

. . .

I pulled Amatxi's blanket over me and huddled on the sofa, thinking back to what he had really told me that day.

Outside, the wind rose, driving the rain against the window of my little terraced house. Water was gushing from a broken gutter my landlord was too lazy to fix.

I had just enough energy left to turn off the gas fire and crawl back to the sofa where I fell asleep clutching Pop's makila stick to my heart.

CHLOE DISCOVERS MORE THAN SHE BARGAINED FOR

The next morning, I was standing by the kitchen counter crunching my way through a bowl of cornflakes when the phone rang. I checked the caller ID and was tempted to let it ring, but what was the point? Reality would soon catch up with me. I steeled myself, picked up the phone and blurted out a jolly, 'Hiya Carmela! How's things?'

'You're back,' Carmela said uselessly.

I kept up the jolliness. 'Yep, full of beans, raring to go.'

In the glass of the windowpane, my reflection winced back at me.

'Ahem…' Carmela's hesitation prepared me for the worst, or so I thought. 'Listen, I'm afraid it's not good news.'

I focused on a blue tit pecking at a feeder fixed to the wall across my tiny yard, and managed an upbeat, 'What do you mean?'

'I've been summoned by Lady Molyneux.' Carmela pronounced it Molinoo. 'Remember how we were hired to do all the catering for the engagement of her friend's daughter, Harriet Fart-a-Plenty, down in Berkshire?'

Of course, I did. The fiancée from hell. It had taken three

weeks, but we finally had agreed on a menu. Carmela had already hired extra help.

'It's all off now.' Her voice wavered. 'I don't know what I'm going to do. Bloody woman knows everyone.'

Not only had I lost my job, but because of me, Carmela's business was going to collapse. I felt awful.

'I don't blame you, Chloe. I want you to know that. I know it wasn't your fault her oaf of a son went mountain climbing.' She sniffed loudly into the phone.

'We didn't go climbing, Carmela. We were in a forest. Cosmo stood under a beech in a thunder storm.'

'W– what do you mean? The papers –'

'The papers repeated what Portia told them. Now that her brother has turned into a vegetable, Portia wants to give the impression he was daring and intrepid.' *And not wasting his time with a kitchen scullion.* 'We were in a forest, Carmela.'

I began to explain, but distracted – probably rummaging for the tissues she always kept tucked inside her capacious bra – my boss wasn't listening.

'I don't understand,' she blubbered. 'If Cosmo was on a beach, how he could have fallen on his head?'

I lifted my eyes to the heavens. 'He wasn't *on a beach*. He was sheltering *under a beech tree* when lightning struck. Oh, what does it matter anyway, Carmela, I'm so sorry. I really am.'

'It's all right, pet.' Her voice softened. 'I'd had enough anyway. I was permanently knackered.' She blew her nose. I held the phone away from my ear. 'Know what?' She sniffed. 'I'm gonna set a up a little tea-room somewhere. Moly's been really good about it. Gave me a little nest egg to get me started.'

'Moly?'

'Eustace, you know–'

'Eustace?' Carmela was a widow. Who the hell was Eustace?

'Eustace Molinoo and me, we had a – thing.'

I uttered a strangled squawk. My hand flew to my mouth. The sudden movement frightened the bird away from the feeder.

On the wrong side of forty, top-heavy Carmela was well past her sell by date. As for Old Molyneux… good grief, he was at least sixty-five if not seventy! Could people that old still have sex? I gagged. It was too gross to think about.

'He didn't leave me short,' Carmela said. 'I'll pay you the few hours I owe you, but apart from that funeral tea we've got booked at Simpson Village Hall, I'm afraid work's dried up.'

'Thanks Carmela,' I mumbled, desperate to end the conversation. I shook my head in an attempt to dispel images of Carmela's breasts ballooning over Molyneux's baldpate. Where on earth did they 'do it?' She lived with her sister. In the stables on horse rugs thrown over bales of hay? At their age? Surely not.

'I'll miss that love nest we had, Moly and me,' Carmela confided with a ragged sigh. 'The dowager cottage' he called it. It was lovely.'

The regret contained in that sigh filled me with guilt. Poor Carmela. She had, for an all too brief moment, believed that for her too, life could be easy. Beaten for years by a husband who had drunk all her savings, she deserved a little happiness and now, I'd gone and spoiled it all.

'How is Cosmo? Have you heard?' I was still hoping for a miracle.

'He's settled down. Back in his old nursery, quite content apparently. Plays Jenga with the Swedish au pair. Moly says he hopes the boy'll be well enough to play croquet in the spring.'

I apologised again, hung up and had another cry. Later, I returned to the lounge, extracted the Banania tin from my holdall and looked L'ami Ya'bon in the eye.

'Okay, my friend, this is the plan. As soon as I have earned enough money for the fare, we're going back to France, you, me and Pop.'

L'ami Ya'bon gave me a toothy smile. Bless him, he was so easily pleased.

I rustled around for something to nibble on, but my biscuit tin was empty. Leah and Jason had eaten the lot, in bed probably, feeding each other my Hobnobs during foreplay. I forced myself to go upstairs, changed the sheets, stuffed them into the washing machine and called Mrs Hart, my French teacher.

'Chloe, how nice to hear from you! I did think of you last week. You were in France weren't you? Did you carry out your promise to your grandfather? It must have been quite moving.'

Mrs Hart didn't read The Express, so much was obvious.

'Well, no. I didn't and that's why I am calling you. The lake was fenced off and, well, I couldn't get in. I still have the ashes here.' I paused. 'I'm calling you because I have found some documents written in French and in Basque, and I can't make them out.' Aware that I was rambling, I stopped.

'I'd be glad to help.' There was a smile in Mrs Hart's voice. 'Though it will have to be soon. I'm off to Strasbourg at the end of the week.'

'Thank you.'

'Why don't you come over for coffee tomorrow morning? I live in Fenny, by the canal. I'll e-mail you the details.'

I collapsed on the sofa overcome with gratitude. I wasn't alone. I still had a friend.

CHLOE'S WINGS ARE CLIPPED

The décor of Mrs Hart's flat was an organic blend of distressed paint effects, old books, pebbles and dried flowers. Something caught my eye by the canal running below. The place looked familiar somehow.

I went to the balcony and pointed to the opposite bank. 'That used to be my grandad's favourite fishing spot.' I couldn't believe my eyes. 'Seeing it from up here is so strange.'

'This is a brand-new building.'

Ageless, white hair cut in a long bob, Mrs Hart, or Wendy as she insisted I call her, was wholesome. Yes, wholesome was the best way to describe her. A smile always seemed to ripple under her skin.

'This place is convenient for Luton airport.' She pointed to a photo. 'Antoine lives in Strasbourg. We met fifty years ago during a language exchange. He's a physio.' She blushed a little. 'Antoine is widowed now.'

I glanced at the photo. A flowery shirt, a halo of white hair and a white beard gave the 'boyfriend' an air of Santa on holiday. I shuddered at the thought of what kind of massage the two of them got up to in Strasbourg. *Good grief,* I thought, somewhere between horrified and reassured, *Molyneux and Carmela in the dowager cottage and now my old teacher is doing it with Santa. I'm only twenty-three and I worry that I'm on the shelf.*

Unaware of the direction my thoughts had taken, my French teacher embarked on the subject of Europe. 'My grandfather studied in Strasbourg as a young man. He loved that city. Tragically, when he enlisted in the RAF, he was sent to bomb it. The Americans also did a lot of damage.'

'Oh, the poor man! Did he – did he ever talk about it?'

'Never. My father told me just before he died.'

'Why did they do that, keep secrets? As it turns out, my grandad kept secrets too.' I pulled a large envelope out of my bag. 'These need deciphering and I was hoping you could help me.' The table was full of cups and coffee things, so I placed the envelope on a wooden chair straight out of Goldilocks.

'Cute chair,' I said to quash the anguish gnawing at my insides. If there was anything Pop had wanted me to know, he would have told me, wouldn't he? Or did he think he had more time?

'It's an Alsatian chair. Odile – that is my penfriend – gave it to me when we were emptying her parents' house.' Wendy sighed. 'What a heart-rending task that was.'

'My Pop didn't leave much. Only his walking stick and the Banania cacao tin he's in now.'

'Why don't you tell me everything while we're having coffee?' Wendy pointed to the tray she had prepared with a thermos coffeepot, mugs, biscuits and a bowl of tiny pretzels.

'Crumbs, I'm not sure where to begin.'

I took a seat on the linen sofa and laced my fingers around my knees. 'As you know, our name is Etchegaray, a bit of a mouthful here but common in the Basque Country.

Etxe – you say it etchy – means house. Etxe-garay means high house, which isn't surprising really, considering it's all mountains over there.'

'How fascinating. I knew it was a common name, but I had no idea it meant anything.'

'My grandparents came from Jaioleku, a village high up in the centre of the Pyrenees. They eloped together in the sixties and never went back. Well, Amatxi did go back to Bayonne, but she never went home. My grandad never returned to France. Ever.'

Wendy listened intently. 'Sorry, who's Amatxi?'

'That's my grandma. Pop should have been Aitaxi, but he said it sounded too much like a sneeze.'

'I see. How strange that he never returned.' Wendy asked in a soft voice, 'any idea why?'

I shook my head.

'Southern people can be volatile. They fight, but they make up. Life-long feuds are rare. The first baby usually brings people together in my experience. Yes, this is most unusual.'

'I asked my dad once, but he said it was best left alone. He said he didn't want to end up with a horse's head in his bed.'

'The Sicilian vendetta scenario? How intriguing.' Wendy poured our coffees. 'Tell me, have you heard of ETA, the Basque separatist movement? They were quite active in the sixties, quite violent. Could it be that, even for the best of reasons, your grandfather was caught up in the unrest that shook the Basque Country at the time?'

I gave her a dark look. 'Pop wasn't a terrorist if that's what you're hinting at.'

Wendy persisted. 'Sometimes, one has to take sides.'

I knew whose side I was on and I didn't like where this conversation was going. ETA were involved in bombings. Pop wouldn't have harmed a fly. 'I know my grandparents felt strongly about their culture. They were sorry they weren't allowed to speak Basque at school, but that's as far as it went.'

'Yes, that happened throughout France. Teachers were incredibly inventive with their punishments, made children stand on chairs, wear a clog around their neck whenever they caught them speaking dialect, horrid really.'

'When they were caught speaking Basque, Amatxi and Pop were handed a token of disgrace. At the end of the week, the only way to avoid being beaten or having to write lines...'

'Was to denounce someone else. I heard of that in Alsace.' Wendy shivered. 'What a horrendous system, teaching children to tell on each other.'

'Pop never did, you know. He never denounced his mates.' I narrowed my eyes. 'Why did the teachers do that?'

'At the beginning of the nineteenth century,' Wendy switched on her teacher's voice, 'there were over three hundred dialects in France.' She opened her hands. 'The new republic wanted to unite the country, so they jumbled teachers around and imposed a single language.'

I picked up my mug and took a sip, my eyes still on her.

'In Spain,' Wendy explained, 'the repression in the Basque Country was pitiless. It started in thirty-six, during the Civil War. Franco's fascist dictatorship went on for forty years, so you can imagine, informers, torturers... The Basque language and culture were completely banned. Dissidents were imprisoned and tortured. Thousands of new born babies were stolen from troublesome couples.

'Babies *stolen*?' I nearly spat out my coffee.

'Oh yes, but that was only in Spain. Doctors and Catholic priests were in cahoots with the government. Mothers, if they were Communist, were told their child had died. The child was handed over to 'good' Catholic families.'

I lowered my mug and stared at her, my mouth open.

'But that didn't happen in France, right?'

'No, it was worse in Spain. Remember though, French or Spanish, the Basques see themselves as one people.'

I picked a pretzel and snapped it in two. 'You can't seriously think Pop was involved in all that?'

'It must have been hard to avoid. He was young, idealistic perhaps. He might have been naïve, conned into gun-running, relaying messages, found himself harbouring fugitives from Spain, even with the best of motives.'

'Nah.' I shook my head. 'Pop was a carpenter. Amatxi was a cook in a school. They didn't care about politics. They were normal decent people.'

Wendy smiled and handed me the biscuits. 'Of course, they were. I met them remember? I had a conversation with your grandfather about storks migrating from Alsace to Morocco.' She chuckled. 'He assured me that the Basques didn't shoot storks as they flew over the Pyrenees, even if they shoot everything else that comes their way.'

'Tell me about it,' I muttered. 'I was nearly mistaken for a dove.'

She laughed as I recounted my attempts at whistling to warn away the hunters.

Down on the canal, a barge chugged along.

'This flat is great for gongoozling,' Wendy said brightly. 'I can watch barges chug past for hours.'

'Gone-goo what?'

'Gongoozling: watching canal life without being part of it.'

'Good word, gongoozling– I can relate to that.'

'Yes,' Wendy said wistfully. 'Watching life pass one by.'

We gongoozled for a while, Pop's envelope ominous on the three-legged chair. I had looked inside but couldn't make much of it.

A heron lazily flapped past the balcony and landed at the edge of the towpath.

Down by the canal, a dog spotted the bird and ran towards it. The heron flapped disdainfully to the opposite bank. The dog barked.

'How much Basque do you know, Chloe?'

'Not much. I know Hegoak, of course.'

'Hegoak?'

'It's our freedom song. It draws a parallel between a bird and freedom.

I blushed, cleared my throat and sang to the heron. After a few ooh ooohs and lalalas, I tapped a foot and sang a rhythmic, *'Hegoak ebaki banizkio – Neuria izango zen – Ez zuen aldegingo –*

'Gosh Chloe, that was lovely.' Wendy clapped after the very last oohoo. 'It sounded so authentic.'

'My dad was a fan of Bayonne Rugby Club.' I gave a little shrug. 'They sing it during matches.' A strange nostalgia came over me. 'There was another song that made Pop and Amatxi cry.' I put down my cup and cleared my throat. 'It's about a man leaving his home to go to work in Paris because his elder brother's getting married.'

'Ah yes, eldest boy inherits the farm. This is why there are so many Basques abroad.' Wendy tilted her head. 'It must be a very old song. What is it called?'

'Oi Ama Euskal Herri. I pronounced it *'e-ush-kal,'* the way it was supposed to be. 'It means Basque Country, *'ama'* is mother.' I took in a wobbly breath. 'The bit that got to Pop was when it goes–' My lower lip quivered. 'When the chap in the song asks his mother to prepare–' My eyes misted up. 'To prepare a final resting place for him, for when– he –he returns, you know – in his coffin.' I raised damp eyes to her and said in a ragged whisper, 'That's why I have to take him

back, you see. Going home meant everything to Pop. Everything.'

The lament was so melancholy, so heart rending, that I could never have sung it without sobbing. It conjured up rugged exiles staring into their Parisian Pernod, their American whiskey or Chilean Pisco, tears rolling down stubbly cheeks, homesickness gnawing at their hearts and ripping their souls apart.

Wendy took away the tray and placed my envelope on the coffee table. 'Let's see what we have in here.'

She shook out the thin contents. A letter, issued by Jean-Baptiste Gorrotxategi, *notaire* in Bayonne had puzzled me the most. I handed it to her.

While she studied it, I spread out the rest of my meagre find: three postcards simply addressed to Pop as 'Lazarro Etchegaray, Jaioleku - Pyrénées Atlantiques - FRANCIA' and signed Fernand.

I deciphered 1960 on a faded postmark, but that was all. The postcards were written in Basque.

Wendy went to fetch her glasses and picked up a postcard. 'Interesting. It was posted in Chile.'

'Really?'

'Santiago. That's the capital of Chile.'

Chile? Pop had never mentioned Chile. 'How about the letter?' It was in French but I'd not been able to make sense of the legalese.

She pursed her lips. 'This acknowledges a previous correspondence and offers to take on some legal dispute.' She looked up. 'Is it the only letter in your possession?'

I nodded.

'These legal disputes are usually about property. They can go on for years. Perhaps your grandfather could not afford the cost and dropped it.'

A dispute about property? Now that was intriguing. I wondered where it was, that property.

The hoard also contained a faded photograph of a young man in front of a hotel that bore the strange name of Hartzainostatua.

After a frustrating struggle, the best approximation that Google Translate had come up with was *'bear staying.'* Good grief, what kind of name was that for a hotel, *Bear Staying?*

'You're planning to return to France to scatter your grandfather's ashes, is that right?'

'Yes.'

'Will you visit the lawyer who wrote this? He will know what the dispute was about and you will find out where this hotel is. Don't despair.'

'Hmm. Once I've got the money together.' I lowered my head and mumbled, 'I've just lost my job.'

Wendy placed a cool hand on my arm. 'You're going through a rough patch, dear, and I'm sorry for you, but I know how hard you work and how talented you are. You'll get there, of that I have no doubt. You will go back to France.'

I wished I could share her confidence.

TEN MONTHS LATER

I did go back to France. It took me ten months. Ten months of penance at the King's Arms, reduced to kitchen scullion, chopping onions and crying over the mess that was my life, Pop's death, Cosmo's accident, my poisoning, the loss of my job, Leah's betrayal and Mum and Dad's desertion. Yes, there was a lot to cry about.

The crying over, I was back in Euskal Herria, back with a vengeance and back with a plan. After the debacle caused by my photo on the front page of Sud-Ouest, I took no chances. No one would recognise me now. Gone was the-girl-next-door in tame blue jacket and neat bob. Chloe Etchegaray had undergone what the French call *'un relooking'* and morphed into Chloe Moreton, an Aussie backpacker with frizzy hennaed hair, round glasses and hoop earrings.

The new Chloe swore like a trooper, slapped her thighs, knocked back pints of lager and went around in grey AC/DC T-shirt, shorts and walking boots. I'd even sewn a kangaroo badge on the small backpack I carried at all times, just big enough to hold Pop's Banania tin. This week however, Pop and L'ami Ya'bon would be spending the Bayonne festival locked in the hostel safe. As I said, I took no chances.

I had chosen Bayonne as a base because it was familiar. I had spent a few summer holidays there with my parents and Amatxi when I was little. Close to the Spanish border, inland from the Atlantic Ocean, the town straddled two rivers called la Nive and l'Adour. Neither too big nor too small, colonnades, tall white houses and blood-red shutters gave the place a solid feel.

I arrived during the feria. Safety in numbers, I thought. Strewth, how wrong was I. A girl on her own – probably the only person not wearing top to toe white – sent out the wrong message to the drunken revellers, and there were plenty of them about. Throbbing with booze and testosterone, the feria was a free for all. *'Jingoes,'* I grumbled to my Australian self, *'the next yobbo who pinches my butt gets my backpack in his mug.'*

Tonight in Bayonne, night was falling. There was an air of expectancy. Heaving, Place de la Liberté was white with crowds. Crammed like sardines around the Town Hall, the white-clad mob held up red scarves, which undulated like poppies in the breeze.

'Baiona, Baiona!' shouted the good people of Bayonne, clamouring, 'Oh Léon, Oh Léon' for their carnival king to open the fair. I joined in, until at last, on the brightly lit town hall balcony, the stage curtains opened. A nine-foot-tall cardboard effigy was rolled out and gave a stiff wave. That stiff little wave shot straight to the hearts of the populace.

A clump of balloons floated into the night, up up and away, over the port, towards the ocean where it would choke some unsuspecting whale swimming around the Bay of Biscay.

Was I envious? Of course, I was. Half-Basque, half-Australian, all I could do was sing Hegoak, while they could play *pelote,* jump over bullocks, dance mutchikos (sorry, mutxikoak, it's a plural) bask in their Basqueness and crawl home five days later, convinced that their country was the best place in the world for the simple reason that they were born in it. Heck, I'd never felt that way about Bletchley.

Next to Léon, a local celebrity stepped onto the balcony, bringing the screaming to fever pitch. He allowed his ego a few moments of adulation and finally hurled two giant red and green polystyrene keys into the crowd. It was the signal for the Feria to begin. Bliss erupted on the square, fireworks lit up the port and in one synchronised movement, the white-clad locals tied their neckerchiefs around their necks and went off to dance.

I trudged back to the hostel where, earplugs pushed in deep to blot out the drunken ruckus, I slept. I was not part of it. I didn't belong.

The next day, feeling a little better, I decided to check out the location of the lawyer's office, but instead, the crowds carried me to Place Paul Bert, which was fenced off for the famous 'Cow Games.'

The sun was beating down on Bayonne. Forgetting the lawyer, who wouldn't be working on a Sunday anyway, I lowered my bush-hat over my eyes, elbowed a space for myself in the shade downwind from a *churros* stand, and waited, my nose twitching. A hundred calories apiece the *churros* or *chichis* are irresistible. I gave in, bought a paper cone of the fried pastries and watched young men desultorily trawling the sand-filled arena, squirting wine from leather gourds into their mouths, dreaming of becoming heroes.

'Lâcher de vachettes,' said my programme. 'Launch of heifers' sounded safe enough. I imagined dainty cows stepping out like debutantes in Chelsea for a last taste of fun before settling down to the serious business of reproduction.

Debutantes brought Portia to mind, or was it the cows?

After a tumultuous affair with Graf Von-Vollstreckung-zu-Wurtenberg, Portia had reached the end of the alphabet and the end of her options. The Windsors sadly out of reach, she had finally said yes to a Cartier diamond ring presented to her by Viscount Walter Wutherswaithe of Zinfandel. Not exactly handsome the viscount, but the size of his bank account matched that of his nose. I was glad of this arrangement. It would keep Cosmo in jellybeans and Swedish au pairs for the rest of his days. It also meant that, busy with the wedding arrangements, the Molyneux women would forget about me.

The frazzled crowd was growing restless. One foot on the metal barrier, incognito under my Akubra hat, I discovered that the challenge was to detach a rosette from the animal's brow. Simple enough. Nothing too barbaric.

To the left of the arena, oblivious to the impending release of a cow, a group passed the time constructing a human pyramid. I knew that these pyramids were a national sport, but in a bullring? Meanwhile, in the centre, a group was calmly playing cards around a table. I pulled the programme from my pocket. Was I in the right place?

I focused on the card players. The one sitting at the end of the table looked familiar somehow. I removed my sunglasses and studied him. He wore the regulation whites, a red belt and neckerchief but there was something else about the man. Had I seen him before? Bah, I told myself as I licked the icing sugar from my fingers, I'd had too much sun. My mind was playing tricks.

At the top of the pyramid, a youngster was just steadying himself on the shoulders of his comrades when a black heifer galloped in at full speed, slid on its haunches and sat down in surprise inches away from them. The crowds roared.

Were these people for real? I pushed my hat back and watched the scene wide-eyed. Had they never heard of health and safety? I checked the gate, expecting panicked officials to rush and interfere, blow a whistle, wave their arms and stop the cow before it was too late. No. Not here, obviously. Released from modern day jobs with computers and machines, deprived of natural challenges, frustrated young Basque men occasionally needed to get in touch with their wild side.

The cow charged into the pile, sent everyone flying and backed out of the wreckage, surprised at finding a metal chair around its neck. It lowered its head, shook off the chair and found itself plagued by swarms of 'tumblers,' lithe young men somersaulting over its back, flipping and cartwheeling as if nothing had changed since ancient Greece. The animal snorted, spun and tried to skewer them one by one as they landed.

'Ah, this is a playful cow,' the commentator shouted over the tannoy.

Plucked from its daisy field, bundled into a lorry, the cow had had enough, I could tell. It charged at anyone it found in its way. Around me the noise reached fever pitch. The crowd wanted blood.

Here was my man again, behind a wooden island. Where, during my brief stay could I have met that torero? Poised, he was watching the youngsters, not the cow.

A young Eritrean leaped and hung on. *'Bat... Bi... Hiru... Lay... Bost!'* the crowd counted to five. Enraged, the cow shook him off, scooped up the first lad she could find and rammed him into the fence. Once, ouch, twice.

A gasp rose above the arena, followed by silence. The *churro* stopped halfway to my mouth. Huddled in the sand, the boy curled up under the blows, the ring he'd been about to throw clutched against his stomach.

A clown jumped over the barrier and waved a pink cape

to distract the crazed animal. The cattle pen opened. Freed from its nightmare, the animal galloped away to safety.

'Attention s'il vous plait!' Someone pushed me aside. Two *ambulanciers* rushed past carrying a stretcher. Over in the sand, Mystery Man was kneeling by the victim. He wore an armband. No torero then. The paramedics set down the stretcher and took over from him.

Mystery Man stood and glanced around. I caught sight of his face. Fireworks exploded inside me. I knew where I had seen him. He was the ranger who had revived Cosmo after the lightning strike. At last, life opened up. Hope filled my chest. If I could only make contact, I could ask him how to get to Pop's lake. Would he remember me? Shucks, here was the one person I wanted to recognise me and I was camouflaged.

Oh no, he was walking away!

The paramedics carried the victim past me. Grimacing with pain, the boy dropped the ring.

Moved by a wild impulse, I picked up the ring, handed my *churros* to a child who'd been eyeing them, and squeezed into the enclosure just as the barriers were pushed together. Heart pounding, fingers tight around the ring, I hovered at the edge and searched for the ranger, hoping to reach him before another beast was released.

I spotted him across the arena and took a few steps. The gates opened. A new heifer galloped in, a dun-coloured beast with a glint in its eye. I froze. It pawed at the sand, lowered its head, went straight for the first man who barred its way, spun and knocked another one sideways with a blunted horn. I came to my senses. This cow was dangerous.

The feel of the ring took me back to the times Pop and I played quoits in the garden. I was champion at it, but when we played on Pop's lawn, the spike was static, it didn't charge at me as the cow did now.

Panicked, I darted towards the central platform to the jeers of the crowd. One hand over my hat, I ran, backpack bobbing about, the animal's hot breath on my neck. The crowd screamed with laughter. From the platform, hands stretched out to me. The voice on the tannoy shouted encouragement. A dark instinct, a primal rage sprung from nowhere and forced me to face the snorting monster and hurl the ring at its horns.

Only once I'd climbed to safety, did I remember to breathe.

Bull's eye. The cheers were deafening. I stood, arms lifted in triumph. And then it hit me. Did I never learn? From every direction, phones zapped and flashed. I dived down, hunched up into a ball and tried to fathom out why on earth I hadn't stuck to the espadrille-throwing competition.

CHLOE MAKES A FRIEND

I jumped off the platform and ran towards the place where I had last seen the ranger, but he had vanished. All the air went out of me. What was going on? Had I risked my life for nothing? The bizarre card players were still sitting in the middle of the enclosure, but his chair was empty. I jumped back into the fray, elbowed my way through white clusters of dark-haired youths who all looked the same, and slumped on a grass bank in the shade of the city wall, my head in my arms, feeling very alone.

Gradually, the crowd thinned and dispersed. The last of the cattle were herded into trucks taking them back to their meadow. Smells of dust and cowpats rose from the scorching sand. A few drunken cowboys still swaggered about, squeezing jets of warm wine from their leather gourds into their tonsils. Each to their own, I thought. Back in England, after a concert, drunks traditionally smash beer bottles in underpasses. Ostentatious as those gourds may seem, at least they were ecological.

There! My heart did a somersault. Behind a plane tree, my man was picking up *churros* cones and cigarette packets and dropping them into a bin bag. I sprang up and brushed the dried grass from my jeans, about to call out to him... but held myself in check. There was a lot at stake. I slid behind a plane tree and observed my quarry.

He wasn't tall but he looked fit. There was a lot of muscle under the white T-shirt. With those large brown eyes, his was a face you could trust.

I removed my hat and sunglasses, shoved them into my bag, strolled towards him casually and called out in French, 'Need some help?'

He looked up, ran his gaze over me, shrugged some sort of approval and held out a bin bag. We worked in silence in the blistering heat, picking up plastic bottles and candyfloss sticks.

Every so often, he would sneak glances in my direction and shake his head, computing my clothes, the kangaroo on my backpack and my accent, probably wondering why an Australian rodeo queen would want to gather rubbish with him.

'Was there a prize for throwing that ring over the cow's horns?' It was feeble I know, but it was too hot to think of any other opening line.

He straightened up. The penny finally dropped. 'I have met you before, haven't I?'

Bingo. I could cut to the chase.

'You work as a ranger at Lake Irrabia, right?'

There, that wasn't so hard. Why had I not just sidled up to him with that in the first instance, instead of risking death by ridicule?

He nodded. 'The thunderstorm.'

'You saved my friend's life. I don't think anyone has thanked you for that yet.'

'Bah.' He shrugged. 'I heard the poor fellow didn't come out of it too well. I'm sorry about that.'

'Yes, I'm sorry too. He's back in England now, with his parents.' I didn't know what else to say. If he had read the paper at the time, he wouldn't trust me. I couldn't blame him.

'Dis-moi, ce lac...' I had to find out about the lake before he vanished again.

After a moment's hesitation, he indicated the grassy bank. We sat down in the shade, our bin bags at our feet. I shook off my backpack and leaned on my elbows.

'Do you know why it's fenced off, the lake? I mean, do you have access to it?'

He tilted his head to one side and studied me, still trying to make his mind up. 'No. I patrol the forest. Why do you ask? If it's a lake you're after, there are plenty of other lakes. Saint Pée sur Nivelle for instance, is lovely to swim in.'

'Non, le Lac Irrabia. C'est très important. Il faut absolu-'

Damn, he'd already stopped listening. Something behind me had caught his eye. He stiffened up and jumped from the bank.

A buxom blonde in red and white was charging towards us, brow lowered, platform espadrilles twisting with each step.

From the angry air blowing from her nostrils, I feared I was in for a rerun of my earlier rodeo. That young heifer did not want me near her stud.

'Ah, Xavier, there you are.' She stamped. 'We've been waiting for *hours*. Everyone's wondering where you are.'

She didn't even look at me, her fury directed at her boyfriend, or was he her fiancé? I checked her ring finger. Boyfriend then. So, he was called Xavier. Nice strong Basque name.

'You were supposed to meet us *hours* ago.'

How could she do this? Maul the poor chap in front of a stranger? What a cow. Dairy too, I could tell from the milky flesh spilling over her Wonderbra.

Struck by a sudden impulse, I clutched my middle and winced in obvious pain. 'Oohh.'

She looked down at me and snorted. *'C'est qui cette nana?'* 'Who's that girl?'

Xavier answered in Basque. *'Australian da.'* I deduced from the signs he was making with his fingers, that he was telling Daisy I was either concussed or not quite right in the head.

My hand left my stomach and flew to my head.

She cast me a withering look.

Before I had time to get Xavier's details, she hooked her arm in his and dragged him towards town.

'Wait, could we –' I protested weakly. Too late. He was gone. I collapsed on the grass with a defeated sigh and closed my eyes.

A rustle of plastic jolted me. Xavier was back. He grabbed our bin bags and casting a furtive glance at the girl, whispered, 'Bar Victor Hugo tomorrow during the *corso.*' He handed the rubbish to a man shovelling cowpats, and headed for the town centre in Daisy's wake.

I addressed a prayer of thanks to my guardian angel. At last, I was getting somewhere.

The *corso*, I had read in the tourist brochure, was a traditional procession of King Léon's courtiers through the streets. Every morning, six giant figures were paraded along the quays towards the town hall to wake up the king on the stroke of twelve. They were, the brochure said, the King's Mistress, the Doctor, the Governess, the Marshall, the Jester and the Chocolate Cook. Never having had a King worth celebrating, the good people of Bayonne had made up their own.

Rue Victor Hugo was perpendicular to the quays and looked easy enough to find. All I had to do was wait.

That night, buoyant and filled with purpose, I agreed to

join my hostel mates – all dinkum Aussies – to 'knock back the grog' and join in the Feria.

Goodness, could those girls drink. I staggered out the following morning and found Bayonne heaving and the quays impassable. Pushed deep into a medieval labyrinth of narrow timber-housed streets, I lost my bearings and ended up by the old market in the middle of the World Omelette Making Championship. *'Omelette au piment d'Espelette.'* Omelette with pimentos? I'd never come across that before, but then again, Mum had not liked spicy food.

My mother, where was she when I needed her? Probably sunbathing on Warrnambool Beach, with nothing more to worry about than funnel spiders and salt water crocs.

Pressed inside the tight red-and-white human swarm, I wondered for the millionth time what I was doing here.

I woke from my trance under the cool stone arches edging the river and, just in front of me, tucked inside a classic stone building was the Bar Victor Hugo. My heart flipped. He was here. I halted, punched by a blast of hormones. Ten months of celibacy had taken their toll. I reminded myself that I wasn't here to find romance but to help my grandfather reach his final resting place with dignity.

A hand around the back of an empty chair, the other cradling a beer, Xavier was casting desultory glances at a nine-foot-tall puppet in cook's garb rolling past, waving a giant spoon dripping with chocolate.

I needed to calm down before I approached him and, under a window leaching aromas of tomato and basil, I fished out my 'Feria' programme to search out the origin of The Cook. 'Bayonne is famous for its link with chocolate.' Ah, there it was. 'Jews chased out of Spain in 1609 brought with them to Bayonne the secrets of chocolate. Mixed with pimentos, it was thought to be an aphrodisiac.' I inhaled a cleansing lungful of tomato and basil and set off again.

In an attempt to look friendly, '*sympathique,*' a touch helpless perhaps, I had swapped boots and shorts for sandals, khaki skirt, halter-top and my disguise of red glasses.

Nose in the air I casually ambled onto the terrace where Xavier sat with his friends.

Xavier looked surprised.

'*Bonjour.*' I swallowed hard.

'*Bonjour.*'

Oh dear, the way he said *bonjour*, the velvet softness of his eyes, his voice messed with my vital organs. I pulled a chair to his table and signalled to the waiter.

'*Un Perrier menthe s'il vous plait.*' I hoped mint and water would dispel last night's excesses.

In front of us, the parade was slowing down as it approached the square. Bells rang twelve times. The crowd burst into song. It was time for King Léon to wake up. '*Debout Léon...Oh Léon...*'

'We're having 'pintxos,' Xavier said. 'Would you like some, *euh–*'

'Chloe, my name's Chloe.'

'Xavier.' We shook hands. I shook hands with the other musketeers but struggled to take in their names, such was the din. One might have been called Jean-Phi, the other something like Patchy and the third one's name sounded like an unguent.

Over on the town hall balcony, King Léon was waving to his ecstatic subjects to the rousing tune of la Peña Baiona.

I remembered Cosmo ordering pintxos in Biarritz. Similar to the canapés I made up for Posh-nosh, they could be anything from mini pizzas to quails' eggs on toast… two mouthfuls to keep you going until lunch or, if you ordered enough of them, they could make up a whole meal.

'There was a *pintxo* competition last May,' piped the plumpest of Xavier's friends, whose name I'd heard as Patchy, probably spelled Patxi. 'There were some very odd combinations.'

I checked out the men. The only difference between them was height, bulk and the state of their shirts. Patxi's sported dashes of ketchup and mustard. 'You would not believe what they came up with.' His chins wobbled at the memory.

'I remember, I was there.' Xavier indicated the sliced baguettes topped with salami and cheese our waiter had brought in on a tray. 'These are so tame. Back in May, the competition carried *pintxos* to a new level.' His face lit up. 'Fried anchovies filled with paprika, prawn and bacon–' he listed dreamily, 'pork and polenta, squid wrapped in Bayonne ham.'

I sunk into my chair. Oh ... My ... God. Xavier was a foodie. His words pinged inside me like pinballs, lighting up every nerve centre.

'The gold medal winners, I got to taste them, were shaped like small logs. On a base of corn bread –' the memory still burned bright inside his eyes. '*Foie gras* with a rhubarb bavarois and a mushroom duxelle topped with a parmesan crumble and...' he opened his hands, '–the whole thing covered in dark chocolate.'

His smile said it all.

'Yuk.' His friends retched. 'It sounds disgusting.'

Patxi made a face. 'Chocolate and mushrooms, oh God, that is so wrong. And what the hell is a duxelle of rhubarb anyway?'

I chuckled. The silly boy had got his duxelles and his bavarois mixed up. I met Xavier's gaze and rolled my eyes. The glance we exchanged was the equivalent of a Mason's handshake.

For me, pintxos opened a world of possibilities, an

enchanted universe of pyrotechnic flavours and artistic compositions, tastes that might only last for two mouthfuls but lingered in the mind forever. My body tingled, flooded with creative juices. Perhaps it wasn't sex I needed most but, after months of chopping onions in the Kings Arms' kitchen, stimulation of the gastronomic kind.

I reached out for a slice of baguette topped with tomato, goat's cheese and ham. It wasn't bad, though I wished I'd just ordered water. That mint cordial confused my taste buds.

Letting the tastes and noise of the fanfare wash over me, I mulled over how I could best direct the conversation to what really mattered: the lake.

Xavier pre-empted me. 'So, can you now explain to me why you're so keen to get to that particular lake?'

I debated how much to tell him and decided that if I couldn't trust a man who knew his duxelles, I couldn't trust anyone.

'My grandfather's dying wish was to have his ashes scattered over Lake Irrabia. I thought perhaps you'd be able to sneak me in.'

He tilted his head. Oh, those large puppy eyes. 'I'd love to but I don't hold the key.'

'Oh no!' I recoiled from the crushing blow. 'What on earth do they do in there that's so secret?'

Xavier shrugged. 'I've no idea. There might be a solution. My father goes shooting in that forest. He has contacts. I'm sure he'll be able to tell you.'

'Merci, c'est super.' My spirits lifted considerably.

The boys' conversation resumed in Basque and I watched the procession. The Cook had gone, followed by the Marshall and the peace-keeper. I selected a small roll of ham wrapped around a mild *piquillo* pepper and was just about to tuck in, when above the partition of the café terrace, I spotted Xavier's girlfriend tottering against the flow. Really, could the man have no peace?

Xavier hadn't seen her yet. I thought I'd better leave before she noticed me.

She was still fifty yards away. My eyes popped. It was clear even from where I stood that she wasn't wearing anything under those white trousers. Her dark triangle proved too much for a randy *festayre* who lunged at her crotch. She slapped him, and in one continuous move, stamped on his foot and kneed him in the groin.

I made a mental note not to upset the girl, grabbed Xavier's pen, scribbled my mobile number on his napkin and pushed it into his shirt pocket. His chest was like concrete.

My heart trying to jump out of my ribcage, I steadied myself on the back of a chair.

'What's that?' He lifted his face to me.

'Mon numéro de portable.'

I slung my backpack over a shoulder, dived into the procession and, safe in the shadow of the Marshall, let the crowd carry me to the Town Hall, secure in its embrace.

CHLOE AT THE LAWYER'S

While Bayonne was recovering from its festivities, I put my plan into action. I had so little to go on, the strategy was simple.

Firstly, gain access to Pop's lake and scatter his ashes. I didn't for a moment imagine he'd be too happy to spend eternity inside chain link fencing, but it wasn't up to me. *Hitza hitz*, a promise is a promise and if his ghost took to haunting the Iraty forest, chain link wouldn't hold him in. The fence was buried deep, I couldn't crawl under it, and since I didn't know what was kept in there, wire cutters were out of the question. I'd just read that American scientists had 'edited fourteen woolly mammoth genes into a living elephant cell.' I wasn't too sure what 'editing genes' entailed, but just in case a genetically modified mammoth was kept in the lake enclosure, I would take no chances. My only course of action was to find out who owned the lake and ask for permission to enter. I had delegated this part of the plan to Xavier, confident that his father would provide an answer in a matter of days.

The second part of the plan was more delicate. I was

determined to discover what Pop had done to earn him a lifetime in exile. It had become an obsession with me since the toadstool incident. Someone had threatened my life and I would have no peace until I'd found out who and why.

While he was alive, I'd never given Pop's past much thought. We went about our daily business, met at the pub, looked forward to little things like watering his petunias, picking asparagus or playing cards. Only now did I notice that some things in Pop's life didn't add up – the fact that he never came to France with us for a start – and I'd always believed him when he said he had to stay behind to tend his vegetable garden. To my young mind, the tale of their elopement was enough to give Pop and Amatxi's lives a frisson of mystery. They had eloped, they said, because Amatxi was to be married to a rich farmer whose land her father had designs on.

After my first trip to the Basque Country, I had called Mum and Dad and asked them what they knew. They had told me to let sleeping dogs lie and scatter Pop's ashes over the nearest pond. He'd never know the difference.

Since they were not willing to help, I had made an appointment with the lawyer whose details I had found in the letter, whose name was pronounced, so his secretary told me, *goro -tchat- eggy*. It was a shot in the dark, and an expensive one at that. The thirty-minutes I had booked of Maître Gorrotxategi's time was going to cost me the equivalent of a week's wages at the King's Head.

For the occasion, I had purchased a suit from the Galeries Lafayette, with a view to wearing it carefully and returning it to the shop straight after the meeting.

I teetered on borrowed heels to the large half-timbered block where the lawyer's office was situated, right in the heart of town.

I loved the *Petit Bayonne* medieval district, its shady

arches, and the way the town had spiced up its provincial steadfastness with chilli-red shutters.

Next to an imposing red door, a ridiculously long brass plaque announced 'Maître Gorrotxategi & Fils,' father and son legal team. Muggle that I was, I had pictured a kindly gentleman smiling at me over half-moon glasses as he explained the pitfalls of Napoleonic law and, when time came to pay, would tut and shake his wise head. I'd obviously read too many Harry Potter books.

Brisk, sinewy and all of forty years old, Maître Gorrotxategi strode out of his office, a hand extended in greeting.

'*Monsieur.*' I supressed a curtsy and turned on my best smile.

'*Maître.*' He corrected, crushing both my fingers and my self-confidence. I followed him into a large book-lined office, perched on the edge of a metal chair and held out the letter I had found in Pop's case.

He patted the copy I had forwarded to him and read it again. I bit my lip and waited like a naughty schoolgirl in the headmaster's office, scanning the shelves that groaned under the weight of all the lawsuits the *Maître* had to cram into his brain to follow in his father's footsteps. It can't have been easy. Bursting with legalese, his forehead rose like Bart Simpson's and bulged over the rimless glasses. It was obvious that he would not part with one iota of information without a fee.

We had not exchanged a single word and already, ten Euros worth of time had gone by. My body heat rose. The suit clung to my chest and in the back of my neck the label itched. A clock callously ticked my savings away. A strand of hair fell across my face. I pushed it behind my ear.

At last, the *notaire* cleared his throat, drew an inhalation worth at least three Euros and said, 'in this letter, Maître Gorrotxategi, my father, the lawyer in charge of the case at the time... let me check the date. Yes, nineteen seventy-two.'

That's right, use five words when one would suffice, why don't you? I'm made of money. I wanted to shake him.

'The letter simply states that he cannot take the query further without your grandfather's instructions. I am sorry, but it is impossible to tell from this what the query was about.'

Really? Was that all he had to say? I stretched my lips into a smile and remonstrated in approximate French.

'*Maître,* I realise this letter tells us very little, but I was hoping that my family's files would clarify the origin of the dispute.'

I hoped the files were not in some labyrinthine underground basement. To my relief, he pulled out a faded dossier and fixed his greedy eyes on me. 'How much of your family history do you know?'

'Nothing. That's why I'm here.'

I took measured breaths and smoothed out my skirt. If I couldn't return the outfit, it would be a very expensive morning indeed.

'Your grandfather, Lazarro Etchegaray, was born in Jaioleku in 1946, right?'

Unsure, I compromised with an affirmative shrug.

'His father, Alphonse Etchegaray, had two sons, the afore mentioned Lazarro –'

My heart rate increased. I leaned forward.

'– and Fernand, the elder by five years, born in 1941. The family ran an inn. When Alphonse died in 1969, the property was left to his wife and two sons.'

The word INN lit up inside my head and flashed in letters of gold. An inn. A restaurant. My blood shot around my veins like rocket fuel.

'Do you know where it is, that inn? Does it still exist?'

'Yes. It's in Jaioleku. The name is Hartzainostatua.'

My eyes popped at this volley of Basque. I swallowed hard.

'I see. Who ran it, that inn?'

'After their father's death in 1969, the two brothers, Lazarro and Fernand, ran the hotel with their mother.'

'They both inherited it?' I'd read a few Agatha Christies in my time and knew that wills could spring all sorts of surprises. Not in France, obviously, as I was about to find out.

'The French Revolution did away with the law of primogeniture, Mademoiselle.' The *Maître* dripped with scorn.

My mouth fell open. What language was he speaking now?

A surreptitious glance at the clock revived him. He leaned forward and made a bridge with his fingers.

'French law does not allow a child to be favoured. Every offspring inherits exactly the same amount – after death duties are disbursed of course.' He sat back and crossed his legs. 'Legitimate children and illegitimate children are all entitled to the same share. It is not possible to disinherit a person except...' he paused and said pointedly, 'except if he has broken the law.'

The ensuing silence wormed its way into my conscience. What did he mean by that?

I was both infuriated and thankful for the slow delivery of his speech. At least I could understand him, but although I understood his words, I couldn't fathom out what they meant for me.

'On Lazarro's death, his children –'

'His son, my dad's an only child.'

'His son should – according to French law – be entitled to a part of the estate.'

I wondered if Dad knew that he could, if he wanted, claim

a chunk of a French hotel with an impossible name perched on top of a mountain.

I asked in a small voice, 'Does he have children, huh, Fernand?'

'Yes, he has three daughters.'

'Really?' My eyes opened wide. I had three French aunts – or whatever they were – and probably a whole crowd of second cousins who knew nothing about me.

He frowned. His sinuses bulged over the glasses. It was not a pretty sight.

'You must be aware of the fact that the circumstances in which your grandfather left the country were not altogether clear.'

'What do you mean?'

'Your grandfather disappeared. The address to which we sent this letter is in Paris.' The small eyes shone with an ominous glint. 'He gave no sign of life for fifty years.'

I gripped the edge of my chair. I didn't like where this was going.

'Lazarro Etchegaray was wanted by the police for a very long time.' His eyes lasered through me. 'He was never found.'

XAVIER COMES TO THE RESCUE

I left the lawyer's office, hurried to the hostel, changed out of the suit and rushed to the Victor Hugo bar where I had agreed to meet Xavier. I really needed to know about that lake. In spite of the early hour, I ordered a beer to help me recover from the revelations.

'Klo-é?'

Xavier signalled to the waiter for an additional lager and pulled out a metal chair opposite me. 'I saw you rushing past in a suit this morning. Were you working? You said you were on holiday.'

An electrical storm started in the centre of my body and spread from my toes to my head. The way he pronounced my name, his brown arms, and the Bermuda jeans… I dabbed the foam from my lips, scanned the bridge for signs of his limpet and relaxed slightly. He was alone.

'No, I wasn't working,' I sighed. 'It's a long story. As a matter of fact…' I shifted on my seat and urged my brain into gear, 'I'm a little confused, and I was hoping you might help me piece that story together.' Or at least, it was what I had intended to say. My French was ungrammatical, tainted with the slang I had picked up on holiday, and I kidded myself that if I spoke fast enough, no one would notice the mistakes. Because my vocabulary didn't extend to 'I'm a little confused' or 'piece together,' I garbled something like *'C'est compliqué... c'est un mystère'* and remembered that we were here to discuss the scattering of Pop's ashes.

I concluded with, 'Did you find out how I can get to the lake?'

He gave a helpless shrug.

'Oh, for God's sake.' I threw up my hands. 'What can be hidden in a lake that size, that would warrant so much security? A Yeti? A nuclear submarine on loan from the Swiss navy? Is that it?'

'It can't be army related,' Xavier replied, completely missing the irony, 'my dad said the Ministry of *Environment* held the key.'

'The key to the mystery?'

'No, the key to the gate.'

I closed my eyes in frustration. Why was life so complicated? Why had Pop not asked me to scatter his ashes over the Atlantic Ocean? I would have had the choice of four hundred kilometres of white sandy beaches. I wouldn't be here today, trying to puzzle out why he had pretended to be dead. I took in a deep breath. Through my eyelashes, I caught Xavier peering at me, his face strangely soft. Ah well, perhaps Pop had done me a favour. I was becoming very fond of that ranger and, well, he seemed to like me.

The waiter brought two beers, which Xavier insisted on paying for straightaway. He lifted his glass. *'Topa!'*

I followed suit. 'Cheers. So, not working in your forest today?'

'No. I've got the day off. I'm heading to Biarritz later on for a spot of surfing, but my mother needs a hand during the school holidays. She's a childminder. I have to pick some of them up from their holiday club in an hour or so.'

'Right.' I nodded knowingly, though I hadn't understood everything he had said. It didn't matter. That Xavier should agree to help his mother only added to his already impressive list of qualities. From what I'd seen so far, I could not fault him for anything – apart from his taste in girls and his poor sense of humour, that is.

'Thank you for finding out, you know, about the lake.' I leaned forward. 'Now, there is something else I need help with.'

He put down his beer and gave me his full attention. *'Le mystère?'* His eyes sparkled.

Oh my. A man who listens. Is he for real? I shook myself. *Stop dreaming, Chloe. He's not available.*

I attempted to explain. 'I need to find out information about my grandfather and his family. Do you have any idea where records of births are kept?'

He pushed his lower lip forward. 'Hmm. We keep them in town halls usually. Do you know where he was born?'

'He was born in Jaioleku.'

'That place is too small to have its own town hall. The records are probably kept in the Herriberri *mairie*. I think the process is quite straightforward.'

Straightforward? Really? Herriberri was dangerous. I was once poisoned there.

I narrowed my eyes and whispered. 'I need to go incognito.'

'Incognito? Why?'

'Last time I went there, claiming to all and sundry that I was the granddaughter of Lazarro Etchegaray, I had the distinct impression that I wasn't welcome.'

'Herriberri isn't the Wild West you know. I really don't see –'

'There's something fishy going on there. Until I get to the bottom of it, I want to play it safe.'

'I see.' Bless him, he believed me.

'I'll pass myself as an American.'

With a frown, Xavier jutted his chin towards the kangaroo. 'Not Australian?'

'Okay, it's like this: there are hundreds of thousands of Basques in the States, loads in South America and only a handful in Australia.'

He nodded thoughtfully. 'That's true.'

'If I say I'm American, no questions will be asked.'

'That's true too. So where will you say you come from?'

'Elko.'

'Where?'

'Elko Nevada. There's a huge Basque gathering there every year.' That festival had been right at the top of Pop's bucket list. The familiar pain scalded my solar plexus. We had planned to go this year. In fact, had Pop not kicked the proverbial bucket, we would just be back from the States by now. My voice wobbled. 'We – we were going to go there together, my grandad and I.'

'To Nevada?' Xavier said softly. 'Why Nevada?'

'Around the time of the gold rush, Basque shepherds went over to The States to graze sheep in the Sierra Nevada–'

'And they have a Basque festival? I've never heard of it.'

'Oh yes. Cow races, strong man competitions, omelette competitions, the lot!'

As I said this, I realised why Pop had so badly wanted to go, and it broke my heart. Since he could never go back to his village, in Elko he would have been feted as the *genu-ayne* article, free to speak his mother tongue and mingle with his 'haplogroup' without any fear of retribution. Poor Pop. He never made it. The least I could do was make sure he returned to his lake.

I stared ahead through misty eyes. The bridge lost its contours and dissolved into the muddy river.

'Klo-é, are you Okay?'

I dissolved too. 'Sorry.' I grabbed a napkin. 'I get a bit tearful whenever I think of him.' I blew my nose and squeezed the tears back into their ducts.

'Do you want me to go with you to the *mairie?*'

'Yes!' I jumped out of my chair... shook my head sadly and mumbled, 'it's very kind of you to offer. I will be fine. I'll borrow a baseball cap and sweatshirt from one of the Americans at the hostel and take the bus.'

I added with a half-smile, 'There is something you can do for me though, but I don't know if –'

'Yes?'

Oh, now that 'yes' was keen. Had I imagined it? I waited for a moment, focused inwards, checked the vibrations on my man-o-meter and tested that 'yes' for signal, strength and clarity. Hmmm, rather solicitous for an attached male, even a male attached to a strumpet. Should I raise my hopes or, simply bored with driving around a lonely forest, the ranger needed a change? There was only one way to find out. I took in a deep breath.

'I would like to invite you for dinner at a restaurant called –' I made a face and stuttered, 'Hartz-ain-ostatu-a? It's Basque. Does it make sense? I need to check the place out, but I'm not sure where it is and, I don't have a car to get to it.'

'The Bear Inn in Jaioleku?'

'The Bear Inn? Oh, is *that* what it means? Yes, *'Bear staying.'* Pfew, my goodness, the Bear Inn. Of course. You know it?'

'Sure. My cousin got married there in May.'

Things were looking up. 'Really? What is it like?'

'It's the traditional *ostatu,* nothing fancy. It serves traditional home cooking. The food they did for my cousin's wedding was good but it's a little out of the way.'

I remembered Xavier's enthusiasm for the *pintxos* and hoped he wouldn't be disappointed.

He put his hand over mine and said in a soft voice, 'Chloe, if you want me to take you to a really good restaurant, I can recommend something nearer.'

I pulled my hand away as if burned. 'Thank you,' I said, polite but firm. 'I'm afraid it has to be the Bear Inn. You would do me a huge favour in accepting.'

Xavier sat back and studied me. I could hear the cogs whirring inside his mind, wondering what I was really after.

'Listen,' I lifted a hand. 'I know how it looks and I realise that it might put you in an awkward position, so I will put the cards on the table. I have just found out that my grandfather, the one who recently passed away, was unable to return to his birthplace during his lifetime for a reason I yet have to find out. The *notaire* told me that his family – my family too I suppose, owns the Hartza – sorry, what did you call it?'

'The Bear Inn.'

'Right, the Bear Inn. I had planned to take a taxi and go with my Australian friends, but they're leaving tomorrow and, I don't know anyone else here. I'm sorry if I sound forward.'

Xavier gave me a bashful smile. 'It's not every day that I'm asked out by an Amer– an Australian girl, so yes, I accept. I'll pick you up tomorrow at eighteen-thirty.'

Heat rose from my neck upwards. My hand went to pull my hat down to hide my blushes. I wasn't wearing it.

He looked at me intently, lifted his glass and said with a cheeky grin, 'You know, what you said earlier on?'

'What, about Nevada?'

His eyes twinkled, dark and mischievous. The trace of a

smile hovered at the edge of his lips. 'No, about the lake and the Swiss navy.'

'What about it?'

'It was really funny, and quite unexpected coming from an – ahem – American.'

Oh gawd, so he did have a sense of humour. A sinking feeling hit the pit of my stomach. I was bewitched.

CHLOE AND XAVIER DISCOVER THE BEAR INN

Just before eight-thirty, my insides fizzing like a can of newly opened soda pop, I waited for Xavier to pick me up as arranged in front of the Bar Victor Hugo, absently watching the Nive flow by, sedate and brown.

I had been to the *mairie* where a mouse-like employee had led me to a room and left me to dissect the records of births and deaths to my heart's content. Pop's elder brother Fernand's three daughters were mentioned, and I now knew their names. Back at the hostel, I had looked up my three aunts on the Internet with varying degrees of success. I hoped Xavier would help me find out more.

Going to the *mairie* in Herriberri by public transport, sixty kilometres from Bayonne, had been quite a trek. The inland train went as far as Saint Jean Pied de Port right inside the mountains, and the last ten kilometres of the journey had taken longer even than the first leg. The rickety bus stopped at every farm, café and stone cross. Hunkered down in my seat, baseball cap pulled over my face, I had watched the scenery roll past for what seemed like forever.

Tonight, I was grateful to have secured a lift. For the restaurant outing, I decided I would be neither Australian nor American, but a tourist all the same. My frizzy hennaed hair and red glasses were disguise enough. I completed the attire with a little black dress and gold sandals. Not exactly discreet but, as the Chinese say, 'the darkest place is under the candle.'

Expecting the French forestry Range Rover, it took me a while to notice Xavier waving from behind the wheel of a small Renault. I opened the passenger door, unimpressed to find his girlfriend next to him. I grumbled *'B'jour'* and flopped on the back seat. Was she coming with us? I didn't remember inviting her.

'Charlène, Chloe, Chloe, Charlène,' Xavier said by way of introduction.

So, she was called Charlène. It figured. Aspirationally named after an American soap star I shouldn't wonder, or the Princess of Monaco. Amazing the fascination the French have for royalty, probably to make up for having beheaded their own king, or so Amatxi thought.

Charlène was predictably chewing the cud, blowing bubbles of strawberry-scented gum. She slouched in the front seat, her feet on the dashboard. She reached out, cranked up the radio full volume and sang along to French rap. After thirty minutes of this torture, Xavier turned onto a steep rocky path and stopped by a half-timbered farmhouse crushed under a tiled roof.

Ignoring a flock of mean looking geese, he headed for a large red arched door, while Charlène fussed with a sheep dog.

An old woman came out and kissed both of them. They exchanged a few words and after another round of kisses Amatxi used to call 'a fricassee of snouts,' Xavier returned to the car and called me to the front.

'Les grandparents de Charlène.'

He switched off the radio, fastened his seat belt and drove off.

'Do, hum, Charlène's grandparents run the farm alone?' I asked with magnanimous selflessness, her name catching in my throat.

'Yes. It used to be much bigger, but they're getting old. All they have left now is a couple of fields, a vegetable garden, a cow and a few hens.'

'How old are they?'

'Monsieur Arroztegui is about seventy-five, I think.'

'Huh?' I spluttered. 'What did you say their name was?' Were they related to the mad pharmacist?

'Arroztegui. Why?'

'It's just – it's just that –' Was I about to make a fool of myself? 'They seem to be everywhere, the Arroztegui.'

'They are everywhere, Klo-é.' Xavier smiled. 'Arroz means forge. It's a very common name here. It's the equivalent of Smith. It's my name too.'

'It is?'

'Yes, why?'

'Just wondered.' I changed the subject. 'My grandmother was from around here. She used to tell me about witches, have you –'

'Ha, our famous *Lamiak? Oh la la,* try and convince Charlène's grandmother that they don't exist! Did you notice? Her barn door is covered with thistle flowers to ward off the evil eye. The poor woman lives in fear of the supernatural.'

'Really?' My voice went up a pitch, filled with scorn. 'They still believe in witches here?'

'You'd be surprised.'

'Pff!' I guffawed.

I knew I was hexed. How else could I explain the quivering, the palpitations every time Xavier changed gear? I had no right to feel proprietorial, but after ten long months of solitary confinement, I was ripe for enchantment.

I crossed my arms and leaned against the car window. To clear my mind, I looked at the sky and focused on large birds floating on thermals.

'Those birds circling up there, are they eagles?'

'No, they're griffon vultures. Eagles fly alone.'

'Vultures?' It just went to show how little I knew about the country of my ancestors.

'They're very useful, vultures. They clean up the carcasses of dead sheep in no time. Now that it's illegal to leave dead animals outside because of the fear of BSE, finding food is harder for them. Sometimes though, they get lucky. A few years ago, a German tourist fell to her death. When the rescuers came an hour later, all they found were her shoes.'

I shivered and watched the scenery roll by, my mind filled with a host of 'what ifs'. What if Pop had been able to come home to Jaioleku? He was such a nature buff, he would have told me about the vultures, taken me mushrooming, pointed to every peak and river and told me their names. Amatxi would have taught me Basque. I would now be visiting my aunts at the Bear Inn, exchanging recipes. I would be welcome here and not have to pass myself off as a tourist, but what could I do? 'With enough 'ifs' you could put Paris in a bottle,' Amatxi used to say.

I watched Lower Navarra unfurl, the *Nafarroa Beherea* my grandparents had carried in their heart, wild, majestic, and so removed from Buckinghamshire. No wonder they were homesick.

We left the main road for a one-lane track. France, Xavier informed me, was the country with the most tarmacked roads in the world. Narrow but purposeful, the ribbon of tarmac dipped over brooks, threading its way through forests and fields with the confidence of a road that was going somewhere, a confidence I didn't share. I was sure we were lost. Bar a few sheep, there was little in the way of civilisation.

I switched on the radio, twiddled the button and stopped when a soulful male choir filled the car.

Xavier turned to me. '*Tu préfères pas la musique pop?*'

'*Non, non, j'adore les choeurs basques.*' I lied. I'm an Enrique Iglesias fan – those latino eyes – but in that magical setting, it would have seemed crass to request Fun Radio.

As we drove through mountains, the choir sang the soundtrack to Pop and Amatxi's life. Male voices rolled out pictures of green velvety slopes, crisp white and red farms, white cattle and sheep. Green red and white were the colours of the flag, of Pop's nostalgia, the colour of his pain, now swelling inside my chest and threatening to spill over.

I sniffed.

'*Ça va?*' Xavier asked with concern.

'Hmmm.' I pushed my glasses into my hair and surreptitiously wiped a tear.

'*T'es sûre?*'

I nodded. I wasn't sure, but how could I explain, bowled over as I was by a tsunami of emotions on a scale I'd never felt before. The vastness of the sky, the mass of the mountains, the song's sorrow were branding Pop's homesickness into my soul. Back home, I had felt sorry for him in a 'there-there-pat-on-the-shoulder' sort of way, but I'd never understood. Not really.

How could I have? When I gave up my terraced house and left Bletchley – was it only last week– I'd watched, detached, the landmarks of my twenty-three years of life roll by for the last time past the taxi window. The Manor at Bletchley Park was grand – I'd spent a month there making fish-paste wartime sandwiches – but it was surrounded by a sea of prefabs where all the decoding had taken place during the

War, a view, which on a dull day, would have destroyed the soul of anyone not hell-bent on saving their country.

Would I ever miss the ugly railway bridge, the Enigma Tavern and its plastic fascia board, the crumbling façade of Plumbing and Heating? What had there been to miss? I had felt a small twinge as we drove past the Irish club where Leah and I had celebrated many a Saint Patrick's Day. The twinge, mostly caused by her desertion, was nothing like the ache now gnawing at my bones.

The music touched every fibre of my being. My body throbbed with longing. Melancholy wormed itself inside me with every *adios, tristura,* and *maite,* the Basque word for love.

Unable to hold back the tears, I whispered, 'I must get to that lake.'

He slowed right down and glanced at me. 'He must have been some man, your grandfather.'

'Yes. Yes he was.'

It wasn't just about my promise to scatter Pop's ashes over Lake Irrabia. It was more than that. I knew in that moment that I had been sent here for a reason.

I had seen how my grandparents lived and I had seen how they died. They were Good People. Whatever had kept them away from Jaioleku wasn't deserved. I was convinced of it. I wiped my eyes. The melancholy lifted. I had a purpose.

Night was falling. The last of the sun rays brushed the valley, sprinkling it with gold. Under their low eves, gleaming white farms clung to slopes inside neat square patches of vines and cornfields.

The road led up to a hamlet and splayed out into several tracks. Up ahead a small church with a square steeple rose above a mess of higgledy-piggledy houses set inside walled yards. Xavier nosed up to the cemetery wall between two pollarded mulberry trees and declared, '*On est arrivé.*'

Arrived where? Not at the Bear Inn surely. I'd always

been taught that to get trade, inns had to be on the way to somewhere, and we definitely were *not* on the way to anywhere. We had driven for the best part of an hour through hills and dales without encountering anything other than cattle. I had obviously missed something.

I looked around. The sun was dying against a tall pink wall, the *fronton* where *pelote* would be played, backing onto the cemetery.

'Where are we?'

'Jaioleku. That's where you wanted to go, wasn't it?'

'Yes but… the Bear Inn?'

'It's here, Chloe. Right in front of you.'

THE BEAR INN

A white half-timbered house stood obscured by a large tree. Above the door, *'Auberge de l'Ours'* was written in decorative script and in faded letters below, its original name, *'Hartzainostatua.'*

'Ostatu is the Basque for inn,' Xavier explained as I stood open-mouthed. *'Hartz* means bear. We like to glue words together.'

I rummaged in my bag for the photo of Pop. On it, the large tree was a sapling, but apart from a few modern tables outside, nothing had changed. The red wooden shutters, the small wrought-iron balcony above the entrance door, everything was the same, down to the sheepdog asleep on the road. A shiver ran through me. So, this was the Bear Inn, the place where Pop was born.

'Shall we go in?'

I pushed my glasses down, fluffed my hair over my face, in case anyone remembered me from the newspaper article, and followed Xavier into the cool dark hall.

'Un apéro?'

'Oui,' I squeaked. An aperitif would give me courage.

Heart in my mouth, I took my first step into my family's past. On one side of the oak-lined wall was a dresser crammed with painted china and copper implements. The hotel desk was in the right-hand corner. Ahead, a twisting staircase called to me. I reached out for the banister and lifted my foot.

'Chloe?'

Xavier's seductive Klo-é pulled me back. I turned away. To the left was a cosy bar, just a zinc counter and four tables where he ordered a beer for himself and for me, after much reflection, a glass of local cider.

'I'll pay for the drinks.' Xavier offered.

'No, I'd like to.'

'Hé, salut Xavier!' One of the locals called out before I had time to protest.

I grabbed a tourist brochure from a shelf and slunk onto a seat, hair over my face. In the conversation that followed, I picked out three words in Basque, *'Australian, turista* and *Camino.'*

In a corner of the bar, a bear of a man presided from a carved chair, late seventies perhaps, thick features topped with a white crew cut. Something about him reminded me of Bayonne's King Léon. I'm not sure whether it was the way he commanded the space, his large red nose perhaps, or the procession of courtiers who went to shake his hand.

I watched him covertly. From the greetings and conversations, I deduced he was called Fernand. Fernand was the name of Pop's brother. Good grief, I gawped. Could it be him?

He didn't notice me, too busy regaling a flatterer with his tales. Though he spoke Basque, his puffed-out chest, knowing glances and raised voice told me it was a battle he had won. One of many I imagined. This was a man who liked to have his way.

I was relieved when Xavier touched my shoulder and suggested we go to our table.

We crossed a panelled dining room with a grey tiled floor and thirties wall sconces. My mind was in a whirl. If this was the house where Pop grew up, the house he ran away from, the old man could be his brother. What had Pop done to alienate him?

I trailed behind Xavier into a long, glazed veranda where he chose a table overlooking the darkening valley.

A middle-aged woman greeted us and reeled off the menu in the southern singsong of a troubadour reciting a poem.

The words *Poêlée navarraise, chicken basquaise* and something like *cider apple jelly* floated around the fog growing inside my mind. The mythical valley Pop had painted for me was just on the other side of the glass, but he had never told me he lived in a hotel.

I dragged myself back to the present, though even that made little sense. Here we were, on a Tuesday, on top of a hill, an hour from anywhere, and the dining-room was full to bursting point. I loved the place already.

How did they do it? Back in England on a Tuesday, even during what Leah called 'crappy hour,' all the King's Arms could muster was a couple of derelicts clustered around the 'pie and pint' on offer for a fiver.

Our entrées arrived, but so moved was I with the hotel, the setting sun and Xavier's legs brushing against mine, that I couldn't do the food justice. I toyed with the artichoke hearts while my own melted and, on the horizon, mountain peaks were turning from purple to black.

'Tu n'aimes pas le jambon de Bayonne?'

I did love Bayonne ham. I didn't want Xavier to think I was fussy, but my throat had closed up.

He reached out for my plate, spooned my food into his

and cocked his head to one side. 'Chloe, I would like to ask you something.'

If he looked at me like that, the answer would be yes.

'I need to practice my English. I know you want to improve your French, but your French, it is good and my English, it is bad.'

Of course, I agreed, though for the purpose of this story, his errors – and there were many – will be glossed over.

We said nothing for a while. Below our terrace, village life was following its course. A stout woman came out of her farm, called to her geese, grabbed one under her arm and carried it indoors while the rest waddled obediently into a barn.

'Is she going to feed the poor goose with a funnel to make *foie gras?*'

I wasn't sure about *foie gras*. Some recipes called for it but I balked at the idea of turning the fatty liver of some poor force-fed bird into a luxury food.

'Nah, she's just getting it in.' Xavier read my face and applied a diversion tactic. 'Look! The ewes are coming back for milking.'

A small flock of sheep ran below us. A ewe strayed, soon yapped back into the fold by a shaggy black and white dog. You couldn't dream of a more pastoral setting. Nothing had changed for centuries, and yet, around us, the restaurant was buzzing. Crikey, how *did* they do it?

The answer came with the second course. Our chicken *basquaise* came laid out on a bed of red white and green vegetables criss-crossed in the manner of the *Ikurrina*, the Basque flag. It looked fantastic. The portion was just right for a light evening meal and I managed to eat most of it.

After this meal, all the good people now crowding this veranda would go home and tell their friends, 'Go to The Bear Inn in Jaioleku. You will eat well there.' It was the only recommendation needed to convince a French person to get into his car and drive for an hour in the hope of pleasuring his taste buds. Food mattered in a country where McDonalds were attacked with bulldozers.

But it wasn't just that. Here, at the Bear Inn, the *patronne's* motherly attentions made you feel that you were invited to dinner by a favourite aunt. Forget London, forget Michelin stars, this was exactly the kind of place I wanted to work in. I'd always enjoyed cooking, but what had driven me to make it my profession was the privilege of making people happy. When I was younger, I'd dreamt of being a fairy. I loved the magic, the simplicity of cooking to uplift the mood. Feeding the multitudes was the closest I would ever get to waving a magic wand... lighting up smiles as I went.

Working at Posh-Nosh, I would walk around and offer canapés that I had concocted to induce maximum happiness and, invisible inside my waitress pinafore, watched the faces brighten one by one.

My magic potions were gazpacho shots in tiny glasses, crunchy vegetables with their dip in hollowed-out baguettes, bite-sized concoctions served in china spoons and spicy chicken fortune cookies. The magic was in that first burst of taste. It would explode, gel with other ingredients such as friendship, love and a sense of place, and linger long after the party was over.

Here at the Bear Inn, I recognised a kindred spirit in the *patronne,* the way she fussed over her guests, the way she glowed from their joy.

Was I related to her? Would she turn out to be my fairy godmother? Perhaps. At some point, I'd heard her call the old man in the bar Papa.

I felt silly coming here camouflaged as a tourist, angry at the pharmacist who had scared me away and forced me to go under cover. Tempted to drop all pretence, I wanted to run to her and confess who I was. After all, if these people really were my family, why would they not welcome me?

I hesitated. They might remember me from the newspaper article printed at the time of Cosmo's accident. How would I explain? Until I knew more, I decided to keep my counsel.

The chef was a young man called Frédéric, apparently making a name for himself in the region. I'd caught sight of him behind the bar. A chip off the old block. The nose gave him away. Important tool for a chef, a good nose.

The whole thing was driving me mad. I dabbed my lips with a napkin and focused on my companion. 'Xavier, who did you say I was to that chap you met in the bar?'

'Ah yes. I wasn't sure of the character you wanted to play tonight, so I said you were an Australian pilgrim on the way to Santiago. I hope I did the right thing.'

I sat back, intrigued. 'Santiago?' I'd heard of the Santiago pilgrimage but knew very little about it.

He opened his hands. 'It was the first thing that came to mind. We're only a few kilometres away from Saint Jean Pied de Port. Saint Jean is the most convenient pass into Spain, it's where pilgrims cross over the Pyrenees on their way to Santiago de Compostella. The Camino, the pilgrimage to Santiago, is hugely fashionable at the moment.'

'A pilgrimage? Fashionable?'

'Sure. This year, about fifty thousand people did it.'

'Fifty-*thousand*? Jeepers. How far is it, this Santiago?'

'It is over seven hundred kilometres away.'

'You're joking, right? Fifty thousand people want to walk five hundred miles?' Was he serious? 'How long does it take?'

'Depends how fast you walk,' Xavier answered sensibly. 'Anyway, I thought it would be your best cover.' He ran his eyes over my fluffy hair, red glasses and black dress. 'You look like a tourist and I thought –'

'It's Okay. It's a great idea. I'll swat up on this Camino pilgrimage and use it as a cover. Brilliant. Sorry, what did you say the town was called?'

'Saint Jean Pied de Port. We drove through it on the way here. You commented on the ramparts.'

'So I did. Very picturesque. I might try to find a room there. Hidden amongst foreigners is probably the safest place for me.'

A commotion in the car park below attracted my attention. The local King Léon was getting into his car.

'Adiou Fernand!' Someone called out to him.

'Listen.' I leaned over and whispered to Xavier, 'Could you find out who that old man is? Look, he's getting into his car now.'

'Sure. Why, who do you think he is?'

'I think he's my great-uncle.'

I was interrupted by the *patronne* carrying in our desserts, a very light cider jelly which slipped into my stomach of its own accord, unimpeded by the way Xavier's eyes seemed to caress me, an impression brought about I imagine, by the two glasses of rosé I'd blithely consumed on top of the cider.

We had coffee, and while I paid, Xavier went in search of information. Out in the hall, I noticed a photo on the dresser and peered at it. From the clothes, it had been taken in the fifties. A couple stood in front of the Bear Inn together with two boys wearing berets. One of the boys – I could tell by the nose – was the old man, aged around thirteen. As for the small cheeky one, I had a pretty good idea.

Outside, the old sheep dog, probably an offspring of the dog in the photo, struggled to his feet and came to greet me. By the time Xavier came out, we were firm friends Old Shep and I.

'Was your grandad's name Lazarro?'

My breath caught in my throat. 'Yes, yes it was.'

'I talked to the *patronne,* the lady who served us. The couple in the photo are her grandparents, now resting in the cemetery.' Xavier pointed to the church behind me. 'The boys are her father, Fernand, the old man you saw in the bar. The younger one is his brother, Lazarro.'

'So, she is my aunt.' I was glad. 'What did she say about Lazarro?'

'Well.' Xavier frowned. 'According to her, he died in the seventies.'

'Really?' My voice went up one notch. So, that lawyer was right. 'Did she say how?'

His answer knocked me for six.

'He moved to Paris and died there in a car accident.'

TO BE A PILGRIM

'*He who would valiant be-ee/'gainst all disaster/ Let him in constance-ee/ Follow the Master.'* At the top of my voice, I sang the Bunyan hymn I had so loved at school, lathering my hair in the shower. Just outside the bathroom window, pigeons cooed along with me. *'There's no discoura-agement,'* I warbled, *'Shall make him once relent –'* I took a deep breath, *'His first ava-owed intent,'* I rinsed out the shampoo and boomed the last notes in treble bass, *'to be a pilgrim.'*

I had found lodgings in Saint Jean Pied de Port in a converted attic at the top of an ancient building on rue de la Citadelle. I loved the vastness of my room, the smell of wood, the whitewashed beams and wide floorboards. Outside, the jumble of roofs I peeped from my little window was pure poetry.

In the two days I had been in Saint Jean, I had rambled around the old ramparts, visited every church and the Bishops' Prison. When it rained, I hung around souvenir shops fingering berets, jars of Espelette pimento, striped tea towels and sheep key rings, feeling more and more Basque by the minute.

Once I had seen all there was to see, I realised with a pang that my money wouldn't last much longer. There was only one solution. I had to find a job. Unfortunately, it was the end of the tourist season and jobs were hard to come by.

On the upside, I now had Xavier's mobile number and a promise that he would get me into Pop's lake before the week was out.

On the downside, I had skyped my parents and given them my address. My father, uneasy at the idea that I was about to disturbed a hornet's nest in a land where memories were long and guns plentiful, had announced that a single ticket to Oz for the beginning of October was on its way. I had just one month to meet my French family and exonerate Pop.

I rinsed my hair and hummed the Bunyan hymn again, inspired by the pilgrims I had seen, treading their weary way to Saint Jacques de Compostelle, dusty and weather-beaten, backpack adorned with the distinctive scallop shell. The French for scallop is *coquille Saint Jacques.*

Today, I would pretend to be one of them. As I towelled my hair, I tried to put myself in the shoes of someone preparing to walk seven hundred kilometres. *'There's no discouragement/Shall make her once relent/ Her fictitious intent* – deep breath – *To be a pilgrim.'*

When I was at school, I never saw the point of drama lessons, uninspired perhaps by having to 'stand like a tree,' or communicate anger using nothing but the word 'cabbage.' Now there was a point to the masquerade, I hoped my acting would be up to looking like a wannabe pilgrim.

I had discovered that the youngest of Fernand's daughters, Viviane, a teacher volunteered in the pilgrimage office on Wednesdays when French schools were closed, and I wanted to meet her. Would Aunt Viviane be friend or foe? I was about to find out.

It was 'raining ropes' as the French say for cats and dogs. Halfway up a cobbled street, the small Camino office was filled with damp pilgrims proposing to set off over peaks, ravines, rivers and mesas in an attempt to discover themselves.

I had read up on the Camino and understood that its appeal was to tread in the footsteps of all the penitents that had walked The Path for over a thousand years, and to catch a glimpse of that Eternal Truth, so lacking in our ever-changing world.

'Bah!' Pop would say, for he was very wise, 'all you have to do is switch off your phones and go fishing.' He was right, of course.

I too was searching for the dimension lacking in my life, but I would not search for it on the way to Santiago. I knew it was right here and to find it, I would follow Pop's advice and go fishing in the bog mire of my family history until I discovered the truth, for there *was* something very fishy about the tale of Pop dying in Paris.

They say you're only truly dead when no one talks of you. My mission was to talk about Pop and Amatxi and bring them back from the dead.

By the time I was dressed – a thick jumper under a brown anorak – and clattered down the stairs in muddy boots, it was nearly lunchtime.

For the pilgrims, the day's walking was over. Trudging over glistening cobbles, stick in hand, the caped wayfarers were hurrying to their hostels. They had begun their journey further north, in Vézelay perhaps, in the centre of France, or as far north as Germany.

The Camino office smelled like a sheep pound. I pushed past the damp mob and hovered at the back, studying the notices on the wall. My original plan – to take a chair opposite Viviane and have a cosy chat – was dead in the water. I hadn't counted on such a demand for pilgrims' passports. September was a popular month.

Behind a row of tables, Viviane and her colleagues were dispensing advice, sympathy and comfort to the sodden multitude. Stocky, of average size, she wasn't pretty – that nose again – her hair was neatly razored at the back in that sober cut French women prefer, but her face was kind. She was a Good Person, I could tell, and I was confident that we would get along.

Viviane glanced at her watch, pushed her chair back, and signalled to her colleagues that she was going on her lunch break. She slipped on a raincoat, opened her umbrella and set forth into the rain.

I drew my hood over my face and followed her to a small restaurant backing onto the ramparts. The place was buzzing. She crossed the long stone corridor-shaped building, took a seat in the glazed extension abutting the old town walls, gave the menu a cursory glance and pulled a book from her bag.

I let a large party of Germans take up the remaining tables and put a hand on the free chair opposite her.

'Do you mind if I sit here?' I said in French.

She looked up. 'Not at all,' and returned to her book.

The rain was pounding down on the glass. I sat down, heart beating wildly, wondering what to say. Everything I had prepared seemed silly.

Xavier and I had cobbled together a story on the way back from the Bear Inn. The nearness of him and the amount of wine I had consumed had made concentrating on the plot rather a challenge at the time. Though I'd had the leisure to refine it as I lingered around Saint Jean's old walls, it now seemed blatantly implausible.

I cleared my throat. 'Excuse me. I'm sorry to disturb you during your lunch break. You work at the Camino office, yes?' I had planned to say much more but though fluent, my French was childish, colloquial and not at all adapted to polite conversation with strangers. I spoke French, as the saying goes, like a Spanish cow, *une vache espagnole,* which Xavier assured me, started life as *un Basque espagnol.* Go figure.

She looked up from her book. 'Yes, I work at the office.'

'I wanted to ask you a question.' I bit my lip. 'I'd planned to leave for Santiago this week, but I don't have enough money for the trip.'

Her face fell. Drats, she thought I was asking her for lunch money. 'I don't want money.' I quickly waved a hand to reinforce the point. 'I just need advice.'

She relaxed slightly.

'I need a job and, well, I was wondering if you could tell me where to start looking for one.'

It was the end of the season. Jobs were impossible to come by, and it was exactly what Viviane told me, using words I'd never come across before.

'C'est la fin de la saison. On débauche les employés saisonniers.'

Debauched employees? Seasoned employees? I drew a blank and repeated dumbly. *'Les employés? Débauchés?'*

She repressed a smile and explained that in a couple of weeks, casual employees would be let go. '*Embauché* means hired – *débauché* means let go.

Obviously when idle, one became debauched, who knows.

The waiter came to take our orders. Viviane ordered *garbure* soup. I did the same, though I had no idea what it was.

I explained to her that I had worked in kitchens. I did not admit that I was a chef. The French distrust everything about

English cuisine, from bacon in the morning to the sugar in baked beans. Unsure of how to describe my career path, I garbled that I had worked as a salad girl, which I translated as '*fille de salade.*'

She burst out laughing. Oops, not *fille de salade* then. Never mind, the ice was broken.

'I'll give it some thought, but as I said, it's September.'

'Is helping the pilgrims your job or do you volunteer?' I wanted to find out what made her tick.

'I'm a primary school teacher. I volunteer here on Wednesdays.'

'You don't teach on Wednesdays?'

'In France, schools are closed on Wednesdays.'

We talked about this and that until I managed to shoehorn the question I had been wanting to ask all along.

'Is your family from around here then?'

'Yes, I was born in Jaioleku, a few miles from here.'

'The Camino, have you ever walked it?' I was itching to know more about her family but I made a point of sticking to my brief.

'Yes. I walked it in 2010. It was a holy year because St James's name's day fell on a Sunday. Santiago means Saint James. It was very special.'

The soft glow radiating from her face told me that Viviane was kind, devout and could not possibly have had a part in the cabal mounted against me when I had first arrived. I felt I could trust her.

While I dithered as to whether I should tell her who I was, Viviane enthused.

'Walking,' she brought her hands to her heart, 'you transcend everyday life, connect with the divine and find answers to questions you hadn't even asked. It's all very simple really.' She smiled. 'What moved you to attempt it?'

'Attempt what?'

'Your pilgrimage.'

Oops. I'd been caught napping. I hated lying to her, she was so lovely.

The waiter brought our soup, a thick broth with vegetables and beans.

It gave me time to compose my answer.

'I've just finished my catering training and I'm still not sure what I want to do with my life. I thought walking the Camino would help me figure it out.'

Viviane's nod was so sympathetic, I was itching to blurt out everything. Substituting the Camino for my own quest, I said, 'The pilgrimage will enable me to find out who I really am. I'm sure –' I made up in fervour what I lacked in grammar '– that the time spent in the kitch–, hum, in the mountains will help me find the secret of – of –' I picked up my spoon and stirred the vegetables around my bowl, wondering what secret the mountains would unlock.

'Yes!' Viviane took over. 'The mountains will unlock the secrets you have been searching for all your life. It is impossible to explain but,' her smile was warm, 'it will make sense to you as you walk. You'll see.'

God bless the woman. I took a sip, keeping my eyes on her as she spoke.

'When you start off, your backpack feels heavy – mine weighed eight kilos – but you get used to it and as time goes by, you understand that what was really weighing you down, the problems you had been dragging like a ball and chain, were in fact problems of your own making.'

'Do they become lighter?' I willed her to say yes.

'They burn themselves out. You'll see, when you reach your goal, when you enter the Santiago Cathedral, when the bells ring and the huge incense burner swings –' Her eyes misted over.

'Wow.' Any more of this and I was off. However, I genuinely did not have the funds.

'What job would you like to do? Your French is very good.'

'My job? Do you mean now, or in the future?' I tore a chunk of bread and pondered the next step.

'As a profession.' She specified.

'I'd like to work in a kitchen. *'Fille de salade'* was only a first step. I want to be a chef. France is famous for its gastronomy. That's why I studied French.' I hoped this was a convincing explanation.

'A chef huh? Very commendable. Did you know,' Viviane lifted her spoon, 'that the world's best chef is a Basque woman? She is called Elena Arzak. Have you heard of her?'

Who hadn't heard of Elena Arzak? The Picasso of gastronomy, my role model, my muse, the zenith of my dreams. Her father, Juan-Mari, arranged his dishes like a Miro painting. A stint in her San Sebastian restaurant would set anyone's career on a path to glory, though I doubted her fame had gone quite as far as Botany Bay. Remembering I was supposed to be Australian, I pursed my lips and shrugged.

'Nah. Can't say I have.' I cringed and caught myself thinking, *Crikey, Chloe, you're ready for am-dram.*

'Her father is Juan-Mari Arzak. They have a restaurant in San Sebastian.'

'Really?' I cocked my head to one side, well aware that a taste of their techno cuisine would cost me a month's rent.

We chatted on. The rain drummed on. The restaurant was turning away customers.

I excused myself and went to the bathroom. When I came back, Viviane was chatting into her phone. She looked up at me, ended her conversation and leaned over the table, rather pleased with herself.

'Your prayers to Saint Laurent have been answered.'

'Saint Laurent?'

'The patron saint of cooks.'

I should have known better than to ask Viviane how the man had acquired that privilege.

'He was martyred on a grill.'

Leaving me to struggle with the image of our venerable patron saint roasting on hot coals, Viviane said, 'my sister runs a restaurant a few miles from here. It's called the Bear Inn.'

I managed to squash my elation into a look of polite enquiry, while inside me, a hallelujah chorus exploded and my blood pressure trebled.

'We've a wedding coming up this Saturday. I'll be waitressing, but we'd welcome some help. We're short staffed in the kitchen.'

'Oh, thank you!' I had to stop myself from reaching out and kissing her. 'What will I be doing?'

Viviane called for the bill and replied with a grin, '*Fille de salade,* what else?'

CHLOE IS INVITED TO A TXOKO

The next morning, I was singing, *'My first avowed intent to be a scullion,'* when my ringtone stopped me mid-warble. The caller ID sent the molecular composition of my body into overdrive. My head swam, my grip relaxed, my towel dropped to the floor.

Smooth and southern, Xavier's voice liquefied the few parts of me that were still functioning. 'Klo-é?'

I sank into an armchair, swallowed hard, forced air into my lungs, and managed a carefree *'Bonjour Xavier!'*

'What are you doing tonight? We're having a *txoko*. I thought you might like to join us.'

'A *txoko*?' Heck what did it matter what it was. Even if a *txoko* involved walking on burning embers, I would consider it.

'A group of friends are getting together for a few drinks, some food and a bit of dancing.'

A party! I must be dreaming. Xavier was inviting me to a party. *Careful, Chloe, don't sound too keen.*

'I'd love to come, but I've no transport and I have to work

tomorrow. You're not going to believe this, but I got myself a job as a–' I hesitated.

'*Chef de cuisine?*'

'More like *aide-de-cuisine*.' I paused for effect. 'At the Bear Inn.'

'*Hé hé*, well done. One foot in the door. *Waouh*. How did you manage that?'

'I'll tell you when I see you. I'll try and make it, if it's not too far. Where is it, that *txoko*?' I realised I was naked and retrieved the towel. Nudity suddenly didn't seem appropriate.

'It's in Esterençuby, just on the other side of Saint Jean Pied de Port.'

'Okay… tell me more.'

'There's a large farm overlooking the Nive on the right side of the road as you come in, advertising Ossau Iraty cheese. We'll be in the cellar. It starts at seven.'

'Thank you for that. I'll try to be there.' God, was I cool.

A party in a cheese cellar might not sound exciting, but for me, poor Cinderella trapped for *months* in the King's Arms' kitchen, it was as exhilarating as a grand ball.

My day passed in a frenzy of preparations. I trawled the sales for a pretty dress for the *txoko*, and a dark uniform for the Bear Inn kitchen. My dinkum Aussie mates had gone. I couldn't dip into their luggage for fashion accessories any more. Struth, how I missed those girls.

I studied bus timetables and, confused, eventually took a taxi to Esterençuby, a few miles away. Atop its hillock, the church was just chiming seven when we drove up to the village. The sun was already setting over a valley strangled inside steep craggy highlands.

A cheese sign pointed us to the yard of a traditional farm at the edge of a field sloping down to the river. The taxi driver stopped by a long drinking trough, let me out and drove off, leaving me standing alone amongst sheep droppings, feeling a complete twit. Why had I not asked the driver to wait until I'd checked I was in the right place?

Above me, the stars twinkled. Inside me, it was another matter.

My panic subsided when I caught sight of an elderly couple out for an evening stroll. I went out on the road and waited for them.

Thin and kindly, the man reminded me of Pop. His wife was a standard issue French housewife, grey hair neatly cut at the back. Slightly dumpy, she wore a straight skirt and dark blue cardigan.

'Bonsoir M'sieur-dame.'

'Mademoiselle.'

'I'm looking for the – hum - *txoko*. Do you –'

The man pointed to a dimly lit staircase at the side of the farm.

'Le txoko?' I repeated, thinking he hadn't understood.

'Oui, oui, c'est là.' They headed for the door and invited me to join them.

So, this was the place. No wild rave then, not with guests that age anyway.

'Ahem,' I hesitated. 'I was invited, but I don't really know anyone here and I'm not too sure –'

'Please, come with us.'

I followed them down musty stairs into a long, vaulted cellar. Along the stone walls, trestle tables covered in gingham were set with plates, cutlery, salt, pepper, bottles of white and red wine, carafes of water and baskets of bread. I relaxed slightly.

At the end of the room, I caught sight of Patxi wiping his face with a length of kitchen roll. Flooded with relief, I walked up to him.

'Salut. I'm looking for Xavier, is he here yet?'

Patxi ran his eyes over my skimpy floral dress and licked his lips. 'Hmmm. He sure is. He's been here since morning. I'll tell him you're here.' He pushed a door. I went to follow him.

The lady who came in with me touched my arm. 'Sorry. Women are not allowed in the kitchen.'

'But,' I mumbled, 'my friend…'

The old man pointed to a bar set up along a wall. 'Why don't you get yourself a drink? Your friend will come out in a minute.'

'What is going on in there?'

His eyes sparkled in the candlelight. 'Behind that door is the kitchen.'

'Ahh. I see.' I didn't, but smiled as if I did, and went to the bar.

A handful of old boys had clustered and, beer in hand, were discussing sport. I ordered a Kir – white wine with blackcurrant liqueur – and looked out for Charlène.

Feeling horribly awkward, I stood, sipping my Kir, willing Xavier to come out.

'Klo-é, you made it.' Xavier wiped his hands on his apron and kissed my cheeks. His face was damp. 'We're cooking up a feast in there. I hope you'll be impressed. Listen, I'm sorry, but I've got to get back.'

'Can I do anything?'

'No!' He laughed. 'Women aren't allowed in the kitchen.'

'You're all kidding me, right?'

'Not at all. In a *txoko*, men do the cooking.'

'It's a great honour for you ladies to be allowed here at all,' the man I had met on the road butted in. 'In the olden days, these gatherings were for men only.'

'José, this is my friend Chloe, over from hum… Australia. Chloe, this is Monsieur Loyola.'

'José. Please call me José.' The man said. 'We've already met.'

Loyola? Now that was interesting. Amatxi's name was Paloma Loyola. I wondered if Loyola was a common name.

'Good.' Xavier cast a glance towards the kitchen. 'Then you can update Chloe on the details. We won't be much longer. Sorry, got to get back. I've left Imanol and Patxi in charge of the sauce. Anything could happen.' He rushed back to his post.

'So, Chloe from Australia,' José smiled, 'what brings you to the Basque Country?'

His consonants were rougher than the mild local accent, his Rs rolled like pebbles inside a drum. I pushed my red glasses up my nose, got in touch with my inner Aussie and got into character.

'I'm taking a year out to travel around Europe. I really like it here, so I decided to stay for a while. I was thinking of doing the Camino, but I need to earn a bit of money first.' Having got this out of the way, I went on to ask in my best French, 'I'm surprised at this division between men and women. I thought you Basques were egalitarian in that respect.'

'Oh, we are, don't worry.'

'Your accent, it's –'

'I'm Basque,' José said with a hint of pride, as they did.

'But –'

'José was born on the Spanish side. He came to France for love.' A man butted in to our conversation. About Pop's age, he looked like a school teacher. 'He came for a holiday and ended up marrying Jacqueline.'

I looked at the woman I had met on the road, and was trying to imagine her as a young girl, when Charlène made her entrance in skin-tight jeans and candy pink blouse loosely knotted above her belly button. She strutted past us, rapped on the kitchen door and summoned the musketeers. Two of them filed out, sweaty and dishevelled.

Patxi couldn't refrain from groping her butt as he kissed her – she took it with good grace – as for the one with the name of an unguent, he held her neck and glanced into her eyes. I thought back to Xavier in the kitchen and cringed.

He came out at last and gave her a brief peck on the cheek. She rummaged inside her handbag, pulled something out and handed it to him. His face lit up. He wiped his hands on his apron, hugged her, took whatever it was, and rushed back.

A roar of *'Imanol! La sauce!'* got them all scurrying back into the steam room.

Charlène tottered to the bar and joined a gaggle of girls freshly emerged from the bathroom.

'Sorry, where did you say you were from?' I turned to my new friends.

'José comes from Hegoalde, that's how we call the Spanish side,' said the teacher who was called Michel.

'I was told the Basque country was just one country,' I ventured. 'Is it how you see it?'

If José Loyola was Spanish, I couldn't be related to him, could I?

'That's right,' José said, 'the Basque Country straddles the Pyrenees. Traditionally, we don't recognise the border.'

'I heard things were bad on the Spanish side, am I right?'

I had an agenda. As a tourist, opportunities to talk to locals were rare. Keen to find out as much as I could about the region, to build a portrait of the country as it was when Pop lived here, I had tried to strike up conversations in cafés, but it was frustrating. The men who prop up bars are not normally history buffs and, what was worse, many mistook my intentions.

I needed someone to paint a picture of the region at the

time of Pop's flight. I knew that until the French Revolution, it was usual for the elder brother to inherit the farm and for the younger one to emigrate, but all that had changed in 1800 when, as the lawyer had pointed out, all children inherited equally.

In the eighteenth century, young couples did elope, but why had Pop and Amatxi eloped in 1971? Was she engaged to another? Was he suspected of a crime? What kind of crime could one commit, for God's sake, in a country whose wealth was based on cheese? It was bamboozling.

'Have you heard of General Franco in Australia?'

My eyebrows rose above my red glasses. I decided to play dumb.

'Franco was the dictator that made our lives hell for over forty years.' José's French was rocky, every R and J catching in his throat. I struggled to understand him, but hung on. 'You see, if you are a Protestant, you can give up your religion, but if you are Basque, how can you stop *being* Basque, even if you want to? It is like asking you to stop being black. You can't. In San Sebastian, my family were bullied daily. The Guardia Civil stopped people in the street for the slimmest of reasons.' His face crunched into a mask of pain as he got deeper into his story. 'The police could keep you for ten days without charge, and torture was routine. Even now, some Spanish police stations still have a bath with electrodes.'

'No!' My hand flew to my face.

Jacqueline nodded with a pained sigh.

'My mother was hit by a cosh while shopping, and my uncle kicked so badly by the police that he lost a kidney,' José said.

'So, your traditions became all the more precious.' I was beginning to understand.

'Exactly. Our Basque ways were outlawed, so we became more attached to them. We refined them, like singing for instance, or walking in the mountain; because you can't prevent people from singing, walking or eating. Gatherings like these,' he twirled a hand towards the bright tables, 'took on a deeper meaning. By punishing us for being who we were, the fascists strengthened our identity.'

'How about violence?'

'Ah ETA. The Freedom fighters.'

Ouch. I had touched a nerve.

I anticipated José to reply that the bombings were in the past, that they had all moved on. But I *did* want to talk about the past and I *couldn't* move on, not as long as Pop was trapped inside his tin, banished and vilified. In order to know about the climate in which he had grown up, I needed a lead.

It occurred to me then that Pop might have told me all I needed to know while he was alive but that, like all young girls, I'd paid no attention. Now I was hanging onto José's every word.

'The violence, when it came, erupted like a geyser. It was unavoidable, it was liberating, even if we didn't agree with it. In Spain, the violence was directed mainly at the fascist police, the bullies, the ones who tortured us. Some of us did use violence, but I won't tell you how many thousands of innocent people *they* maimed and killed in their attempt to destroy us.'

'Hey José, what are you telling this young lady?' An ancient man in a beret put a hand on José's shoulder. 'You know it's forbidden to discuss politics in a *txoko*.'

'This is Chloe from Australia. She speaks very good French and asks intelligent questions. I'm explaining to her how we have General Franco to thank for making us even more Basque than we already were.'

'Ah, yes. I'll tell you something you might not know down in Australia, but when I was at school,' the ancient one said to me, 'if you spoke Basque, you were given a piece of wood.'

I knew about this from Pop and Amatxi, and had discussed it with Mrs Hart, my teacher.

'If you still had it at the end of the week, you got a hundred lines. I always managed to hand it over to a friend,' The old man cackled. 'He he. We all spoke Basque.' He limped away.

Simple but effective, the technique had nearly wiped out the language.

'Tell me one more thing!' I called out as José rose from the bench to greet a friend. I couldn't lose him, not when I was so close to finding out whether the conflict had touched this region. 'Did the violence spread over the border; did it spread to France?'

José settled back and gave my question some thought.

'In the seventies, yes, there were bombs. Extremists targeted the police, tourist organisations, politicians.' He cast a glance in his wife's direction.

'Didn't something happen here?' The man called Michel butted in. 'In 1971? I remember because we'd just go married.'

Jacqueline shuffled uncomfortably and dismissed it with, '*Bah, des têtes brûlées.*'

Burned heads? Good grief, what was that about?

She placed a hand on my arm. 'It isn't who we are. It's over now. Tourism is a lifeline for us and we are glad of it. You are welcome here.'

'I see you've finished your Kir.' José took my empty glass. 'Can I get you another one?'

I didn't reply, feeling like I'd just missed something crucial.

'Thank you, I'll just have a coke. I've to get up early tomorrow.'

Michel took a seat opposite me and pointed to Jacqueline. 'Did you know that this lady is the mayor of our little town?'

I glanced at the woman. Mayor, huh? She could have been anyone's mum.

'In Australia, a mayor is mainly a ceremonial role.' I ad-libbed, adjusting my glasses to appear knowledgeable. 'I met the mayor of Herriberri last week. He seemed to wield a lot of power.'

'Old Etchegaray, huh?'

The look José and his friend exchanged spoke volumes. I only wished I could translate it. I had enough trouble deciphering what people were saying. Tonight the challenge was deciphering what they were *not* saying. It was exhausting.

The cellar was filling up. Unsure of how long I could I keep our desultory conversation going, I ploughed on. 'He holds court in that bar. I can just imagine him under a tree, dispensing favours and punishments like a medieval lord.'

A wry smile ran over José's face. 'That's right. The old rascal has his finger in every pie.'

Jacqueline took over. 'Fernand Etchegaray owns the Bear Inn. He's got a perfectly good *mairie* in Herriberri but he uses the bar as his office. As a mayor, I'd say he's a bit of a–' she struggled to tone down the qualifier she was itching to use, and settled for 'demagogue.'

She didn't like Fernand much, I could tell.

'A demagogue?'

'Yes, giving favours, calling on favours, using threats, that sort of thing.' She faced me fully. 'I don't want you to think that is how all our French mayors function. That man's hubris is unbelievable. But what can you do?' She opened her hands. 'We're a democracy and they keep re-electing him.'

WHAT IS CHARLÈNE UP TO?

Finally, the door to the kitchen opened. Xavier and his gang filed out in a cloud of steam, bearing earthenware dishes they placed on a long table along the far wall. Charlène and the girls took over the waitressing.

Xavier removed his apron and called me over to his table.

'So, what are we eating tonight, Chef?' I beamed.

'*Merlu à la plancha.*'

'*A la plancha,* fantastic.'

'And for main course, a wild boar shot by my uncle.'

Did it get any better? I hopped over the bench, buzzing with anticipation. Someone poured white wine into my glass. I raised it and addressed the heavens a prayer of thanks for sending me to this cheese cellar. For me, it was the equivalent of an early Christian secret place of worship.

Freshly caught hake grilled in its own juices sprinkled with *piment d'Espelette,* salt and a little garlic, cooked over a hot metal plate went a long way to demonstrate what food meant to my new friends.

When a Basque tells you that food is important to him, it isn't about Sechuan pepper, star fruit, pink Himalayan salt or wine in every sauce. No, it is about celebrating the honest flavour of local ingredients. The wild boar, fed on acorns, had practically walked into the pot and only yesterday, the *merlu* was still swimming off the coast of Biarritz. Eating was a celebration of the seasons, a communion with the land and sea that had sustained the Basques for millennia. I had to admit, though they were a little too carnivorous for my taste, I admired their devotion.

'Xavier, did you ever have aspirations of becoming a chef?'

The corner of his eyes crinkled. 'What? Work ungodly hours tied to a stove? Never having any time off? No way. I'm too much of an outdoors man. I love the forest. I'm lucky to have a job near home. Very lucky. Jobs are hard to come by here. That's why I need to practice my English.'

'So, you can talk to trees in English?'

'Ha ha.' He nudged me affectionately. 'When I meet a poacher, I won't be arresting him in English, but it'll be one more string to my bow. We're very big on eco-tourism here.'

'How about your friends, the three Musketeers, what do they do for a living?' I addressed a smile at Patxi, who was following our conversation.

'The three Musketeers, yeah that's us,' Patxi spluttered, his mouth full of bread. 'We've been together since primary school.'

'Thick as thieves, aren't we?' Xavier slapped Patxi's back. 'Patxi works in a bank.' He pointed to the tall silent one. 'Jean-Phi is a sports teacher in Paris, and Imanol is doing his last year of agricultural college. Then he'll be looking for a woman with a farm, won't you Imanol?'

Imanol shrugged. Macho, cool in a vest that showed off his biceps, he sank his large teeth into a boar rib and ignored us.

You can tell a lot about a person from the way they eat.

Imanol held the bones with his fingers and tore off great chunks of meat. Strong, rugged and daring, he was the type who got drunk and would throw himself into a river for a bet, though it did puzzle me that he didn't drink more than he did.

Plump Patxy needed love. Vegetables just didn't hit the spot. I watched him dip his bread in the oil of the hake, the sauce of the boar and, at the end of the meal, gobble a second helping of cake. He might have been ignored as a child, perhaps he was the 'middle one' in a brood of three. Insecure Patxy was a clown, a crowd pleaser, a follower.

There was a military streak to Jean-Phi. He lifted his hand whenever the wine came around, his intake strictly limited to two glasses. He favoured the vegetables and ignored the dessert. Jean-Phi was the kind of guy you wanted around when stranded on a desert island.

Xavier, my epicurean D'Artagnan, chewed slowly, discussed the ingredients and inhaled the aromas. Creative, organised, he was the leader. The way he swooned over his food promised a fantastic lover. The four of them complemented each other and I was beginning to like them. A lot.

The girls had finished serving and came to sit with us, Charlène far enough away for me to relax. I didn't follow all the banter but basked in their warmth, Xavier's thigh against mine. He made a few attempts to draw me into the conversation, and even translated the jokes. Bless him, he wanted me to be part of his gang.

Between the cheese and the gateau, Charlène got up and leaned against Xavier's back, wrapped her arms around his neck and simpered in Basque in a little girl's voice. Like a cat on heat, she went on to snuggle between Patxi and Imanol, taunting poor Patxi with a plunging view of her décolleté. What Xavier saw in her, I really could not fathom.

The cheese – I was told – came from the ewes now asleep

above our heads. The meal drew to its end and once the gateau was served, guests began to drift about. A middle-aged man kicked up a jig on his accordion, accompanied by a drummer. Charlène took to the floor with another girl. Xavier returned to the kitchen.

Soon, the 'dance-floor' was full of Basques a-leaping, their intricate steps bringing back memories of St Patrick's Day at the Irish club. Bottles of Cognac and Patxaran liqueur were passed around. At the back, José, Jacqueline and their friends had thrown a piece of green baize over a table. José was dealing out the cards for a game of *'mus.'*

For me, it was time to go. I took my leave of the card players. Unable to find Xavier, I told Patxi I was going, and called the taxi that had brought me here.

I stepped into the yard, removed my silly glasses, inhaled a lungful of warm grassy air tainted with lanolin, and looked up at the stars. A half-moon dimly lit the valley. Below us the young Nive skipped over rocks and rushed towards Bayonne and the sea. Songs rose from the cellar. Over in the large barn, ewes were baahing in their sleep. I closed my eyes, replete and mellow and listened to the noises of the night.

From the side of the farm rose giggles and sighs. I tiptoed to the corner and stopped with a jolt. Standing against the wood stack, pink arms clutched Imanol's white vest and a long jean-clad leg was clamped around his thigh.

I shot back into the shadows. Heck, what was going on? My heart went out to Xavier. I couldn't imagine a worse scenario: the poor chap spends all day cooking while his best mate shags his girlfriend.

'Chloe?'

Yikes. I rushed back to the door, hooked Xavier's arm in mine and pulled him towards the river, away from the rutting. 'I'm sorry I have to go, but you understand how important tomorrow is for me. I'm starting at the Bear Inn.'

'I do, Cinderella.' His eyes twinkled in the moonlight. 'Listen, you don't have to pay for a taxi. Imanol will give you a lift. Wait here. I'll go and find him.'

'No!' I drew him away from the house. 'He's been drinking.'

'He can't have. He drew the short straw. He's Sam tonight. Listen, he can't be very far. He's probably gone out for a smoke.' Xavier headed for the wood shelter.

I gripped his arm. 'Sam? Who's Sam?'

He placed both hands on my forearms. At his touch, my body fizzed like a can of Guinness after it was just opened, the one with the widget.

'Sam is what we call the one who doesn't drink. It stands for Sobriety And Moderation, or is it Security and Moderation, I'm not sure.'

'Yeah well, so much for Sam. I've just seen him down a glass of Patxaran.'

I'd drunk two myself against my better judgement. That stuff was amazing. Strong too, my head was swimming, or perhaps it wasn't just the liqueur.

I shook myself. 'I've called the taxi already. Why don't we go back down and listen to the music while we wait?'

A car drove up the hill. 'Okay, Prince Charming, here's my coach. Thank you for inviting me. I've had a fantastic time.' I babbled on as loud as I could. By the woodshed, the sighing had reached fever pitch. 'The food was amazing. Tell me, the sauce you made for the wild boar, what was the secret ingredient? Couldn't put my finger on it.'

He smiled. 'Chocolate. I'd forgotten to bring it. Charlène had to go home for it.' He drew me to him and ran his fingers through my hair, a question in his eyes. 'Chloe, I–'

I sank into him, overcome by the deadly mix of chocolate and magical summer nights.

The beam of the taxi illuminated the yard. I bit my lip.

Behind Xavier, the headlights brushed Imanol and Charlène clinging furiously to each other. Xavier's words struck me. Had he said Charlène had to go *home* for the chocolate? Jeepers, did they live together?

The bubble burst. I came to my senses. Two wrongs didn't make a right. I plonked a sisterly kiss on Xavier's cheek and escorted him to the top of the stairs, relieved when someone called him from the cellar.

He skipped down the steps, unaware of his friend's betrayal. I trudged to the car and collapsed on the back seat with a groan, my head and my heart in a mess.

CHLOE GETS A JOB

The Bear Inn was a place of light and shadows. The long veranda windows framed rural scenes of such timeless beauty that for the visitor, here at least, time stood still. Warmed by the setting sun, the veranda was an oasis for souls that pined for the old world.

In this cocoon, my aunts Muriel and Viviane – who did not know they were my aunts – pampered our guests, tenderly suggesting, a hand on the back of their chair, that they might perhaps fancy a slice of cheese before dessert, and hinted, eyes half-closed in pleasure, that the *gateau basque au chocolat* was to die for.

While our guests gazed over Paradise Lost, inside the dark north-facing kitchen, we minions toiled. Heated by an ancient oven spewing the fires of hell, the kitchen was ruled by Frederic, my cousin, who did not know he was my cousin. The modicum of talent Fred had inherited had gone to his head, and he saw it as an obligation to be temperamental.

So delighted was I to have secured a job at the Bear, I'd never imagined I could dislike my own cousin. From the moment I'd stepped into his kitchen, the label 'Aussie scullion' written on my forehead, Fred's eyes gleamed at the chance of another female to bully.

Did we *really* cut green beans on the slant in Australia? Had the spiralling of courgettes not yet reached our shores? His scorn tagged with *'Putain, elle est con cette nana,'* 'Christ, is she dumb,' never failed to send his evil valet Urko into fits of sniggers.

Fred objected to everything I did. He would yank things from my hands with such contempt, that I was inches away from punching his big nose.

'Chloe,' he would sigh, 'this is *magret de canard...* Duck breast. Duck is to be treated with respect, it's not kangaroo.' How often had I dropped my knife as if it was on fire, gripped the edge of the worktop and breathing deeply, counted backwards from ten to calm my murderous impulse.

Last night, after the wedding, we'd finished at two in the morning. Today, my head was swimming with exhaustion. It was Sunday and I had to return to the kitchen early to cater for a party of cyclists. I couldn't see the attraction of cycling here myself, it was always uphill, but piqued by the challenge, and with the help of electric bikes, Parisian Middle-Aged-Men-in-Lycra came in droves.

The menu, Frédéric the Great had declared, would be simple. The MAMILs didn't come all that way for molecular cuisine. They would expect regional food, therefore a classic Bayonne ham and melon combination would make a good starter and, for main course, *lomo* and *ratatouille*. Fred might have been a small-time tyrant, but he knew his onions, and that pork-loin tasted better in Spanish.

Lomo carried enough exoticism to tease the palate. I had learned from Cosmo that just as words of love are the sweetest foreplay, a well-written menu whets the appetite.

All it may take for us Brits to enhance our food is a clove

of garlic and a glamorous French name, but what do the French do when they want to add that *je ne sais quoi* to a dish? They are stymied, since it's already French. To that purpose, Spanish came in handy around here. Everyone spoke it and it was a lot easier to pronounce than Basque. So, if you are French, all you need to spice up your food is a pinch of Espelette pimento and a sprinkling of Español.

I was prepping the melons when Urko, Fred's valet, crawled out of the cellar, dragging up a bag of aubergines. He dumped it on the worktop and leered at me, uncovering teeth like gravestones. He tipped the aubergines out, pushed them towards me and slouched back down to the cellar.

The other salad girl, Maia, was wan and exhausted. With dark circles under her eyes, she looked like of one of Dracula's victims.

Maia and I scooped up a pile each, sighed in unison and we began to chop.

Ratatouille is a dish that can't be hurried. Every vegetable must be thoroughly fried or the stew will taste insipid. Frying uses a lot of oil, so to minimise the calories, I like to roast my aubergines, courgettes and peppers separately in the oven beforehand.

Fred glowered at me. 'Chloe, what are you doing?'

I had a knife in one hand and a pile of aubergines in front of me. What did he *think* I was doing?

I replied through gritted teeth, 'Prepping the veg for the ratatouille.'

Urko emerged from the cellar, emptied a box of courgettes on the worktop in front of Maia with a smirk.

Fred narrowed his eyes. 'Maia's doing that. I told you to prep the *karrumbol*.'

Of course, he hadn't. Altering instructions is a well-known bullying technique.

'Sorry.' I stepped away from the aubergines, scanned the

kitchen for a clue as to what the *karrumbol* could be, and drew a blank. All I could see were apples, pears and raspberries.

Fred pointed to the fruit. Urko sniggered.

I dropped my knife, the urge to stick it into him impossible to resist. 'I don't speak Basque,' I growled, 'and I've never heard of *karrumbol*.'

The two idiots tittered. Fred shook his head in disbelief. 'It's English, stupid.'

I grabbed a pen and pad and pushed them towards him. 'Please write it down.'

He scribbled 'Krumble,' pushed it back to me with a sneer and tilted his head as if to say 'happy now?' before swaggering to the bar where, undaunted by the early hour, a posse of workmen were waiting for their first white wine of the day.

I sank my head into my hands and silently murmured a prayer.

'Pop, give me a sign, will you? I'm not sure how long I can bear to work with this arsehole.'

Fred returned, pulled a packet of Gauloise out of his top pocket and signalled to Urko, who shambled after him.

Opposite me, Maia was sniffing over onions. I felt sorry for her. She really looked tired. Her hair was lank and her neck and elbows bore great swathes of eczema. I swept her pile of onions towards me and attacked them with all the rage I hadn't been able to direct at Fred.

The pungent smell drew me back to the King's Arms, to the frustration and loneliness that had been my constant companions at the time. I wiped my eyes and gazed out to the mountains still under their blanket of mist, to the view Pop had carried inside him all his life, reminding myself why I was here. Yes, I had come a long way. Ten months ago, I didn't even know about the Bear Inn.

I pushed the chopped onions towards Maia, washed my hands and went to the window for a breath of fresh air, but instead, inhaled Gauloise smoke. I leaned over. The hotel was built on a slope, which fell away at the back. A staircase led up to the kitchen.

Below me, Fred and Urko sat on the stone steps, making life plans, dreaming big, as boys do.

'Christ, I'm pissed off with these mountains.' Fred said.

'Shit man, if you fuck off to Paris, you're gonna leave me without a job. If this place closes down, I'm in the *merde,*' Urko replied in the same vein.

They spoke French, *Euskal* probably too short of expletives for their purpose. For once, I was glad of the slang I'd picked up on the beach.

'What's so great about Paris anyway?' Urko grumbled.

'I've got myself an apprenticeship with the best fucking chef in France, dickhead, that's what's in Paris. I'm not spending the rest of my life here cooking *poulet basquaise*. I'm worth more than that.'

Paris? Wow, Fred was indeed dreaming big. Plucky of him, considering how the family's livelihood rested on his shoulders.

'You're leaving us in the lurch, man.'

'My old woman used to cook, didn't she, before I took over. She can do it again.'

I wondered who he was referring to, and remembered that Muriel was his mother.

'Don't worry,' Fred was saying, 'she'll manage well enough until the end of the season. As for next year? Yeah, you're gonna have to find yourself another job if this place gets sold. Sorry mate.' Fred bent down to put his cigarette out and said something I didn't hear.

'You really think it's going to happen?' Urko sounded worried.

'Sure. It was her idea. She got me the apprenticeship in Paris. Dunno how a pharmacist gets to know a famous chef, but there you are. I've got his offer in writing.'

Fred slapped Urko's shoulder. 'Urko my man, you're looking at the next great Basque chef. Watch out Arzak! Fred Etchegaray is on his way!

Pharmacist? Which pharmacist? I mulled over the word. Then it came back to me. Of course, the pharmacist, the witch who had tried to poison me was his aunt. Why was she sending Fred to Paris?

'The shit will hit the fan.'

'*Putain*, Urko, stop fretting like a girl.'

The click of a lighter. The smell of Gauloise grew stronger. Fred sucked in a lungful and said, 'Talking about girls, what do you think of that new Aussie broad? *Elle est bandante hein?'*

I gagged. Untranslatable, the adjective conjured up a picture I simply did not want in my brain. Those two sex-starved pillocks had included me into their private fantasies. Hoping to cleanse away the image, I stared out at the clean wisps of clouds lifting into the morning sky. Still, their filth floated up towards me, together with the stink of unfiltered cigarettes.

'She's hot,' Urko enthused. 'I bet she's up for it.'

In your dreams mate. One false move and their balls would be floating in white sauce with the *ris de veau* sweetbread planned for Monday's menu.

'Oy! Hands off, okay?' Fred invoked his *droit de seigneur*. 'You can look but not touch. She's mine.'

A hand over my mouth I leaned against the wall, not knowing whether to laugh or cry. Below me, the conversation carried on in Basque. I singled out one word. '*Aitaxi*.'

In the bar, Aitaxi was pontificating to the postman,

unaware of his grandson's plans to desert the family hotel for Paris.

Puzzled, I returned to the *karrumbol.*

LIFE AT THE BEAR INN

At lunchtime, Maia, Urko and I took our meals with the family in the original oak dining-room. Every morning, our hotel guests had their breakfast there, and it was sometimes used as a spill-over room for functions when the veranda was full.

Sitting at the head of the table, Uncle Fernand was regaling us with a story I struggled to follow, something about a bridge between our village and nearby Esterençuby.

'So, I said to her,' the old man boomed, 'Madame Loyola, have you not heard of regional grants? The woman was fully expecting *me* to pay for repairing the bridge!'

Interesting. Loyola was the name of the couple I'd met at the *txoko*. Was Jacqueline not mayor there? I tuned in.

'But Papa, is that bridge not within the confines of your *commune*?' Viviane piped up. 'Why should Jacqueline have to pay?'

Fernand glowered at her. 'That bridge is coterminous with her *commune*.'

'Coterminous? Don't you mean contiguous?'

I was glad Muriel had asked. I'd never heard of coterminous, but then again that applied to most words.

Contempt skimmed across her father's face. '*Coterminous* means that it has a common border. Jacqueline Loyola –' Fernand uttered her name like that of a poisonous plant '– did not know what it meant either, silly woman. Because it is coterminous, the responsibility falls on both of us to carry out repairs.' He spat, 'a woman mayor, ha! Why can't she stay in her kitchen?'

'Papa, your *chipirons* are getting cold.' Viviane reproached gently.

Fernand ranted on, ignoring the tiny squids congealing on his plate.

'You can say what you want, shabadabada law and all that, women aren't cut out to be mayors.'

'Shabadabada?' I repeated, round-eyed.

Viviane whispered, 'the law that ensures that the same number of men and women apply for positions.'

My squid dangled half-way to my open mouth. 'Huh?'

'It comes from the song, 'A Man and a Woman?'

I chewed slowly, digesting the information.

Across the hall, guests were dropping into the small bar. Urko went to serve them.

What were the chances, I pondered, in a region so proud of its roots as a matriarchal society, that I would find a dinosaur at the head of my own family? Fred was bound to follow in the footsteps of his flawed role model. No wonder Fred's father had made himself scarce.

Tired of listening to Fernand, I went to the kitchen to fetch the ratatouille.

'So, what do you think of our Harzainostatua?' Old Fernand bellowed as I filled up his plate.

I nearly dropped the dish. Had he noticed my existence?

I cleared my throat. 'Ah it is surprising – ahem, it is

wonderful that the restaurant is so out of the way and yet filled so consistently, hum, with happy customers.' I was honest. Heck, where *did* they all come from?

The old man beamed at his grandson. *'Frédéric est un grand cuisinier*, a great chef. Yes, people come from miles around to eat his food. Soon, we will be famous.'

Muriel buzzed with such motherly pride, the air crackled with it.

Fernand winked at Fred. 'That boy' will put the Bear Inn on the map. By next year, he will have doubled the number of customers, won't you boy?'

Fred shuffled uncomfortably and stared into his plate. To his left, Urko had turned the colour of beetroot.

I watched the two of them squirm as I served my two aunts, toying with the idea of revealing what I'd overheard. What a bombshell that would be.

'Was this always a hotel?' I asked sensibly.

'No. My father was a shoemaker. My mother loved cooking and villagers came to her whenever they had a baptism, a first communion or a funeral, and she would cook for them. This was our home.' He lifted his eyes to the ceiling. 'I was born up here, in the room above. I inherited the hotel and ran it with my wife. When she died–' he pointed to his daughter with a dismissive gesture, 'Muriel and her good-for-nothing husband kept it ticking over.' He patted his stomach with a proud grin. 'Now we're going places.'

Fred had turned puce. He pushed his plate away and went to the bar.

I could not believe the look of filial devotion on Viviane and Muriel's faces. It seemed so undeserved. My own father, Matteo, had had no patience with Pop. Whenever Pop reminisced about his birthplace, Dad would roll his eyes and say, 'Oh, here we go again.' No wonder I did not know anything about my Basque heritage.

I carried on pleasantly, 'I read that families were very large here in the Basque Country. *Monsieur,* did you too have many siblings?'

Fernand poured himself a glass of wine, took a sip and slowly shook his big head.

'Hmmm. I had a younger brother.' His eyes were vague. 'Following our local tradition, he went to seek his fortune in Paris.'

'And, did he find it?' My smile was a little forced. Would he confirm the tale Xavier had been told?

Fernand tore a chunk of bread, dipped it into his sauce and mumbled so low I could hardly hear, 'No. He died.'

'I'm sorry.' I said disingenuously.

The old Bear returned his full attention to his ratatouille.

'My grandmother opened up rooms and cooked for guests,' Viviane explained. 'In those days, just after the War, commercial reps would take the train to Saint Jean Pied de Port. My grandfather picked them up from the station in his car and brought them up here. They'd stay for a week and *walked* to wherever they had to go.' She nodded thoughtfully. 'Poor chaps. It's hard to imagine, isn't it? They walked everywhere, those reps.'

In all our minds, the image appeared of a lonely rep pulling a vacuum cleaner down a winding road, across the Jaioleku bridge coterminous with Esterençuby.

'Why the name, the Bear Inn?'

Fred came back from the bar and leaned on the doorjamb. 'An ancestor on my grandmother's side once shot a huge brown bear because it was attacking his sheep,' he explained, 'that's when we still had bears in the Pyrenees. He had the head stuffed. It used to be here on the wall, but we had to take it down. Too much flack from conservationists.' He sat down and added with a sneer, 'They've been re-introducing bears up on the peaks. The last Pyrenean bear was shot in 2004, so they had to bring them in from Slovenia. Local farmers are up in arms about it, you know, worried about their sheep.'

I lifted my gaze to the discoloured patch where the trophy used to hang. Crikey, that Irouleguy wine was strong. I'd only had one glass. The paint wobbled, bubbled, and a hologram of Fernand's head looked down at us as we ate.

Viviane took over. 'The bear my great-grandfather shot was a female. It had a cub. He caught it and sold it to someone in a valley near Andorra where they were known to teach bears to dance. That bear went to America, to the Barnum Circus.'

I swallowed hard. I didn't know how to feel.

'Shooting's big around here.' Fernand wiped his mouth. 'We're expecting a large shooting party on Wednesday. Fifty of them.'

'Them and their muddy dogs.' Muriel grumbled. She caught my eye. 'Chloe, would you be able to help out on Wednesday? It makes life so much easier for us, having you around.'

'I'd love to.' My heartbeat went up a notch. If I could stop myself from castrating my cousin, I might get somewhere in my fact-finding mission.

I left them to clear away the plates and, under the pretence of looking for a bathroom, sneaked upstairs. A small corridor led to the bright guest extension Fernand had added to the side of the hotel a few years back. To my right was a dark oak-panelled landing and three doors marked 'private.' Dim light bounced off copper kettles and waxed furniture.

I tiptoed along squeaky floorboards, and projected myself back to the War years, when Pop's family lived here. I quietly opened one of the bedroom doors. The picture that came to me was the day Baby Lazarro was born.

. . .

Great-grandfather Alphonse is nervously pacing the landing, his steps heavy on the parquet floor. In the bedroom, his wife Marthe is grunting. A baby cries, hurled into the world, furious at being dipped into the blue and white basin on the washstand. Five-year-old Fernand pushes the door and runs to his mother, exhausted and radiant in the big bed. He finds himself confronted with that monstrous creature, who just by existing, has supplanted him in his mother's affection, a brother called Lazarro.

Sibling rivalries heal. This one never had. Why else would Fernand pretend that Lazarro had died? Why would he want to 'kill' his brother?

XAVIER DECLARES HIS HAND

I had been working in the Bear Inn kitchen for two weeks, and what did I have to show for it, I wondered, pacing my attic like a caged bear. Yes, what had I learned? I sat down to write a list of my findings, but it was difficult. I couldn't concentrate. I checked my phone again.

I hadn't dreamt it. Xavier's text was there, in deliciously ungrammatical English.

'Hello Chloé. I have news for the lake and if you have the time, we can do a pique-nique. I will take the food.'

I read out the message to Pop and L'ami Yabon.

'Listen you two, I'm going to the lake, right. I'd love to take you with me, but I'm not sure we'll be allowed in just yet.' I lifted a hand. 'I'm just going to check it out, so don't get your hopes up. Pop, I don't blame you for leaving that bully of a brother behind. Listen, what I don't understand is why he told me that you had died.' I ran my fingers through my hair. 'I'm trying my best, you know, but I haven't exactly got much to go on, so why don't you give me a sign?'

A ray of sun caught the yellow chocolate tin. L'ami Yabon smiled brightly, but then, he always did.

I pushed my thumbs into my jeans pocket and carried on. 'I have two lovely aunts I didn't have before. They're cousins once removed really, but they're so much older than me, I think of them as aunties. You'd love them. They're Fernand's daughters Muriel and Viviane. I love the Bear Inn, though there is a problem. Fernand's eldest daughter, Arrantxa, the pharmacist. She wants it sold.'

The sound of my ringtone distracted me. I'd chosen *Show'm what you're made of* from the Backstreet Boys. I should have outgrown those boys years ago really.

'Xavier?' I whispered breathless.

'Did you get my SMS?'

I swallowed hard and injected a little formality into my voice.

'Yes, I did, thank you. I was just about to reply.'

'Are you free this afternoon?' His voice was warm and carefree. I was glad he was still carefree. It was only a matter of time until he discovered Charlène's infidelity and Imanol's betrayal. Should I tell him what they were up to behind his back? Perhaps not. These things had a habit of backfiring.

'Did you say we could go to the lake? Do you have news?'

'Yes, I do.'

'Well?'

'I will pick you up at four o'clock.'

'What should I bring?' We were speaking English, and conversing on the phone in a foreign language was a challenge Xavier had yet to master. Still, we persevered.

'Just you.' Xavier said.

'Not Pop?'

'No, I have a radio in the Jeep.'

'Huh? Sorry, I meant should I bring the Banania tin?'

'No, I have a thermos.'

'A thermos?' What was he talking about?

'For the hot chocolate.'

I gave up.

Time stretched like bubble gum, spent in a frenzy of bathing and getting dressed, trying to make sense of the vibrations I had picked up from him. I was not an expert on French men. Was Xavier simply being helpful, or did he have an ulterior motive? Surely, the appeal of Charlène's creamy breasts would wane when he finally realised that she didn't have a brain. Was he one of those rats who played the field, preying on tourists? Were we just friends?

I plumped for the latter, though when I opened the door and saw him standing there, it took all I had not to drag him into my lair and rip off his denim shirt.

'Hi.' His smile went straight to my womb.

Calm down Chloe. Deep breaths now. Think of the bigger picture.

The trip to the lake was a blur. We didn't say much. Every so often, he would glance at me. In a trance, I stared out of the window, my heart pounding inside my chest. If his affair with Charlène was over, how soon could I offer to comfort him?

Was I even in with a chance? I wasn't sure, so I tried to concentrate on the lake, trying to imagine what I would find there, but whenever I broached the subject, Xavier simply shook his head, saying I would see for myself.

He parked the jeep as near to the lake as he could.

'Xavier, why have you brought me here, if not to scatter my grandfather's ashes?'

He removed the key from the ignition, grabbed a carrier bag and invited me to sit on a large tree trunk.

I breathed in his scent of shampoo and clean cotton. He rested soft brown eyes on me and his hand strayed towards mine. We were so close, I thought he might kiss me.

He let out a long breath and said, 'Let me show you something.' He took out his bunch of keys and separated one from the rest. 'This, is the key to the jeep.'

I huddled closer, wondering where this was heading.

'This, is the key to my Renault,' and so it went on until the last one, a tiny padlock key. 'And this,' he concluded with an apologetic glance, is the key to the lake.'

'What?' I jumped back with a murderous glare. 'How long have you had it?'

'I am a ranger here. I always have it.'

My mouth fell open. 'But, you – you said your father knew –' I stammered. 'Why? Why did you keep me hanging on, why did you tell me you didn't have it?' I shook my head. 'Christ, what is *wrong* with you people?'

'Klo-é,' he cooed my name. 'Klo-é, you have to trust me.'

'Trust you? Why would I do that?'

'Here, have some hot chocolate and brioche.'

'Chocolate? Now?'

'Yes, you said you wanted Banania.'

I sunk my head into my hands with a groan.

He unscrewed the thermos, poured steaming cocoa into an enamel mug, handed it to me, poured himself another, and calmly dunked his brioche into the chocolate. I don't know what it is with the French and dunking.

He dropped his cup to the ground and smiled. 'You told me that you once saw the Basajaun in there, remember?'

'The Basajaun.' I sneered. 'So that's who they're keeping behind that fence. Sorry. I'm not amused.'

'The Ministry of the Environment,' Xavier ignored my cynical comment and explained in French, 'has initiated a programme of reintroducing brown bears to the Pyrenees.'

'That's all well and good, but what does this have to – aaargh.' I didn't finish my sentence. Something was moving in the undergrowth. I nudged Xavier. 'Look!'

A huge brown bear had shambled to the gate. It stopped, stood on its hind legs, and wriggled its nose, scenting the air.

'He's after our brioche.' Xavier whispered.

I stood rock still. The monster sniffed around, lowered its huge paws and looked straight into my eyes. It knocked the breath out of me. He held my gaze for what seemed an eternity, then turned away and lumbered back into the bushes, leaving me flushed with awe.

'Fancy going after him?'

My heart knocking against my ribs, I shook my head, unable to believe what I'd seen.

'Wow.'

Xavier's face softened. 'That was the patriarch. They've been in there so long, they've multiplied.'

'Why are they in there?'

'The Environment Ministry and conservationists want to reintroduce bears into the wild, but the shepherds are up in arms, worried that they'll go after their flocks, and threaten to destroy them. The dispute has been going on for years.'

'Oh dear, what about Pop?' I asked, both elated and crestfallen.

Xavier picked up his mug. 'It's not as if your grandad is going anywhere, is it? Don't worry. It will happen.' He patted my hand. 'You'll just have to be patient.'

'I can't be patient. You see, my parents have sent me a ticket back to Oz. Even if I come back, I've discovered that the hotel might be sold.

'The Bear Inn? Why? From what I hear, it's doing really well.'

'My horrid cousin, the one who works in the pharmacy, wants to sell the hotel.' Cousin Arrantxa definitely did not deserve to be upgraded to auntie.

'Horrid cousin? Who's that?'

'Arrantxa Arroztegui. She's the pharmacist in –'

'You mean Arrantxa? The chemist in Herriberri is your cousin? What a coincidence, she's my aunt.'

His aunt? Was Xavier my cousin? No! 'How are you related to her?' I asked urgently.

'Her husband, Bruno, is my father's brother. They've fallen out. Bruno keeps borrowing money and never pays it back.'

Arrantxa was his aunt by marriage. Phew!

'She's much older than him. Calls herself a cougar.'

Except she looked like a griffon vulture. 'What else can you tell me about them?'

'Her husband's a womaniser. There have been rumours, but she always forgives him.'

'What does he do for a living, this Bruno?'

'Entrepreneur. What business he is in exactly, no one knows. He is one of these people who have great ideas but they never get anywhere.'

'I don't understand why she tried to frighten me off when she found out who I was. What threat can I possibly be to her? Did she think I was his bit of totty?'

'I don't know, Miss Marple,' Xavier shrugged after I'd explained 'totty.'

He took the cups, hesitated and said, 'Come on, we tidy up and now I show you my forest.'

He opened his backpack. I handed him the cups. Our fingers touched. The cups fell to the ground with a soft clang. In slow motion Xavier pushed the backpack out of the way and shuffled closer. He put a hand around my waist and drew me to him. The enchanted clearing, the tall trees above us spun away. Dizzy, I held on to him and dissolved into his kiss.

CHLOE MAKES A DEAL

I had been working at the Bear Inn for three weeks when Cousin Fred made his move. It was my afternoon break. The weather was fine and I had gone across to the churchyard to commune with the souls of my ancestors. Basque life, we are told, used to revolve around the house, '*etxe,*' and in life as in death, families stuck together. In the little churchyard, while most graves were cluttered with porcelain plaques bearing pictures of sheep and cattle, Alphonse Etchegaray and his wife Marthe rested under a dignified slab of granite right behind the tall pink *fronton.* Though Pop was supposed to have died in Paris in 1971, there was no sign of him.

I sat on a bench. Eyes closed, bypassing the sounds of crickets and cowbells tinkling around the valley, I had relived Xavier's kiss many times and was now testing my body for signs of home-sickness, conjuring up the patter of the rain, the roar of the A5, the screams of police sirens and voices of my neighbours arguing. I found none. I didn't miss England one bit.

How I envied Pop for being born here. The bulk of the

Pyrenees and sloping fields, so green and velvety in the afternoon sun, gave him a dimension I lacked.

While my mother took her Australian fun and sun with her wherever she went, I felt incomplete somehow and wished I'd been born *somewhere*. It would give me kudos, provide me with that *'Appellation d'Origine Contrôlée'* label of consistent quality without which a wine is never worth much.

That label was so important that the nearby town of Espelette was fighting to have it slapped on its pimentos. Did it matter to anyone where exactly the pimentos were grown? Yes, it mattered to them.

I too wanted to know that I had been finely crafted, not churned out on the assembly line of some large maternity unit. I don't know why I felt that way. Perhaps it was simply that I had not yet found my tribe.

Such were the thoughts flitting around my mind as I sat on the bench and gazed down at the Bear Inn. Ageless, solid, the building oozed steadfastness and generosity. On the way to nowhere, its only purpose was to make people happy. How could Arrantxa even *think* of selling it? It was criminal.

Fred came out of the main door, stopped under the tree and lit up a Gauloise. He took in a long draft, caught sight of me, smiled, swaggered across the road and lurched up the four steps into the churchyard.

'I was looking for you.' Thumbs in his pockets, fag dangling from his lips, he put a foot on my bench and said, casual-like, 'Whatcha doin'?'

I indicated the church behind me. 'Thought of going in to pray.'

He squinted at me through the smoke and smirked. 'Why, have you been a naughty girl?'

I had been naughty, but it was none of his business. 'I'm praying for your salvation, Freddo.'

He removed his foot from the bench, sat down and covered my hand with his. He stank of fags, cheap aftershave and ratatouille. My skin crawled but I didn't take my hand away. I bided my time. His predatory eyes mistaking my passivity for a come-on, he saw me as easy bush tucker. He shuffled closer, ran a finger along my face and played with my hair.

I felt sick.

'You're beautiful, you know. I want to kiss you.'

As courtships went, it was brief and to the point, the French version of the 'Sheila, do you fuck?' purported to turn Aussie women on.

I met his eyes and smiled. Encouraged, he leaned over and breathed cigarette smoke all over me.

I placed a firm hand on his chest and purred, 'Why me? Why now, Freddo? There will be plenty of girls when you get to Paris.'

He shot back. 'Huh? What are you talking about?'

'Girls dying to go out with someone with such good prospects. An apprentice at Paul Bocuse's restaurant, hmm, you'll pull easily.' *Even though you're a skunk.*

He eyed me with suspicion. 'Have you been talking to Urko?' He barked, 'If that prick's told you anything, I'll smash his stupid–'

'No.' I put a hand on his arm. He yanked his arm away, singed by my touch. 'I overheard you the other day…' I kept the loving look pasted on my face, 'which is why I was praying for your salvation.'

He crumpled. 'You heard us? Oh shit. If my grandad finds out I'm leaving, I'm dead.'

'I know.'

His panic was lovely to see. His eyes darted between the hotel and me, deciding on a course of action. He took deep drags and tapped his foot, unsure of what to do next. He had come to me charged with testosterone, somehow convinced he was in with a chance, only to find I'd pulled the plug on him. I let him stew for a while, relishing his misery.

'Freddo, *mon chéri*, you've put yourself in a very big *merde* but, I can help you out of it.' He relaxed slightly, only to tense up again when I said, 'First I'd like you to explain something to me. Your aunt Arrantxa, the one who works in the pharmacy, what exactly *are* her plans for the hotel?'

Fred stared at me. 'Are you some sort of witch? How do you know that?'

'I *don't* know. That's why I'm asking you. Don't worry,' I teased, 'I can always ask your mum.'

'No!' He was livid. 'Who are you? What are you doing here? What do you want from us?'

I could tell him the whole story, but I didn't trust him. Raised by a mother who thought the sun shone out of his *derrière*, Fred had modelled himself on a grandfather for whom manipulating people was second nature. Not only did Fred lack Fernand's stature and life experience, but because he had never been hurt, he didn't have the killer instinct. In a way, I felt sorry for him. He might be a weasel, but he was my cousin, a passport into my family, so I spoke his language and 'did a deal' with him.

'I'll keep what I heard to myself if you tell me what your aunt plans to do. Then I will help you.'

'How?'

I shook my head. 'Tut tut, you first.'

He threw his cigarette onto the gravel, crushed it with the tip of his trainer and waggled his head. 'All right, but what I tell you is classified information. If Mum and Viviane find out –'

'They won't.'

'Ataitxi owns the hotel, but before I came along, Mum had

to take out a loan to keep it going. They borrowed from my Uncle Bruno, Arrantxa's husband.'

'Tell me about him.'

'Well, there's a bit of a betting tradition in these parts, you know. People bet on the outcome of a pelota match, or who'll win when they play *mus*, but Bruno's gambling's got out of hand – he was really well-off at the time – and he lost all his money. He can't wait for Aitatxi to die so he can call in Mum's loan. If he does, we'll have to sell.'

I glanced at the doomed hotel, a cold feeling in the pit of my stomach. 'I see, so your aunt has plans for the hotel after your grandfather's death, but she is sending you away to Paris now.'

'Yeah well, he's got a dodgy ticker. Perhaps being a pharmacist, she knows something we don't.'

Good grief, give me the Adams Family anytime. Nice relatives I had. An old tyrant, a gambler, three daughters, one of them a poisoner, and a young weasel. I'd landed in a nest of vipers. No wonder Pop had never made the effort to rekindle with them.

'The real reason she wants me to train is that, if I come back for a season, it will increase the reputation of the restaurant and its value. With a ready-made clientele the place is worth twice the building on its own.'

Selling the Bear Inn. Under the *fronton,* I thought I could hear Alphonse and Marthe turn in their grave.

'But your mother and Viviane would never agree!'

'They won't have a choice.' Fred added with feeling, 'I'm sorry but I want to go beyond traditional cuisine. I really don't want to spend the rest of my life here.'

I opened my lips to reply, but struggled to produce a sound. 'Ho-how can you do this? Leave your family in the lurch?'

His weaselly chest caved in with a long cigarette-scented

sigh. He waved a hand towards the valley. 'I'm trapped here. I can't take it anymore. I'm worth more than this.'

Christ, how could he say that?

I thought back to Fernand's three daughters. While the pharmacist was plotting her father's demise, it was in Muriel's interest that the old man should live forever. We'd better go easy on the crème fraîche and make sure Aunt Arrantxa didn't feed him mushrooms.

'Okay. You said you could help me.' The weasel tried hard to look cool. He realised he was biting his nails and tucked his hands under his thighs. He looked so like a little boy, I nearly felt sorry for him.

'I trained as a chef. I can take over from you if it's any help.'

His eyes popped out of his head. 'But if you're a chef, what's all this crap about a salad-girl? Why the fuck did you say you were *'aide de cuisine?'*

'It got me in, didn't it? Would you have hired an Australian chef?'

'Hm. You have a point. I still don't see why you want to work *here* in this dump of all places? I really don't get it.'

'We'll get to that in a minute. Listen, here is the plan. You will teach me your basic dishes, then I can take over when you go, and then your desertion won't seem so bad.'

His eyes narrowed. 'What's in it for you?'

'I'll tell you why.' I touched his arm and leaned seductively towards him. 'We are related you and I.'

His mouth fell so wide open, I could count his fillings.

'The man who died in Paris a long time ago, I am his granddaughter. Freddo my boy, I'm your long-lost cousin.'

'B–but you – you said you were Australian.'

'I am. My mother is Australian, but before he 'died' in Paris back in the seventies, your uncle Lazarro had a son, my father. This, you will keep to yourself or I will spill your beans.'

'You really are my cousin?' His face lit up. 'That's great. Why didn't you say so in the first place?'

'Last time I broadcast who I was, Arrantxa tried to poison me.'

'What? Why should she do that?'

'I was hoping you would tell me, though I'm beginning to have a little idea.'

He sat back and studied me, a flicker of joy dancing in his eyes. 'Wow, to think you're my cousin.'

'I'm your second cousin.' I lifted a hand. 'And no, you can't kiss me.'

'Sorry about that.'

I stood to leave and turned back with a word of warning. 'And it doesn't mean that because you can't, that plonker Urko gets to try his luck, okay?'

Cousin Fred had the good grace to blush. There was hope for him yet.

CHLOE BECOMES A CHEF

Any insecurity I might still have harboured about Xavier's feelings for me fell away when he offered to lend me his moped. Without it, getting to work would have been impossible. Cross-country buses did not run at night and taxis would have eaten away most of my earnings. What man parts with his wheels? Xavier was an angel.

That Wednesday morning, I straddled the moped and pulled his helmet over my head. His scent took me right back to our encounter in the forest. I stroked the handlebars, sank into the saddle and closed my eyes, wondering whether I had dreamt it.

After we had seen the bear inside the lake enclosure, Xavier had driven me around his forest and shown me the most magical places. The oldest trees, the deepest ravines, he knew them all, the whole forest belonged to him, my Sindarin Elf of the Woodland Realm, my very own Legolas.

After he had dropped me outside my flat, I had rushed upstairs to tell Pop and L'ami Yabon all about the lake, the bear who now ruled over it and the news that Pop would have to wait inside his tin until the conflict between Basque shepherds and conservationists was resolved.

To tell the truth, I had got used to having Pop near me and was not looking forward to parting with him. I would quite happily have arranged his ashes on a small altar as they do in Japan, and placed offerings of Irouleguy wine and churros, but what could I do? *Hitza hitz,* a promise was a promise. Eventually, I would have to let Pop go.

The following day, Xavier had arrived with the moped, followed by Imanol who would be driving him back. I felt awkward with Imanol. Was Xavier still going out with Charlène? I hadn't yet had the heart to broach the subject.

The moped was now mine for as long as I wanted it. The morning was cold. I zipped up my anorak, kicked the moped into life and set off o'er hills and dales to prepare the hunters' dinner.

It was rush hour in the valleys. I encountered four cars. What a commute that was. *If my friends could see me,* I giggled to myself as I parked at the back of the hotel and shook my hair loose. Jason and Leah would never know, would they, enslaved as they were in their galley kitchen. Well, good luck to them.

The old sheepdog came to me, as he did every day, and wagged his matted tail. I was patting him when the postman stopped me.

'Are you going in? If so, could you give Monsieur Etchegaray this letter?' He handed me a letter for Fernand, simply addressed to the Bear Inn, Jaioleku. France.

I checked the stamp and did a double take.

'It's from Chile.' The postman said. 'Does he know anyone in Chile?'

'A satisfied customer I imagine.' Nosy bugger.

I remembered the postcards from Chile I had found in Pop's things and wondered about the connection.

I stuffed the letter into my bag and ran up the stone steps to the back door. Something was different today. The kitchen felt brighter, lighter. The sun snuck from under a cloud and bounced off the steel surfaces. Classical music poured from a radio and Maia was laughing.

'Where's Freddo?' I tied on my red apron.

'Frédéric is away on an errand,' his mother said. 'I didn't really understand where he was going. As for my father, he has finally agreed to go and see a doctor about his heart.'

I nodded.

'Papa will be back for the hunters' dinner. He wouldn't miss it for the world.' She headed for the veranda. 'Can you come and help me with the tables in a minute?'

Humming a little song, I pinned back my hair, put on my round white *toque* and checked out the bar where four old boys were sitting around a game of *mus.* They were shepherds, probably the last men in the region to wear the traditional berets. The tradition would die with them. They had received their first beret when they started school and would be buried with them. The fashion had moved on. Only tourists wore berets now.

'What's the matter with the *patron*?' An old boy lifted his empty wine glass towards the vacant throne.

Crikey, how did they cope with wine so early? I'd heard of Champagne breakfast, but the local stuff was rather hardcore for ten o'clock in the morning.

I refilled their glasses. 'He'll be around later on, when the hunters arrive.'

Urko shambled in. I could tell from the shifty glances he threw in my direction, that he had talked to Fred. I grinned brightly and pointed to a basin filled with *chipirons*, the baby squid the Basques are so fond of stuffing. With a twirling index finger, I intimated he should do just that.

He lifted a different finger, intimating I was the one to get stuffed. As they say, seventy-five per cent of communication is non-verbal.

Maia came in from the veranda. 'I've peeled the apples for the croustade. I'll be okay with Urko for a while, if you need to help Muriel.'

Fred away, that girl was a different person. Had he tried it with her too? I wouldn't be surprised. 'Hot rabbit,' *'chaud lapin'* was how the French described men who couldn't keep it in their trousers. That boy was his own worst enemy.

I joined Muriel, his saintly mother, on the veranda. Through the open windows, the sound of cowbells and bird-song wafted in on a grass-scented breeze. Who would ever want to live anywhere else?

'Will you be making *'salmis de palombes'* for the hunters?' I asked by way of an introduction. 'Do they give you their surplus doves after the shoot?'

I remembered how, during shoots on the Woburn Estate, we were inundated with pheasants. Plucking one was fine but plucking fifty pheasants was downright unpleasant.

'Bah, they don't catch much anymore.' I took note of the fact that Muriel was placing the silverware face down and the glasses centred to the plate. 'Anyway, this is just a gathering. The shooting season doesn't start until next week.'

'I was told they have nets and ping pong bats to lure the doves down, is it true? It must be quite a massacre.' I picked a bunch of forks and followed her example.

'The number of birds goes down every year. They'll be lucky if they bring down a brace each. Shame really. *Salmis de palombe* is Frédéric's signature dish.'

'He's very talented.'

She crossed her hands over her heart in gratitude for having borne such a gifted son. 'Frédéric is so hard-working.' Ah, a mother's love. 'He has big plans for next year, you know.'

He sure did.

The poor woman, it took all I had not to take her in my arms and squeeze her.

I said, 'I'm thinking of a career in catering myself and Frédéric has agreed to mentor me, as it were, b– before I, ahem– leave.' God, how I hated lying to her, though the lie was partial. I would indeed be gone in three weeks' time, to Santiago-de-Warrnambool.

The thought of leaving seared my solar plexus. It meant leaving Xavier, and I couldn't bear it. My ticket was on its way and with it, no doubt, yet another admonishment to forget the Bear and let sleeping dogs lie.

I shook myself and returned to the present. 'Frédéric will show me how to cook a few Basque dishes.'

The Weasel's generosity did not surprise his mother at all. 'He is such a good boy. They all say he'll go far.'

'Oh, he will.' All the way to Paris for a start.

'You know, Chloe, we do appreciate your help. I was wondering – my father's birthday is coming up. Will you still be here next week?'

'Yes. I'll be here until the end of September. You close for winter in October, right?'

'Yes.' Her face fell. 'This birthday may be his last. We don't know how long we have got Dad for, you know, with his heart. He needs a bypass, but he is so stubborn.'

'You father seems –' I searched my inner lexicon for some uplifting comment, something like the equivalent of 'well-thought-of,' and came up with '– *apprécié*.'

'Oh yes.' Muriel clearly adored her father. 'He is appreciated. He's led such an interesting life. He knows everyone.'

I perked up. Whenever Pop was fishing and noticed his float suddenly dip into the water of the canal, he would whisper to me, *'See this, Chacha? I think we have a bite.'*

I had a bite. 'An interesting life?' I let her have the line.

She threaded her fingers through a few wine glasses and set them down one by one.

'Oh yes. Straight after his military he went to Chile.'

'Chile?' Oops. The letter the postman had given me was still in my bag.

'There are a lot of Basques in Chile. Dad was young. He wanted to prove himself, as they do at that age, a bit like you going to Santiago de Compostella.'

Would she be so philosophical when Fred announced that he too needed to prove himself in Paris?

'How long was he there for?'

'Four years I think.'

'What made him come back?'

'His father fell ill. His younger brother was doing his military at the time and someone had to look after the hotel.'

'So, he came back and ran the hotel with his mother and his brother, right?' I was anxious to shoehorn the brother – Pop – into the conversation.

'Well...' Muriel set the glasses down and leaned a hand on the back of a chair. 'It didn't go smoothly.'

I felt the fish wriggle at the end of my line and hoped that, because I was transient, she would not hold back.

'My grandmother hired a cook, a girl from Esterençuby. She was very good and soon, the Bear's reputation spread. My father was so confident, that he built the upstairs extension and doubled the size of the hotel.' She pointed to the modern guest rooms at the side of the original house.

A pile of napkins clutched to my chest, I prayed nothing would break the spell.

'Dad and the cook became engaged. They had been engaged for a year, the bans already published when –' Muriel shook her head sadly '– she jilted him weeks before the wedding.'

Rigid, I silently willed her to tell me the name of the girl.

She lifted her eyes to me.

I slackened my face into a sorry mien. 'Oh, how dreadful.'

'Yes, it was terrible. Not only had Papa lost his cook, but what really hurt was that she ran away with his brother.'

'Ha!' I cried out and tapered my cry into a groan of compassion. 'Ha, ha-ow horrible! And the brother ran away to Paris, yes? Did the girl ever come back after he died?'

She pursed her lips. 'We've no idea where she went. We don't talk to her family. You heard Dad ramble on about the lady mayor of Esterençuby the other day. She was from that family, the Loyolas.' She snorted. 'No love lost between them.'

The Loyolas and I were related? I was seething with frustration. There were a million questions I wanted to ask, but I couldn't, stuck as I was in the role of the innocent bystander.

'Then he met your mother.' I said brightly, unable to think of anything else.

'That was much later. He took his brother's betrayal very hard. The sad thing is, because Lazarro died, they were never able to make up. I think it still hurts. Papa seems intolerant perhaps, and I think it's because he is sad.'

I wondered how hard Fernand had tried to make up with Pop at the time.

At last, I knew why Pop and Amatxi had eloped. There had been no rich farmer. Amatxi had first been engaged to Fernand. From what I'd seen of him, I could not blame her for deserting him. He was a bully.

What made little sense was why my grandparents had broken all ties with both families, why they had never returned to Esterençuby, to Amatxi's family.

According to Muriel, Pop had betrayed his brother and conveniently died in 1971. It was a neat story, but it was just that, a tale. History is written by the victors, I knew that, even when they make themselves out to be the victim, so why had Fernand made up that particular tale?

I went to stand by an open window. A memory surfaced. Pop and I in the Woburn woods...the two badgers fighting near their sett. The smaller badger trundling away down a ploughed field, head low, defeated.

'Remember what you've seen, Chacha. The young one's just been banished from his home. He will never be able to go back. If he does, he will be killed.'

A PICNIC ON TOP OF THE WORLD

I woke up late the day after the hunters' dinner and lay in bed, hands behind my head, listening to the pigeons strutting over the roof tiles. It was a windy day. Above the Velux window, a cloud temporarily obscured the shaft of sunshine highlighting Pop's bright yellow tin.

The hunters' dinner had been a raucous affair and King Fernando in his element, recounting tales of fabulous bounty, of the days when there were still birds in the sky, wondering where they had all gone as he tucked into his '*salmis de palombes*.'

I'd caught scraps of conversation in between refilling bread-baskets and bringing in fresh bottles of wine. Car dealers, farmers, civil servants, policemen, Mayor Etchegaray had baptised and married them all, registered the births of their children and buried their dearest. He had approved planning applications and distributed regional grants. He was a very big fish in a very small pond.

Fernand was a man's man. He had, he claimed, caught sight of the last Pyrenean Ibex in 2000. He knew the farmer who had shot Cannelle, the last brown bear, only seven years ago, a farmer who had become the most hated man in France. Fernand had even spoken with Ségolène, the ex-wife of the then President of the republic, the patron of the reintroduction of bears to the Pyrenees.

Now that Fred had calmed down, we worked well together. The atmosphere in the kitchen had dramatically changed since our conversation and overnight, my cousin went from jealous to zealous, touching on generous. I became his accomplice, a role I wasn't comfortable with, but since we were in the same boat, I tried my hardest to emulate him. He was good at his job, give him his due, and I was keen to learn.

That day, he had showed me how to bake macarons. In Bayonne, whole shops were dedicated to them.

'We call them *musu*, it means a kiss, *un baiser*.'

Urko had sniggered. *Baiser* is the slang verb for fuck.

Fred had reprimanded him with a stern glance. Oh yes, the dynamics had shifted. Only last week, Fred and Urko would have had a field day at my expense. Usurped in his master's affections, Urko hated me, and did everything he could to trip me up, but I didn't really care and anyway, I was too busy to notice.

I bunched up my pillow. My phone pinged on the bedside table. An SMS from Xavier. I allowed that blissful ping to travel around my body, light up every nerve ending and buzz around my nether regions. I was not alone anymore. My life was now punctuated with texts, SMSs and emojis. At last, I was loved, desired and adored and boy, did it feel good.

I picked up my phone with a moan of contentment.

'Fancy a picnic on top of a mountain? Pick you up at eleven.'

The buzzing inside me turned to a throb. I couldn't even remember the last time I had sex. My mind grappled about and returned to my last day with Cosmo, in another life.

I stretched languorously. Why drive all the way to a

mountain top when I could stay in bed and welcome Xavier here, tousled and half-naked in an enticing negligee?

I didn't own a negligee, just a large kukuxumusu T-shirt with a Basque cow printed on it, so I turned over, hugged my pillow with a lustful groan, kissed it, tore myself from the bed and removed the T-shirt. I hadn't bought it, I swear. I'd found it under my bed at the hostel, probably left behind by one of the Aussies.

I stepped into the shower and sang *'I want it that way'* from the Backstreet Boys. (*'You are my fi-re, my one de-sire.'*)

After washing and drying my hair, I wove it into a short French plait, tried on a few outfits and wavered between dress or jeans with laced up boots. Hmm, not very conducive to sex, jeans and boots, but Xavier had mentioned a mountain. How much mountaineering could one do in a dress and sandals? I wanted to be sexy but he *was* a ranger and I didn't want to appear precious.

In the end, I decided that jeans would act as a chastity belt. Not to keep him away, Lord no, but to contain my baser instincts. I would follow his lead. This man was everything I'd always wanted and, with the threat of deportation to Australia looming over me – yikes, in two short weeks – I did not want to spoil the little time we had, nor did I want to appear easy.

Xavier drove up in his works Jeep. He had to check out hunting hides and would be mixing business with pleasure.

Oh my… was I glad I'd gone for the jeans! When he kissed me, I was very close to ripping off his khaki uniform.

'Have you found out any more about Arrantxa?' I asked after I had regained my composure, ten miles into the drive.

'For a start,' Xavier grinned, 'I thought it would tickle you to know that Arrantxa means thorn.'

'Thorn?'

'Yes, from the crown of Christ.'

'Good name.' My hand strayed to his thigh. 'For someone who's a thorn in my side.'

He smiled at me. 'We'll never get there if you do that.'

'Sorry. What else can you tell me?'

'Dad reckons that Bruno, her husband, has financially overstretched himself. Seems like his gambling's got out of hand. He has borrowed heavily and it's costing him a fortune. He thought he could invest in the Bear Inn, but now he realises it will never do more than tick over, he wants to get shot of it.'

The road was steep. Xavier geared down, brushing my leg in the process. I closed my eyes and listened to his voice.

'He wants to re-invest in some tourist venture on the coast near Biarritz.'

My ears popped with the altitude. My stomach dropped. I was staring right down into an abyss. The road snaked ever higher towards a grass-covered plateau. I relaxed slightly once the ground levelled out. Every so often, a flock of sheep would slow our progress, led by rams with magnificent horns curling around their ears.

Apart from the odd cyclist, crazy enough to cycle to the top of the world, there was just us, cattle, dun ponies and vultures circling overhead.

'Xavier.' I wanted to close the topic of Arrantxa, keen to focus on the ocean of plateaux and peaks undulating in the distance. 'What threat can I possibly be to them?'

He drove onto the short turf, switched off the engine and turned to me, a hand on the wheel. 'You really have no idea?'

'Of course not.'

'Inheritance. Fernand is old. From what you've told me, he's not got long.' He pointed upwards to the vultures. 'They're after his money.'

'But –' I frowned. 'How does Arrantxa know that she's in

his will at all? If her husband is such a loser, Fernand will have left her out. I know I would.'

Xavier shook his head. 'He can't.'

'What? Sure he can. All he has to do is –'

'It's not legally permissible to write any child, legitimate or –'

'– illegitimate out of your will.' Of course. The *notaire* had explained. Still, it made no sense to me. 'I don't get it. Why is Arrantxa worried that I'm after her share?'

'Desperate people will do desperate things.'

It was ridiculous. What kind of mind did the woman have, to assume – when I had first arrived with Cosmo, innocently proclaiming I was Lazarro's granddaughter – that I was after her inheritance?

It only went to prove that, unlike Muriel, she hadn't quite believed the tale of the brother dying in Paris. Being the older sister, Arrantxa must have heard other versions, before Fernand settled on the accident scenario.

'But I don't understand. I'm only a granddaughter. The family has multiplied and even if I was entitled to a share of that inheritance, which I don't really want, it would be infinitesimal, wouldn't it?'

I could tell from the long look Xavier gave me, that I was still missing the point. I waited for him to enlighten me.

'Your father is an only child, right?'

I nodded blankly.

'He's entitled to half the hotel. *Half,* Chloe. What Fernand did, robbing your grandad of his share, was criminal.'

We were still in the car. The sound of a loud bell to my right brought me back to earth. Inches from my window, a cow lifted its soulful eyes to me. A large bell hung from a solid leather collar.

I waited for things to make sense.

They didn't.

'So just like that, my father could claim half the property of people he doesn't even know?

'Don't these things happen in England?'

'Well, no.' I floundered, confused by French inheritance law. 'I mean, I don't know. People write wills. Makes life a damned sight easier. Leave their fortune to hedgehog hospitals.'

Xavier had never heard of St Tiggy Winkle, so he leaned over and kissed me. 'Come on, let's go. It's lunchtime.' He reached for the cool-box in the back of the Jeep.

The cow blocked my exit. I slid out over the driver's seat, turned into the wind and let the breeze clear the last cobwebs from my head.

The view was incredible. I shielded my eyes and scanned the great waves of peaks fading towards the horizon in various shades of grey.

'Pottok ponies.' Xavier pointed to a family of plump bay ponies. 'They've been around for a million years. There are sketches of them in caves. Same with us Basques. We've been here forever. Experts try to trace us back to everyone from the Berber deserts to the Caucasus Mountains, but they're wrong. We sprung from these mountains.' He tapped a heel into the soft grass. 'This is where we're from.' He drew me to him, kissed my forehead and rested his chin on my head, his heart beating loudly against mine.

'How can you be so sure?' I whispered.

'Our word for knife and axe have the same root as our word for stone. No one else has those words. We have been here since the Stone Age.'

'Wow. A Stone Age man.' I hugged him tighter, eager to absorb his essence, his authenticity.

He slipped a hand inside my windcheater and caressed my back with a calloused hand. I lifted his fingers to my lips and ran my thumb inside his palm. It felt like leather.

'I play *pelote*,' he said by way of an explanation.

'Oh? Does the *chistera* not protect your hand?'

Pelote players normally tie a long basket-like scoop to their wrist to send the ball spinning faster.

'I play *pelote à main nue.* We use our bare hand. You can come and watch us tomorrow if you want. We're playing in Esterençuby.'

I nodded, nestled into his arms and we kissed for a very long time. When I opened my eyes, I didn't know which way was up.

There was something I wanted to do in Esterençuby, but for the life of me, I couldn't remember what it was.

'Come on, let's check out this hide.'

I zipped up my windcheater, bent into the squall and followed in his slipstream, glad of the jeans and boots. By now, my dress would have been wrapped around my ears.

The wide grassy plane surface we crossed surprised me. As a child, I had always imagined that mountains were pointy, with only enough room at the top for a flag and the man holding it. Though further east, the Pyrenees rise to eleven thousand feet and offer good skiing, the west, where we were, is sheep country, with plateaux level enough for sheep to graze during the summer.

'In the olden days, the shepherds used to lead the sheep up here in great trails in the spring. It was a wonderful sight. Now they use lorries. Shame really. Another tragedy is that wool isn't even worth what it costs to shear it. It's so sad.'

Xavier stopped in front of a small shooting post with a narrow plank as a bench. He picked up a few empty cartridges and drew air through his teeth.

'The season doesn't start till next week. They shouldn't have been shooting.'

'Muriel says fewer and fewer wood pigeons come this way, is it true?'

'The *palombes* are beginning to realise that flying over the forest is marginally safer. This stretch is dangerous for them. They either get shot or caught in nets, so yes, I suppose they are learning.'

I thought the whole thing barbaric, but knew better than to voice my townie's opinion when for millennia, the locals had relied on these mountains to survive. So, I told him about my whistling incident in the forest last year.

Xavier whistled a few tunes and went on to demonstrate the *irrinzina*, the famous cry local shepherds used to communicate from one mountain to another.

'Yikes!' It was deafening. I put my hands over my ears to block his eerie combination of Arab ululation, hyena laugh and car alarm.

'Useful when there's no mobile reception.'

'Come on, we're near the perfect spot.' Xavier hurtled down the slope and disappeared from view with another blood curdling shriek.

I stood against the wind and scanned the grandiose ravines and expanse of shorn grass. I'd never been on top of a mountain before, albeit a flat-topped one and mentally ticked it off my bucket list.

By the time I found him, hidden in a grassy hollow, Xavier had already laid out a striped tablecloth and poured out two glasses of cool Irouleguy rosé.

Sheltered from the wind, our nest was sunny and warm. All we could hear was the meow of eagles and the dull tinkle of cowbells.

'This place reminds me of a series Amatxi made me watch, about a boy and a huge dog called Belle. The pair kept stumbling against smugglers.'

'Belle and Sebastian.' Xavier nodded. 'Wasn't it fabulous?'

'Wasn't it in black and white?'

'Strange you should mention it.' Xavier said, scanning the

immensity of the jagged horizon, 'it's what inspired me to become a mountain ranger. Of course, with Europe, there are no more smugglers. I used to wish I could be Sebastian. That boy had so much freedom.'

'When was it filmed, do you think?'

'That's what was so clever about it. It was filmed in the late sixties, made to look like the time just after the War. Actually, it was filmed in the Alps.'

I couldn't help but grin. 'I bet you were cute when you were little. Bet you looked just like Sebastian.'

His eyes left the horizon and settled on me. The air crackled in the space between us.

Xavier cleared his throat and pulled half a baguette from his backpack. 'I didn't assemble the sandwiches before we left. We would not want the baguette to go soggy, would we?' He handed me a glass of wine and busied himself with the rest of the food.

'Heck, what have you got in there?' I could not believe the spread.

'I'll show you. You spread *fromage frais* on the bread and sprinkle it with a pinch of pimento. Then you pile on the rest.' On a paper plate he arranged lettuce, thin slices of ewe cheese and meat.

'What is this?' I pointed to the meat.

'Duck comfit. Duck cooked in its own fat. You must have had it before. That's how we used to preserve meat for the winter. It tastes fantastic and it keeps forever.'

'I've had duck, but never for a picnic.'

'What do English people eat on picnics, then?'

Bless him. He was serious.

I thought back to our school outings. 'White bread cheese sandwiches with crisps inside and a Twix for afters, what else?'

'You are joking, right?'

I nudged him and lifted my glass. 'Course I am.'

I wasn't. The white bread and processed cheese had been my idea. Mum had wrapped a slice of quiche, cucumber fingers and cherry tomatoes, but I had cried and said I wanted to fit in. Quiche would have been weirder even than Jamila's cold curry.

Xavier loaded a long chunk of baguette with fromage frais, lettuce, cheese and duck and handed it to me. 'Here you are, and for dessert, I've brought some chocolate-filled *musu* from Bayonne.

Oh-My-God. Chocolate macarons. Could it get any better?

'Do you know what *musu* means?'

I did. Fred had told me. I put down my sandwich, leaned over and kissed Xavier to demonstrate my love of foreign tongues, as it were. The world span in a great carwash of emotions to the rhythmic woosh woosh of the blood in my ears as I spiralled upwards, and joined the eagles on warm vortices of bliss.

'I wasn't sure you wanted to do this.' Xavier whispered as he let me go.

'Really?' I stroked his short hair. 'Why would you think that?'

He studied my face. 'You were sending me conflicting messages.'

Good grief, was he blind? I pulled away from him. 'How could I let you know how I felt, with Charlène sticking to you like glue?'

'Huh?' His eyebrows shot up.

The ground went from under me. Had I got it wrong all this time? 'I assumed that you and Charlène –'

He burst out laughing and rolled about on the carpet of grass, shaking with mirth.

'I don't see what's funny.'

He placed his hands on my shoulders, lifted my chin with his thumb and kissed my pouting lips.

'I was the one supposed to stick to her like glue.'

Inside my brain, the cogs whirred in a vacuum.

'She's my foster sister. I told you, my mum looks after kids.'

My stomach melted. A foster sister.

I let out a long breath and said dumbly, 'Charlène lives with you?'

'Yes. Her mother died when she was five. Her father's in the army somewhere. Her grandparents couldn't look after her, so she ended up in foster care. At the moment, she's like a ewe on heat and Mum's really worried. You've seen the way she dresses.'

Against my better judgement perhaps, I blurted out what I'd seen the night of the *txoko*.

'Imanol? No way!' Xavier ran a hand through his hair. 'Wow.'

'Well, you said he was looking for a woman with a farm.'

Not a hundred per cent sure I'd done the right thing by blowing the whistle on his best friend, I kissed him again.

We tumbled onto the soft grass. Ravenous, we nibbled and we kissed, and we kissed again, completely forgetting the food.

By the time we returned to earth, the baguettes had gone soggy.

XAVIER PLAYS PELOTE

The leaden patch of sky framed by my Velux window did not bode well for the *pelote* match. Today, for the pilgrims, the path to self-discovery would be slippery and fraught with puddles.

I collapsed back on my pillows with a yawn of disappointment. The match would be cancelled, and I had been so looking forward to seeing my Basque-a-leaping in action.

When I was able to drag myself out of bed, I mussed my hair and pulled on jeans and my Wallabies rugby shirt. I could not wait to ditch the Australian disguise, but rugby was popular in these parts and the shirt always proved a great conversation starter with locals. I would need it as a prop today, for the game was taking place in Esterençuby, my grandmother's birthplace, and I had some fishing to do there.

The whole Etchegaray clan would be there, cheering on their heroes. If Arrantxa, the evil pharmacist, was planning to force her sisters to sell the Bear Inn, she wouldn't want me in her way, disturbing her plans.

Though I was itching to show my true colours and side with my aunts Muriel and Viviane, now was not the time. So once again, Chloe-from-Warrnambool skipped down the stairs and emerged into the drizzle, complete with kangaroo backpack and red glasses.

The dampness wound itself around me. I zipped up my jacket and, just before I slipped on my helmet, checked the sky for signs of improvement. A patch of blue 'large enough to cut out a gendarme's uniform' had appeared in the south. It gave me hope. According to Amatxi-lore the afternoon would be sunny.

In any event, Esterençuby had got it covered. *Pelote* was played inside a large court simply separated from the road by a low wall. No pink *fronton* here, but a space called *mur-à-gauche,* 'wall-on-the-left' and to the right, a curtain of green netting that stopped the ball from shooting out onto the road.

I bumped into Charlène, who seemed genuinely pleased to see me.

'*Tiens, salut!* You're looking for Xavier? The boys are in the bar.' She pointed to the café next door.

Unsure of the protocol concerning mixing mates, *pelote* and girls, I hovered at the edge of the court. Scanning the small groups dotted around, I noticed José in a cluster of old men in berets. I was heading in his direction when the *pelotari* made their entrance to a joyous cacophony.

All in white, Xavier and Imanol strolled in, calloused hand lifted in response to the applause. My heart did a somersault and I buzzed with the crowd.

The Basques are a clumping nation. They like to do things together, and I'd imagined a much larger team. I was surprised to see, when Xavier and Imanol took up their positions, that they were the only two players in the team.

Xavier turned to me and winked. My insides turned to mush. Love distorted my field of vision and the world shrank to the size of the centre court, where my hero's every move lit up my inner Christmas tree.

'Is this your first game of *pelote*?'

'Huh?' I jumped. José was sitting next to me on the low wall.

I blushed. 'Oh hello. Yes, I mean no. I'm afraid I don't know anything about it.' By now the game was in full flow. I winced, stunned by the force of the blows. 'Ouch, that must hurt.'

'It does. When they play *Cesta Punta,* the version of *pelote* with the rattan *chistera,* the ball reaches speeds of two hundred miles per hour.'

'Really? How do they cope with that sort of speed when they play bare-handed?'

'The ball doesn't go quite so fast in bare-handed *pelote,* just sixty perhaps. They pad their hands with special plasters.'

'Do they?' I remarked innocently, some places still tingling from the rasp of my lover's hand.

José adjusted his glasses and proceeded to instruct me. 'There are twelve kinds of *pelote* games –'

While he lectured, the haze surrounding Xavier dissipated somewhat, and brought into focus a player in a blue top at the back of the court. Nodding absently to José's explanations, I recognised him as Irksome Urko, Fred's minion.

'Falta!' José shouted as Urko stepped beyond the line.

Urko turned towards the voice. His eyes narrowed as he caught sight of me.

Xavier scored again. The building shook with stamping feet, ululations and song. A little way down from us, Charlène was dancing.

I smiled at her. Buoyed up by our devotion, how could our boys not win?

The blues equalised, cranking up the frenzy. The crowd went wild, going back to their roots, back to being Basque. Pop would have loved it.

'Only a few minutes to go. We've as good as won.' José shouted in my ear.

Urko cast several glances in my direction, a strange expression on his face. He had lost his concentration.

The umpire checked his watch. The match ended.

A Basque anthem rose from a sound system. They sang as one voice.

I followed the crowd to the café and remained on the terrace, staring into the swollen river, feeling very foreign. The Nive bounced and gushed joyfully, indifferent to my plight. I turned away and glanced at the village stretched out like a ribbon along the narrow road, and thought back to Amatxi, who was born here.

The church, the ragged mountains, the houses dotted along the road and the Nive had helped her get through our rainy days in England while she cooked, knitted, and prayed.

Stragglers hovered around the court. Urko was in conversation with a man. Handsome in a creepy way, he wore a suit and cravat totally at odds with the locals' overalls and checked shirts.

'Klo-é? Ça va?' Xavier came out and put an arm around my shoulder.

I sank into him, relieved he had searched me out, and took hold of his hand. It was burning hot.

'Does it hurt?'

'Yes, but there is a secret remedy.' He grinned. His fingers crept under my sweatshirt as he breathed in my ear, 'I'll show you later.'

I kissed the corner of his lips and, aware that I would soon lose him to his admirers, pointed to the court. 'That man in a suit over there, do you know who he is?'

At that moment, Urko and the lounge lizard looked in my direction.

Xavier made a face. 'Yep. That's my uncle Bruno.' He pushed me towards the café. 'Come on. Let's go in. I don't want to talk to him.'

I followed Xavier inside, painfully aware that if Arrantxa's husband was speaking to Urko, it could only mean one thing.

My cover was blown. The gloves were off.

The small café was packed. As soon as we went in, Xavier was hailed as the hero he was. I wanted to hail him myself, but like a cherry kernel, he stood inside a thick clump of chums.

Yes, Basques find their strength in togetherness. No wonder the national sport is rugby. Unlike the Parisian, who sees himself as a one-off, a Basque person likes to be part of a whole. From what I could tell, there was a lot of bonding going on tonight.

'What do you want to drink?' Xavier shouted from the bar.

A glass of rosé was passed down to me. I dragged my eyes away from my alpha male and found José sitting with his wife Jacqueline under a television set broadcasting a rugby match. I dashed over before anyone had the chance to reach them with a pack of cards.

'Alors Chloe, la pelote?' Jacqueline smiled.

'Fascinant. José m'a expliqué.' I knew I didn't have long, so I went straight to the point. 'You told me that your name is Loyola, is this right?'

They nodded.

I shouted above the din. 'My mother is Australian, but there were Loyolas in my father's family. It's a common Basque name, especially in the south, isn't it?' I remembered to say *the south* and not *Spain*.

José shouted back across the table. 'That's right, it's a typical Basque name.'

'Remind me when you came to France?'

'I came over from Bilbao at the end of the sixties to visit an uncle who'd left Franco's Spain during the War. I mentioned him to you the other day. He lost a kidney after being kicked by the Guardia Civil. He lived in this village. I stayed with him for a month.' His eyes twinkled. 'I met Jacqueline at a dance and –'

'Very romantic.' I struggled to imagine the efficient mayoress as a young girl.

'Is Loyola your father's name?' She asked.

'No, it was my grandmother's maiden name.'

'I see. What was her first name?'

'Paloma.'

'Paloma?' Her surprise gave me hope.

'Yes. She came from here.'

They exchanged a glance I couldn't decipher.

'Your grandmother's name was Paloma Loyola?' Jacqueline's eyes probed mine.

I didn't know how to proceed. We were speaking French and the noise was such, I couldn't even hear myself think.

José gazed into his beer glass. A deep line creased his brow.

'I had a cousin called Paloma,' he said, 'but she left the country soon after I arrived. Did you say she lived in Australia?'

I toyed with the stem of my wine glass. 'Actually, she –'

The whole bar erupted into song. Jacqueline joined in with a wonderful soprano.

'What can you tell me about her?' I asked her when things had quietened down.

'Paloma. Yes, I remember her, the daughter of José's uncle. We went to school together,' Jacqueline said. 'She was two years above me and left school when she was sixteen.'

'She went to cook at the Bear Inn?'

'Yes, she did. Did you say she was your grandmother?'

Their friend Michel arrived, holding a roll of baize. He was stopped by a couple of men who pointed to the screen above us.

I knew I did not have long, so I blurted out my story. They listened. The lack of surprise on their faces told me that the tale of Pop dying in Paris had never taken hold in Esterençuby.

'Paloma was engaged to Fernand Etchegaray, but from what I heard, she soon realised that what she had fallen in love with, was the restaurant, not Fernand. He was a bully, and still is, but she thought she could make a go of it.'

'She felt indebted to him for giving her that job, and allowing her to do what she loved.' José added.

'What made her change her mind?'

'Two things. His younger brother came home from his military service –'

I nodded and winced as Michel was joined by another card player.

'– and Fernand received a letter from Chile.'

Oh God. The letter! It was still in my bag.

'A letter?' I swallowed hard.

'Fernand had spent time in Chile and had a child with a local woman.'

Good grief. Another potential heir to the Bear Inn. I wondered if Arrantxa knew.

'Fernand refused to acknowledge the boy. Said he wasn't his.' Jacqueline's thinned lips made her opinion of Fernand abundantly clear.

From the name I had glimpsed on the back of the envelope the postman had given me, it was from a Vicente Flores, who lived in Santiago, the capital of Chile. Why would he write to Fernand after so many years?

'It brought matters to a head. Paloma finally saw Fernand for what he was and broke off the engagement.' José pursed his lips. 'She ran away with Lazarro. After that, no one heard from them.'

Jacqueline leaned over and added, 'she did come back, though. She met up with her sisters in the summer.'

José pointed to my empty glass. 'Can I get you another rosé?'

I shook my head. Michel threw the roll of green baize over the table and dropped a pack of cards.

'Sorry,' Jacqueline said with a shrug of apology, 'time for *mus*.'

Michel sat down. I gave the other player my seat. Euro notes were slipped under the baize. Along the bar, the clump erupted into song.

I went out and leaned over the railings of the bridge. Below me, the water gushed over dark boulders that glistened in the evening light. I closed my eyes, tuned out the hubbub and tunnelled back to the past.

I am in France, on the beach. How old am I? Eight perhaps. Amatxi has bought me an ice cream, though this time, I haven't pestered her for it. For the first time ever, she allows me to have three balls, one of them pistachio. It is the first time I have tasted pistachio. She chats with two plump women in summer dresses. They look at me as they would a puppy. I don't know who they are.

. . .

'Ah, there you are.' Xavier came out accompanied by music and a burst of warm air. Imanol followed him, lit up a cigarette and, a little way from us, stood blowing smoke over the river.

Xavier put both hands on my shoulders. His lips brushed mine. 'It's hot in there. I need air. Come on, let's go for a little walk.' A hand around my waist, he drew me towards a path snaking up from the café. At the top of a bend, we stopped.

He swivelled my body to face the valley, stood behind me and rested his chin on my head. 'I love the view from here.'

Against the moonlit sky we faced the dark shape of the church on its hillock, the twinkling ribbon of the Nive, and in the centre, the small lit up café beating like a heart.

Whatever revenge Fernand had exacted on his brother had been exquisitely chosen. Forcing Pop and Amatxi to leave had inflicted a pain he knew would never dull.

'Are you okay?' Xavier kissed my hair. 'You looked so serious with José in there. What were you talking about?'

'Oh, the games people play.' I let out a long sigh and nuzzled his neck. 'I am so sick of mysteries. It's time I faced Fernand.'

Xavier's hand sizzled on my skin, divested of its plasters. Intoxicated, shivering with sensations, I circled my arms around his neck and drank in the present moment, rushing away from us like the waters of the Nive below, on a head-on collision course with the Adour, and me with Australia.

'*Bonsoir Xavier.*' The lounge lizard crept out of the shadows. '*Belle victoire.*' Ice in his voice, he congratulated his nephew on the game, and turned to me. His eyes flickered.

'Well, aren't you going to introduce your girlfriend?'

CHLOE RETURNS TO THE BULLRING

It was time for me to come out and reveal who I was. I'd gone over the battle plan in my head. The strategy was simple, I would catch Fernand on his own, and once the masks were down, demand an explanation as to his brother's estrangement.

I was in luck. The bar was empty when I arrived. Fernand sat in his usual corner with a *café-au-lait*. When I stepped in, full of confidence, I had not expected to face a hundred kilos of angry bull.

'You!' Fernand bellowed. 'How did you inveigle yourself into my restaurant?'

His attack made me reel. What had needled the man? He had been so charming to me last week. A silent shadow slunk around the dark recesses of the kitchen. Urko. Of course. The creep had noticed the change of atmosphere between Fred and me, and fearing for his job, decided to scupper both our plans, whatever he imagined they were, and was now working for Arrantxa and Bruno.

I took in a deep breath and replied breezily, '*Bonjour* Monsieur Etchegaray.'

My smile disarmed him. 'I don't know who you are,' he grunted, 'or what you want from us, but you're here to wash up and wash up is all you'll do.'

So, Urko had snitched that I was sharing the cooking with Fred. This would worry the old boy, whose fragile empire rested on his grandson's reputation as a chef. I wondered what would happen if I told him that Frédéric-the-Great was leaving for Paris. It would kill him for sure, and I needed him alive.

A squeak made me jump. The cellar door. Urko crawling back to his *cave,* his evil work done.

'Did you hear me?' Fernand thumped his stick on the tiled floor. '*Plongeuse* is all you are. You're paid to wash up!'

They had a dishwasher. I had been hired to prep.

I retreated behind the bar. Was this old bull dangerous or were his pawing and snorting just pretence? Just in case, I remained at a respectable distance, turned to face him and, sounding more confident than I felt, delivered the first banderilla.

'You never asked to see my papers, did you? Too happy to get me on the cheap, *'au noir'* huh? If you'd checked,' I inched forward, 'you'd have found out that my name is –' I enunciated clearly – 'Chloe *Etchegaray.*'

He blinked several times and shook his head as if a wasp had stung him.

Had he heard me? I edged closer and threw in another barbed hook. '*Etche-garay,* Uncle. I'm your great-niece.' I narrowed my eyes. 'All the time you were telling your daughters that your brother had died in Paris, you knew Lazarro was alive, didn't you?'

He was thrown. The surprise in his eyes was genuine, but he recovered quickly.

'Ha, what is it to me whether he died in Paris or lived somewhere else! He got his comeuppance.'

'And what exactly did he do? He stole your fiancée?' I added pointedly, 'deprived you of your cook?'

'That pair of rotters deserved each other!' He banged a fist on the table.

I prowled along the bar and raised my voice to make sure my words hit their mark.

'You spread lies so that your brother couldn't come back.' I pinned him with my gaze. 'What tale did you invent, that kept him away for so long?'

Fernand uttered a low growl. 'I didn't have to make up any tales. Lazarro had it coming to him with the company he kept.'

'I don't believe you.' My voice wobbled. 'My grandfather was a good man.'

My confidence was draining away. Fernand was tougher than I had expected. I just couldn't get enough of a grip on him to squeeze out the truth.

Snorting like an old locomotive, he pushed himself on his fists.

'Stop stirring our *merde* and get out of my hotel! One phone call and I'll have you deported back to Australia.'

I noted 'Australia' and countered his threat with a swift pass.

'And I will report you for breaking employment laws.'

'Who *are* you?' He roared.

'I told you, Uncle Fernand, I'm your great-niece.'

I turned my back to him, went to the kitchen and grabbed my apron.

He wasn't finished with me. His mind filled with red mist, disoriented, he lost his focus and attacked randomly. 'My niece, are you? Another harpy to add to the gaggle of women. A sickly wife who gave me three pathetic daughters – one a holy-water-frog, the intelligent one wasting her money on some skirt chaser, and –' he pointed up to the rooms Muriel was busy vacuuming, 'this one so gormless, she can't keep my hotel afloat. And as if that wasn't enough, you –' he thundered '– come all the way from Australia to get your hands on the loot. Well, you're wasting your time. You won't inherit a bean.'

I stopped in my tracks. So, he too thought his hotel was what I was after. What was it with them?

'Out!' He rasped. 'Go back where you came from and tell Lazarro that I won't talk to him. Not now, not ever.'

If he believed Pop was alive in Australia, his information channels weren't that effective.

'They did nothing wrong and you know it. You're stewing in an anger of your own making.'

'Out. And don't ever come here again!' His breath was laboured. He was getting tired.

'You can't get rid of me, Uncle, I work for Frédéric.' I gave the red apron a firm shake to drive the point home.

Fernand slumped forward with a groan, a hand on his heart. The stick clattered to the floor.

Good grief, he couldn't die now, not before he'd confessed, not before I'd taken over from Fred.

I panicked. Should I call for help?

He lifted his face, his small eyes full of life. The healthy flush reassured me that it was a feint. Brow lowered, the old man waited, resigned or bewildered, I couldn't really tell.

My heart beating like a drum, I stood over him and whispered, 'If only you'd had a son, huh? Things would have been so different.'

His mouth fell open. 'What are you –'

I was so close, he could have hit me with his stick, had it not been lying on the floor. I pulled out the letter from my pocket and held it out.

He caught sight of the stamps. All the air went out of him.

We had reached what toreros call 'the moment of truth.' I dropped the letter on his table and plunged the *estoca* to the hilt.

'This letter is from Chile. It's from Vicente. Vicente Flores. The son you never had.'

TIME SLIPS AWAY FROM CHLOE

It was happy hour. I was back at the King's Arms serving chips out of berets to the three derelicts who propped up the bar. 'Last orders!'

The doorbell rang. I surfaced, pushed my hair from my face, staggered out of bed in my kukuxumusu T-shirt – the one with the cow in a Marilyn pose – and shuffled to the door.

I pressed the intercom, and dissolved at the voice.

'Chloe? I've brought you some breakfast.'

Xavier? I wasn't expecting him until tonight. I pressed the buzzer and dashed to the bathroom to make myself presentable, while he galloped up the three flights of stairs.

He pushed a paper bag into my hands. 'I thought you'd like breakfast in bed.' He ran his eyes over my top with, 'Basque T-shirt. Great, keep the economy going…' and went to the percolator.

I dropped at the edge of the bed, my senses in turmoil. 'I thought you were coming over later.'

'I was. I couldn't wait.'

The whole room became charged with electricity. Parts of

me pulsed while others throbbed. I opened the bag of pastries, hid my blushing face inside it and inhaled deeply.

'Hmmm, what have we got in here? It smells divine.'

Without a word, Xavier poured water into the machine, spooned coffee into the filter, every elegant move plucking at my inner strings.

He crossed the room, arranged the pastries on a plate and placed them on the bedside table.

I scooted up the bed. His eyes searched mine, an eyebrow lifted. I lay back and let him come to me. He cradled my face and caressed my lips with his. I sank into him, losing myself in the savours of that kiss.

'Breakfast in bed, huh?' I ran my fingers through his curls.

'I noticed how much you liked brioches,' he whispered against my lips. His rough hands caught on the fabric of my T-shirt. 'Have you any idea how much I like yours… so soft, so delicious.' We rolled over. The energy crackled as his hands grazed my skin, searching for those magic places he believed would heal blisters and callouses; a process, which he said, was not to be hurried. Reverently, he removed my kukuxumusu T-shirt, his eyes filled with wonder. I kissed his fingers and put my magic powers to the test. No inch of skin was left untried. Eventually, after much probing and caressing, the source of all cures was found, both for his ills and mine. God only knew the deprivations I had suffered. Our moans of relief mingled with the sputtering of the percolator and the coos of the pigeons overhead.

Later, much later, amazed and dishevelled I lay back on the big brass bed and soaked up the vision of my man munching on brioches in my all-white room. In under an hour, he would be back in his forest. In ten days' time, I would be on a plane.

I scanned every inch of the room, the limed walls and gnarled beams, Pop's yellow tin on the shelf, the patch of sky above, Xavier's perfect body. I clung to the moment like a drowning woman to a rock in the middle of a river, the weight of time crushing my chest. Inside my shattering heart, the melancholy tune of Oi Ama Euskal Herri rose, louder and louder, blotting out everything else.

'Australia is nine hours and thirty minutes ahead of here. You'll just be waking up and my day will nearly be over.' I slumped on the pillows and closed my eyes, a vision of the future painted inside my lids.

Warrnambool Beach. It's eight am and already, it is sweltering. I'm sitting on the decking of my parents' cabin, disconsolately shovelling cornflakes into my mouth. Mum is belting 'Goldfinger' in the shower. Out front, Dad is checking the sand for empties after last night's *barbie*. There are no cowbells, no manure smells, no mewing eagles, just the heat and the relentless pounding of the waves... and in my head, a Basque lament that refuses to die.

'Klo-é, do you *have* to go?' Xavier carefully placed the tray filled with bowls of *café-au-lait* and brioches in the middle of the bed. He snuggled up to me and stroked my cheek with his hair.

I nodded with a sniff. 'I'm sorry.' I kissed him. 'We've got ten days. Let's make the best of it.'

His damp brown gaze met mine. 'You will come back though, won't you?'

Oh God, he did care. If it hadn't been for the brioches dropping crumbs everywhere and the bowls filled to the brim, I'd have squeezed the life out of him.

'I've never met anyone like you.' He ran a finger along my leg.

'You wouldn't have,' I answered, pretending a great chorus of bells was not ringing inside me. 'Not many Basque Ozzies around.'

'No. I don't suppose there are.'

Cross-legged opposite each other, we munched mindfully, savouring each mouthful of brioche as if it were our last.

'How did it go with old Etchegaray the other day?' Xavier asked in French. It was far too early to speak English and anyway, our lovemaking had zapped our faculties. Sex does that to you.

'Not too well I'm afraid. I thought I could get the old bear to dance to my tune, but I got absolutely nothing out of him.'

'Nothing at all?' He lifted his bowl and took a sip from his café-au-lait.

'Not really. All he said was that Pop had it coming to him because of the company he kept.'

Xavier peered at me over the rim of his bowl. A spark danced in his eyes.

'What? Is it significant?'

'Might be.' He wiped his top lip with his tongue and said something, but so distracted was I by this tongue, that I only caught 'school friends.'

He replaced his bowl on the tray and explained, hands punctuating his words. 'In a *corrida*, the matador has six guys on horses, six guys who watch his back. In Spanish, it's called a *cuadrilla*.'

I had heard the word before. It was the name of a company in England, a fracking company of all things. I remembered Pop grumbling about the cheek of them stealing that hallowed name for an activity akin to rape and plunder. Very ecologically minded, was Pop.

'*Cuadrilla* suggests a group of friends, a gang.'

'All for one and one for all? Like you and the Musketeers?'

'Exactly. Guys you'd put your head on the block for. All you have to do is find out who Lazarro used to hang around with, who his musketeers were, his cuadrilla.'

'How do I do that?'

He pursed his lips and gave the matter some thought. I leaned over and kissed him. There is a special dimension to kissing a French man, and I still couldn't believe that I could just do that, kiss him whenever I wanted, so I kissed him again for good measure.

'You know José Loyola, don't you?' Xavier was onto something.

'Yes, I think I might even be related to him.'

'José could introduce you to some village elders,' Xavier said. 'One of them will know something.'

'Thanks. I might do that. What if they're doolally, or worse, what if they're dead?'

'Come on, seventy isn't that old. Your grandfather died young, probably from a combination of English rain and homesickness. We're tough as old boots here.'

'Okay. I'll call José.' There was something else. 'Talking about *cuadrillas* and Musketeers, have you squared it with Imanol? You know, about him and –' Silly, I know, but her name still caught in my throat.

'Bah. They won't be seeing each other for a while. I drove Charlène to her new college last weekend. It's two hours from Bayonne. It'll give them time to think about how serious they really are.'

'Two hours away?' Surely, I thought uncharitably, there were plenty of hair and beauty courses nearer home.

'It's the only place where she can do a C.E.P. in her field. Ovine management courses are few and far between.'

'Wine management? You mean, oenology?'

'No. Ovine management. Sheep. She wants to be a shepherdess.' He emphasized, '*bergère*.'

My jaw dropped. Prejudices tumbled around my oxytocin-filled brain. '*Bergère,* you said? You mean you can study for an NVQ in shepherding?' Well, wasn't France full of wonders.

'Sure. In Béziers, there's even a bull-fighting school. You could retrain if you find cooking isn't for you after all. You've showed promise. I'm sure they'd take you on.'

'Ha ha. Très drôle.' Crikey, Charlène, a *shepherdess*?

'Our whole economy is based on sheep and tourism. There's a lot to learn in ovine management. Sheep must be tended, wormed, tattooed, milked, sheared and dipped, then there's lambing, cheese-making –'

I tried to picture Charlène running after a stray lamb in white jeans and kitten heels. 'You mean she'll be going up mountains with her flock, on her own, like Manon Des Sources?'

'She won't be on her own. In spring the girls go up to the plateau in groups of six. Every week-end one of them comes down.' He read my face. 'I know, she doesn't look the type. It's just that this summer, she went boy crazy, which is why Mum was worried.'

'But sheep? I just don't get it.'

'You saw her grandparents' farm. She wants to take it over, but first, she needs to learn the job.'

I eventually managed to close my mouth, but still, the question hung in the air.

'And you're okay with Imanol – you know –'

'As you know, Imanol is looking for a woman with a farm. Charlène certainly qualifies, though as you saw for yourself, that farm has seen better days. It'll be hard work.'

He lifted the tray, set it on the floor and whispered in a coffee-scented kiss, 'The good thing with my job is that I don't have to clock in. I rushed it a bit earlier on.' His rough palm flittered over my bottom. 'I want to make it up to you.'

I slid down into the warm bed and drew him to me. A ray of sun beamed down from the Velux and bathed the room in romantic light. Lost in the here and now, languid and serious, I poured myself into Xavier and, together, we made brioche-scented memories of a time when, for a brief moment, everything was perfect.

CHLOE LEARNS THE TRUTH

Xavier had gone off to fight the good fight, leaving me hugging my pillow.

Indifferent to my moods, L'ami Yabon beamed at me from his yellow tin. His irrepressible joie de vivre was grating on me today. Could he not see that I'd failed Pop and with only ten days to go, I was no nearer to discovering the truth?

The day stretched ahead empty and pointless. Arms behind my head, I watched the clouds rush by, turn grey and batter my Velux window with rain. I fell asleep.

The buzzing of my phone woke me up. It was José. Xavier had dropped by on his way to work and asked him to research Pop's school friends. One Bernard Ortegui lived on the other side of Saint Jean, and he had contacted him.

'I was going to work in the garden today,' José said, 'but it's raining. I'll take you to meet him. He would love to meet you.'

'Thank you so much. I really appreciate it.'

I jumped out of bed and feverishly searched for clothes. As my true identity was gradually leached to my new family, the Australian disguise was becoming redundant. I'd ditched the red glasses. After all, who was I afraid of? I held enough information to blackmail Arrantxa, her lounge lizard, Fernand and Fred. I felt like a CIA agent.

It was the end of September and the weather had turned chilly. I had left all my warm clothes in storage in England. I wouldn't need them in Australia, but it was pretty cold right now. I pulled on two T-shirts and a grey tracksuit, zipped up my anorak and ran downstairs to wait for José in the hall.

'The man we are going to see,' José explained on the way, 'has lived in the States until he retired five years ago. You'll be able to speak English with him.'

I lifted an eyebrow. Interesting that like Pop, he should have emigrated.

'Do you know this Monsieur Ortegui?'

'Oh yes, we sang in the same choir for a while, but he's not very well. He doesn't come any more.'

'What can you tell me about him?' I asked with trepidation as we drove along the ramparts out of Saint Jean.

'You want to know about the time before your grandfather left the region, I presume. I asked Jacqueline what she knew about Bernard's family. She told me that his younger brother had died in tragic circumstances.'

'Really? What circumstances?'

Focused on the road, José didn't reply.

'It happened shortly after I arrived in France.' He hesitated. 'There were many theories about that accident. Perhaps Bernard will tell us more.'

Did I really want to find out what had happened? Suddenly, I was not so sure. I had a clear picture of Pop in my mind. To me he was cheerful, polite and mild-mannered. He radiated with a glow that shone from his inner core. and I could not bear to see that picture tarnished.

The rain fell in sheets and the wipers worked overtime to clear the windscreen.

'What is the matter with Monsieur Ortegui?'

'Cancer. He lives alone. His daughter looks in on him.'

José parked outside a modern bungalow. A black and white Jack Russell greeted us with a mixture of yaps and tail wags, unable to decide whether we were friend or foe.

I too wavered. Though I had reached the point I'd been yearning for, I dreaded what I was about to find out.

We ran through the rain towards the open door.

'Loyola, ça me fait plaisir de te voir.' Shrunken, stooped and bald, Bernard Ortegui drew José into the corridor and shook his hand. I remained in the tiny porch.

They exchanged a few words in Basque among which I understood *telefono,* Lazzaro and *biloba,* the word for granddaughter. God knows where I'd picked that up.

I stepped into the narrow corridor. José switched to French. This is Chloe, Lazarro's granddaughter.' 'Chloe, this is Bernard.'

'Bonjour.' Bernard's eyes burned into mine, though his hand was cold as ice. 'Come this way. I made some coffee.'

He shuffled to a shabby conservatory where a triffid-like datura rampaged up flaking wooden trusses. The heat was tropical and it smelled of dog.

'I explained to Chloe that you'd lived in the States, but I couldn't remember where.'

'San Diego.' Bernard indicated green garden chairs and lowered himself into a seat padded with a sheepskin. 'I ran a garage there. Sold up and came home five years ago.' He smiled uncovering stained teeth.

'There are many of us *Euskaldun* over there. We're always talking of going home, but very few do. You get used to the easy life I suppose.' He spoke French for José's benefit.

'Chloe, yes? Chloe, I'm so glad to meet you. I've often

thought about Lazarro, wondered where he was, what he was doing.'

I wondered why they had not communicated all these years.

The old man read my face. 'I didn't – I wasn't very good at keeping in touch.'

I willed him to say more, but he dropped his gaze and fussed with the coffee.

So, I told him about Pop, shocked at how few words it took to sum up his life. I'd wanted to say that with Pop, it was never about what he did, or who he was, but how he made you feel. Pop radiated warmth. He glowed like he'd swallowed the sun. Intimidated, I only managed to say that he had done a bit of carpentry and worked for plastic bottles and containers manufacturer, that Paloma cooked in a school kitchen and that their son Matteo had married my Australian mother, and just retired near Melbourne from being a civil servant. I wanted to say so much more. What a bunch of losers I made us out to be. I know, *'it's not what you do, it's who you are'* and all that, but I simply didn't have the words. I could have spoken English, but it wouldn't have been fair on José.

Bernard listened intently, his face gaunt and dotted with liver spots. 'Cemetery flowers' was Pop's word for them.

Bernard poured out the coffee into tiny cups and handed them to us, together with the sugar bowl. His hands shook slightly.

Unhappy with the portraits I had drawn of my family, I let out a long sigh and with a shrug, concluded in English. 'Pop made the world a better place.'

Bernard studied my face over his cup. 'You don't look like him at all.'

'I take after my mother.'

Mum came from a long line of convicts. I'd always had

mixed feelings about that, though after meeting Fernand, I realised I'd been lucky. Hardy, long-lived and resourceful, my convict ancestors were free from heart conditions, large noses and malice. They killed only when provoked, and bore no grudges.

An album lay on the table. I pointed to it. 'Do you have any school photos? I'd love to see what Pop looked like when he was young. We didn't have photos, you know –'

'Yes. I found this in the loft and brought it down for you.' He handed me a large black and white photo framed in embossed card.

'This was taken when we were at primary school.' He shakily pushed the photo towards me. 'Can you spot him?'

I scanned the rows of children in checked pinafores and pointed to a round-faced girl in the front row. 'Is this Paloma?'

'Yes. Lazarro is right next to her.'

For the school photo, Great-Grandma Marthe had parted her son's hair with a ruler and glued it in place. Slightly puzzled, Pop peered into the future, as if trying to decipher it.

Bernard's claw-like finger stopped on a lanky curly-haired boy at the back. 'And that's me.'

I glanced up at him and said charitably, 'Good looking boy.' His illness had made him unrecognisable.

'This is my younger brother.' A mischievous boy sat cross-legged at the front.

'You can tell he's trouble.' I blurted out before I'd had time to think.

'Oh yes, he was. It is what killed him.' Bernard pushed the photo away. 'I suspect it's what has brought you here.' He opened the album and turned to a snap of four youths posing by the Jaioleku *fronton*.

I knew where it was. I recognised the church at the back.

Three wore white *pelota* garb. Bernard was the tallest. Pop's straight hair covered his ears. The cocky little brother held up a *chistera* tied to his hand. The fourth musketeer, in flared jeans and leather jerkin, had a mop of curly hair and wore thick-framed glasses.

There was nothing dark or nefarious about them. All I saw were four young men engaged in sporty pursuits. When did it go wrong?

'Here's another one.'

In mountaineering garb, the quartet posed in boots and bonnets on a rock jutting out over a valley. Crikey they looked like an advertisement for a walking magazine.

'What was your brother's name?'

'Fabien.' The cup clattered on the saucer as Bernard picked up his coffee.

I turned the pages of the album, trying to decipher photos that meant nothing to me.

Inside the conservatory, the heat was unbearable. I unzipped my tracksuit top.

'Monsieur Ortegui.' I jumped in. 'Something happened in the seventies, something that led to my grandad's exile.' I lifted pleading eyes to him. 'He never returned to France and I want to know why.'

Bernard put down his cup, suddenly alive. 'They were crazy times. A wind of change was blowing over everything. We were young, we thought we could create a better world.' His old eyes shone briefly. 'It's difficult to explain, but it all seemed so close that we could touch it.'

The rain drumming on the glass roof drowned some of his words. I wished he would speak English.

The atmosphere was close; we could have been inside Commandant Cousteau's *Batiscaphe,* travelling under water in a glazed bubble-like submarine.

'Who's the fourth chap?' I pointed to the curly-haired boy in dark-framed glasses.

'Serge. He lives in Paris.'

So, they had all moved away. 'Your brother Fabien –'

A long cough shook Bernard and folded him in two. He took in a long rattly breath.

'It started when Lazarro, your grandfather, came home from the military. I didn't do mine, I – I was discharged.' He paused. 'Yes, Lazarro came home from the army and there was Paloma, working in the kitchen, a very different girl from the one he had known at school. He fell hopelessly in love with her.' Bernard's features softened. 'Oh, the soul-searching, the nights he spent with Serge and me, discussing life and love, quoting Sartre and Camus.' He exhaled. 'In the end, it all came down to one thing.'

I finished his sentence for him. 'What to do about Fernand.'

He opened his hands. 'While Lazarro was agonising over his love for Paloma, I was struggling to keep Fabien from the lure of ETA.'

I remembered José's exposé on the repression during the Franco years. ETA was a terrorist movement if I remembered correctly.

I butted in. 'I have heard of it. José has explained to me how the movement for independence spread from Spain to the French side.'

'Exactly. My brother was an idealist, you see. It was in his nature I suppose, that conviction that he could change the world. But he was impulsive, a *tête brûlée*.'

That expression again. 'A burned-head? What does that mean?'

'Hot-headed,' he explained in American. 'A crazy guy who acts without thinking things through.' He nodded to himself. 'That was Fabien all right.'

My own head was boiling. I searched for a window we could open, wishing we could at least switch off the electric heater plugged in at my feet.

'Fabien became distant and strange. He disappeared for hours on end and would never tell me where he'd been. I guessed what was going on, and I was worried. I – we tried to convince him that the path he was following wasn't sensible.'

Our combined breaths had coated the glass, blotting out the outside world. My clothes clung to me. I removed my tracksuit top and draped it over the back of my chair. It was so hot, the devil's trumpet was drooping. José wiped his forehead with a checked handkerchief.

In cardigan and thick cotton shirt, Bernard was comfortable.

'I want to know why Pop could never return to France.'

'Bernard?' José coaxed gently.

Bernard crumpled with a ragged sigh. It seemed that all that held him together was his pain.

'I've no idea how Fabien got the – there was no Internet in those days – but he found the things he needed to make a –' he whispered the last word so low I nearly missed it.

I sat rock still. Of all the scenarios, a bomb was the very last thing I would have imagined Pop dallying with.

'Fabien's idea was to send a strong message, shock the establishment into change, frighten the tourists away from our Basque Country so that we could return to some sort of purity, to our original state. "Tourism," he said, "was an evil pollutant, as for the police who took orders from Paris, they were the enemy." Bernard noticed his shaking hands and stuffed them into his cardigan pockets. 'I know how it looks, especially now, with Muslim extremists.'

'But I don't see how my grandfather could have had anything to do with this!'

The old man was struggling. I felt sorry for him, but he'd had a lifetime to sort this out, hadn't he? California wasn't exactly short of shrinks. I had just ten days left.

'Were there victims? Was Fabien gunned down by the police? Did they arrest Lazarro, thinking he was an accomplice?' I shot out randomly, about to pass out from the heat.

'No.' Bernard shrunk even more. 'Fabien was the only victim. His bomb went off as he was setting it.' He whispered, 'He was killed instantly.'

'Oh God.' My hands shot to my face. 'I'm so sorry.'

'The police combed the area, looking for accomplices.' He hung his head. 'Their suspicions fell on us.'

'But you hadn't done anything!' I nearly shouted. 'Why didn't you just come out with it?'

Bernard rested his hands on the table and met my gaze. 'We'd been seen together with Fabien that morning. We panicked. At the time, the police were merciless. We didn't think they'd believe us.'

I wiped my forehead with the back of a hand. I could see where this was going.

Bernard whispered the last sentence. 'It happened the day after Paloma told Fernand she was leaving him.'

So, this was it.

'How convenient for Fernand.' I blew damp hair from my face. It was all beginning to make sense, yet the puzzle was still incomplete. 'Could you really not explain? I mean, didn't you have an alibi?'

'A police inspector came to the Bear. Fernand was beside himself with rage, looking for revenge. He told the inspector he'd been suspecting his brother for a while. That night, when Lazarro came home, they had a terrible row.'

I tried to piece the story together. 'What I still don't understand, is why Pop could never return, I mean, after forty years?'

'He was on a list of wanted terrorists. You probably saw it in recent papers? The police arrested the head of ETA *only last week.*' He raised his voice to stress those words. 'They have long memories. From what I read, twenty terrorists were still on the run forty years later. His name was probably on that list. If he had tried to return, Lazarro would have been stopped at the border and questioned.'

'But he was innocent!' I picked up the school photo and fanned myself with it. This was crazy.

'At the time, there were paramilitary groups paid by the Spanish government to eliminate terrorists.'

'What do you mean?'

'Thugs who took it upon themselves to hunt down people suspected of affiliation with the separatist movement. Sort of bounty hunters.'

Was it my imagination or had the temperature dropped?

'These thugs asked no questions. They were given a name, found the person with that name and executed them in cold blood. Rabid dogs. Fernand told Lazarro that if the police didn't find him, those thugs would.'

I felt sick. 'No!'

'We all left that night.'

The rain had abated. A thin rivulet ran down the rotten wood and gathered on the floor along the low brick wall. Bernard's little dog was lapping at the puddle.

After a long pause Bernard said, 'Later, Fernand spread the word that his brother had died. Lazarro's disappearance was very convenient for him. It meant that he could inherit the hotel without having to share it.'

José took over and I tuned in to his Spanish accent.

'Fernand stole your grandfather's share. He had no right to it. There are many things he shouldn't have done, but he's got so many people in his pocket, he's untouchable.'

Bernard nodded slowly. Poor old chap. He really didn't

look well. Hunched in his chair, he had aged another ten years since we had arrived.

I wanted to know so much more, but Bernard was exhausted. We got up and took our leave.

The storm was clearing. My anorak over my arm, I gulped a lungful of fresh air and held out my hand to Bernard.

He thrust several photos at me. 'These are for you.'

'But, Bernard,' I objected, 'they're yours.'

'You have them, dear.' He covered my hand with icy fingers. 'I'm so glad I had the chance to meet you.'

'Are you sure I can keep the photos?'

'Of course.' His sad eyes bored into mine. 'I won't need them where I'm going.'

I managed to thank him, carefully slid the photos into my backpack and wiped a stealthy tear on the way to the car.

We drove away. Above us, in the cleansed blue skies, the vultures had resumed their *danse macabre*.

FERNAND'S 75TH BIRTHDAY PARTY

King Fernand's heart did hold out until his seventy-fifth birthday. A procession of courtiers, well-wishers and arse-lickers worthy of King Léon streamed through the bar all day to congratulate the old rogue. From the kitchen where I was prepping the fish, I could hear their '*zorionak*,' 'congratulations,' another word to add to my lexicon.

First came the *Favorite*. I'd seen her once before. Unlike Fernand's long-suffering wife, whom I could tell from photos had been meek and bland, *La Favorite* was flamboyant, the type who went to the market in her best dress.

Was she Fernand's mistress? Probably. Did people still have sex at that age? I thought back to my teacher, Mrs Hart, and her Santa look-alike boyfriend. And how about Carmela and Cosmo's father? Clearly, they were all at it. And why not after all? Nowadays, with HRT, implants and Viagra, there was nothing to stop you bonking till your hundredth birthday.

Pondering and perturbed, I focused on my fish, their

slithering entrails a welcome distraction from the images cluttering my mind.

After the *Favorite* came the Doctor. With his round stomach, short crown of hair and gold-rimmed glasses, the man couldn't have been anything else. I was relieved when he came in, and realised how ambivalent my feelings were towards Fernand. However vile his actions might have been, I didn't wish him dead, a magnanimity not borne from Christian values, but from self-interest. Once Fred was in Paris, there was nothing to stop Arrantxa from forcing her sisters to sell.

I resented my parents for uprooting me just when I had found my roots. I was in love with Xavier, felt at home at the Bear Inn, and desperately wanted help ensure its survival.

I put the cleaned fish in the fridge and peeped into the bar. After a succession of shepherds worthy of a nativity scene, who wore berets instead of tea towels on their heads, came the Governess. Strapped in a girdle, support tights and sturdy shoes, she was the headmistress of Herriberri school. During my visit with Cosmo, I had noticed that the schoolyard was adjacent to Fernand's mayoral office. Whatever she was saying to him, Fernand wasn't listening, having probably heard it all before.

The bar was filling up. Maia was serving the drinks. She looked good today with her hair up, earrings and a dab of lipstick.

Engrossed in preparing a parsley and dill sauce for the fish, I forgot about the Governess. However, the Marshall who followed her took me by surprise. I knew that Fernand was on friendly terms with the police, but I would never have expected this particular gendarme to kowtow to him.

I dropped my spoon into the sauce. 'Jean-Phi?'

Why was he wearing a gendarme uniform? Was Jean-Phi not a sports teacher and what on earth could Xavier's friend possibly want with the old rascal? I tiptoed to the bar and tried to eavesdrop, but the two men were speaking Basque. I returned to my sauce, thoroughly bamboozled.

The Chocolate Cook, one might have guessed, was standing next to me, busy dribbling chocolate over a cake that would immortalise him, at least in his family's mind. I'd never seen Fred so focussed, so totally in the flow.

The menu was worthy of a king. For his birthday, Uncle Fernand had insisted on a medieval centrepiece called '*un cochon de lait,*' a suckling pig in aspic jelly supposed to wow the guests as they came in.

I'd refused to have anything to do with it. The sight of it made me heave. In the refrigerated cabinet, the grisly piglet lay on a bed of roasted peppers, an apple in its mouth, and stared reproachfully at me every time I opened the door.

The last courtier, the Fool, could have been any one of the other visitors, obsequiously shaking Fernand's hand and laughing at his jokes. What had he done for them, I wondered, and more to the point, what had they done for him?

While Fred was putting the last touches to his chocolate *chef d'oeuvre*, the tip of his tongue sticking out in concentration, I tasted my sauce. Nice, but it needed more parsley. I opened the fridge and once again, was faced with Babe. The poor mite had been boned out, his skin scraped and stuffed with a mixture of meat and mushrooms. Where its heart had once been, Fred had placed his special pheasant-and-duck mousse. We had originally planned to barbecue the piglet, but Fred wanted his family to understand 'what he was really about.'

We made a good team Fred and I. We were not exactly best mates, but the respect that was growing between us went some way to smoothing the angles. Jealous of my influence over his master, Urko hated me.

'Do you know where the word *barbecue* comes from?' Fred said à propos of nothing.

'Sure, it comes from lazy people who can't be bothered to bone out their animals, empty the meat, grind it, mix it with mushroom and herbs, stuff it back inside the poor piglet and sew it up again.'

'*Exactement.*' Fred waved his chocolate-covered spoon. 'It comes from unsophisticated cooking practices.'

'How so?' I lifted an eyebrow, ready to defend Australian cooking practices.

'You take your animal, push in your spit from its beard to its bum, *'de la barbe au cul'* and then you roast it. No skill involved.'

The way he pronounced it – the 'l' in *cul* is silent – I did hear *barbocue*. Ha, Mrs Hart never taught us that one. I would have to e-mail her.

Fred proudly placed his masterpiece to cool on a shelf and took over from Maia in the bar.

I should have known… The last Fool to bow to King Fernand was Maître Gorrotxategui, the lawyer I had consulted in Bayonne. Pensive, I tiptoed out of sight and teamed up with Maia to prep the last of the vegetables. The man's presence was troubling. Was Fernand plotting my demise?

I stepped into the bar, pretending to look for Fred. 'Fred, I say could you –'

Fred had vanished.

'Fred?'

I swivelled. 'Urko?' He too had gone. Were the two boys smoking on the back stairs? I leaned out of the window, but all I could see was Old Shep asleep in the sun.

Strange grunts rose from the depths of the cellar. I lifted the door to avoid the squeak and stood on the first step, taking in the musty smell.

'Fred? Fred, are you down there?'

I treaded down gingerly and peered into the gloom.

Urko was lying prone, his ugly snout pushed down into the sand, Fred on top of him. I went to turn away. Why here for God's sake, when there were twelve bedrooms upstairs?

'Chloe, come and help me!' Fred cried out.

'What's the matter?' I leaned over the banister.

'Huung gglgoo.' Urko lifted his face to me. He looked so funny with an apple in his mouth and parsley in his nostrils, I burst out laughing.

'What's he done?' I clattered down to them.

Urko let out an angry growl and spat out his apple. 'I didn't squeal!' he squealed. 'She's the one who told them, Freddo, you've got to believe me.'

I jumped back. 'What are you talking about?'

Urko's eyes rolled in their sockets. He spluttered. 'I saw you talking to Monsieur Etchegaray. You're the one who told him Fred was going to Paris, I *heard* you!'

Fred loosened his grip, suspicion written all over his face.

'Did you tell Aitaxi I was off to Paris?'

'Of course, I didn't. *Hitza hitz*. A promise is a promise. I do have principles and even if I didn't, it wouldn't be in my interest to snitch on you, would it? I told Fernand who I was. That's all I did.'

'Then who told him I was leaving?'

'I think you're sitting on him.'

'Let me go you bully!' Urko wriggled one arm free. I pounced and caught hold of his hand.

'You told him, I heard y–' I didn't give Urko the chance to finish his sentence. I stuffed the apple right back into his mouth. The air whistled though his nostrils, impeded by the parsley.

'Fred.' I squatted opposite them. 'We have a situation here. The guests have started to arrive. Today is the worst time to make your announcement. Seems to me, barbecuing this animal is the only option, stick a spit up him, *de la barbe au cul*. What do you say?'

Fred settled on Urko's haunches and gave the matter some thought. 'Bah, perhaps he's done us a favour. It had to come out some time. Problem is, the shock might kill my grandad. With his heart, anything could happen.' He got up, brushed himself down and kicked his valet. 'You heard that, worm, if Ataixi dies, it'll be your fault. Now go back to your duties, and not a peep out of you.'

With a look of pure hatred, Urko spat out the apple, dislodged the snotty parsley from his nostrils and scurried up the stairs.

Fred was shaken. 'That useless so-and-so is fired, you wait –'

'Freddo.' I put a hand on his arm, keen to display some British *zénitude*. 'You know what they say. He who plants the wind grows a storm. We must keep calm and carry on. There are ways of dealing with crises such as these in a positive manner. It's called 'people management.' If you want to further your career, I suggest you swot up on it.'

Fred thinned his lips. 'It's 'he who sows the wind reaps the storm.'

'Whatever,' I replied serenely. 'You may be the *chef* here – he knew I meant the boss – but I can still teach you a thing or two.'

I reached the top of the stairs, pushed the door to the kitchen and let out a strangled scream.

There, hands on hips, stood my nemesis.

ARRANTXA

'I knew you were trouble the second I saw you,' Arrantxa squawked. She took a step forward and threatened to send me tumbling back down the stairs.

I jumped sideways and squeezed into the kitchen. Behind her, Urko was smirking. What that worm had done now, I didn't care to think.

'You!' I snarled at him. 'She's paid you to snitch on us, hasn't she?'

He tilted his head with a 'what-are-you-going-to-do-about it' face.

'You imposter. I know what you're after,' Arrantxa clucked.

Defenceless, I checked out the pans out of the corner of my eye and inched away from her. 'You poisoned me, witch!'

'Wish I had.' Her hair bristled like that of a fighting cock. 'We don't want you here.'

'I just wanted to meet my family.'

'Told you she was trouble,' Urko whined. 'She's after your hotel.'

That was it. I'd had enough of those two, their strife, their lying, scheming, poisoning and double-crossing. Yes, I had enough of Urko and Arrantxa, those minions of Satan who did all they could to ruin a perfect Paradise.

'Doing the Camino, huh?' Safe behind Arrantxa, Urko needled me. Big mistake.

'Right, you've asked for it.' The pans were too far, so I grabbed a large marrow and, crouching, I circled them. First I lunged at Urko. He grabbed Arrantxa from behind and pulled her to him like a shield. I lifted the marrow again and struck with all my strength. Urko ducked. I caught the side of her head. She crumpled. He jumped clean away.

I gripped my weapon with both hands, aimed again and with a roar, whacked him as hard as I could. This time, I hit my target. The marrow exploded over Urko's head. He staggered backwards, hit the wall and slid to the floor in slow motion, his face covered in vegetable flesh.

Furious, I dropped what was left of the marrow, fell upon Urko, and spat every insult I'd ever absorbed on the beach. *'Avorton, salopard, couille molle, résidu de fausse couche, enfoiré, crapaud de pissotière!'*

I could have reeled out another five or six, but in ran the Governess, the Doctor and the Marshall.

'What is the meaning of this foul language?' the Governess enquired, as if she didn't know the synonyms for runt and words rhyming with it.

'Don't move, Madame Arroztegui.' The Doctor kneeled next to Arrantxa, now playing dead. 'I think you are concussed.'

The lounge lizard walked in.

'*Chéri*, you're here!' Arrantxa cried out and returned to her swoon.

'Chloe, come with me.' Marshall Jean-Phi grabbed my arm and led me to the bar.

Fred slow-clapped me as I passed by. 'Bravo. I'm

impressed, Chloe. I simply can't wait for that training session on people management.'

I gave him a murderous look.

'*Crapaud de pissotière?*' Fred chuckled. Pisspot toad? Where on earth did you pick that one up?'

I lunged out with a foot but missed. Jean-Phi held me tight, struggling to keep a straight face.

'I don't see what's funny.' I turned on Jean-Phi. 'I'm told the Basques are proud people, straight talkers, that in this country, 'yes' means yes and 'no' means no. *Hitza hitz,* Basque promise, golden promise, huh? Well, all I've heard since I've arrived here are lies and deception. I'm sick and tired of it. You for starters, why on earth did Xavier tell me you were a sports teacher when you're really a cop?'

'It's quite simple.' Jean-Phi answered calmly. 'The French can be very adolescent in their attitude to the forces of order. Back at the *txoko,* Xavier didn't want you to spoil our evening in case you didn't approve. We always get lectured by Parisians. *'You're a cop, quelle horreur!' And 'where the hell were you when I needed you?'* Anyway, I'm not a cop, I'm a gendarme, we're more army related.'

'I don't care what you do, but I'd like to know why you associate with Lucifer over in the corner.' I tilted my chin towards Fernand still in deep conversation with Maître Gorrotxategui.

'There are no jobs in the region,' Jean-Phi said. 'You know that. Monsieur Etchegaray has helped me with my application for the gendarmerie. I'm leaving for Paris at the end of the week and today, I put on the uniform as a gesture of thanks. He's a good man.'

'A good man? Ha!' I shook my head in disbelief. 'Are you out of your mind?' I waved a finger at him. 'That man is a manipulator of the first order. You wait. Soon he'll be demanding favours. Give him a few months and he'll be asking you to hide the bodies of those who stood in his way.' I narrowed my eyes. 'You won't want to do it, but he'll have something on you and if he doesn't, he'll make it up.' I crossed my arms. 'You sold your soul, Jean-Phi. Welcome to Hell.'

Around us, the air had thickened. There was an atmosphere. Fernand lifted his head. His expression hardened. Sensing trouble, the lawyer took his leave. In the kitchen, Arrantxa – who had recovered– was whispering into her husband's ear.

In sharp suit and yellow cravat, the man cut a strange figure in this country inn. He sucked air as if he was about to burst into some Il Divo schmaltz. (Mum loved Il Divo, whose only purpose from what I could see, was to help women through the menopause.) Bruno's dark eyes threw daggers at me.

Arrantxa felt for his hand, but he pushed her away. Ouch. Looked like he wouldn't be helping her through *her* menopause.

I looked to the hall for escape, but Viviane and Muriel were blocking that exit. Their reproachful glares enveloped me with shame and I felt like crying. I wanted to explain, tell them I loved them, that it was all Arrantxa's fault, hurl myself at her and tear out her eyes, but Jean-Phi's steely grip held me prisoner.

Behind the zinc counter, a worried Fred surveyed the scene, glad the spotlight was on me. Urko lurked behind him. The ugly smirk I'd tried to bash off his face regrettably still in place.

Trapped, I prayed to Pop for help, glanced at my assembled family, cleared my throat and stammered, 'You are probably all wondering who I am and what I'm doing here.'

'Oh, we know who you are.' Viviane looked very hurt. I swallowed hard and glanced up at Jean-Phi. He winked in support. Relief washed over me. If he had doubted me, I would have dashed out, jumped on the first TGV train to Paris, six hundred miles away and never come back.

A shadow darkened the door. Xavier stepped in, puzzled by the silence and the scene that stood before him.

My whole world brightened up. Jean-Phi loosened his grip.

The air stirred around me. Pop's face appeared and his presence enveloped me with calm and purpose. I took a step forward.

'My grandfather is Lazarro Etchegaray.' I glanced at Fernand slightly shrunken on his throne. 'Lazarro, who didn't die in Paris in seventy-one but lived in England.'

Fernand's eyes popped out of their sockets when I mentioned England.

My gaze still on the old man, I carried on. 'Last autumn, I came here to meet my family.' I turned to my two aunts. 'Sadly, the first person I met was this woman.' I pivoted and pointed to Arrantxa who cowered next to Bruno, livid with hatred. 'She spread rumours, and to get rid of me, added a toadstool to the crop of mushrooms I brought to her pharmacy.'

'You're not such a saint yourself, are you?' She used up her last arrow. 'We all read the papers at the time. You left that chap to die.'

I countered in a silky voice, 'I did not leave him to die. I saved his life. Xavier was there, he can tell you. Your plan backfired anyway. It made me all the more determined to return.'

'Arrantxa, is this true?' Muriel gasped.

'No of course it isn't. She's making it all up.'

'About the toadstool?'

'It only weighed five grams.'

I opened my hands. 'See? Anyway, I have written proof.

Fungus foedissimus poisoning. Three days in intensive care.' This time the gasp was general. I narrowed my eyes at the pharmacist. 'I think you owe your sisters an explanation.'

Arrantxa sidled up to her husband and grappled for his hand.

'Bruno...'

He growled something in Basque.

'If you don't tell them, I'm sure Urko will oblige,' I said. 'He's had quite a morning of it already.'

'What do you mean?' Viviane twisted the ends of her long scarf. 'Tell us what?'

Viviane and Muriel's attention drifted away from me and focused on their sister and her strutting husband.

From the set of his lips – the French call a hen's arse – Bruno knew he had lost his gamble.

I wanted to explain that we were lucky to have this wonderful place, that Muriel had made it into a bolthole, a haven in a harsh modern world, a place where you felt cocooned and loved, but once again, I didn't have the words.

Bolstered by Xavier's smile, I heard my voice slice through the grumbles of discontent. 'I didn't know I had a family here. So scared was my grandfather of putting my life in danger, he never mentioned you at all. Not once.' Reassured by Jean-Phi and Xavier's presence, I moved to the centre of the bar. 'As soon as I stepped into Herriberri, I realised I'd disturbed a hornet's nest, but still I wanted to know you.' I rested my gaze on each of them and though my stomach was churning, acknowledged their contempt, sadness and bewilderment without flinching. 'I was made to feel welcome by Viviane and Muriel who run the loveliest family hotel anywhere in the world. Their warmth is what makes it special.' Behind the counter, Fred cautiously waited to see where this was leading.

I exhaled. 'Together with Frédéric's cooking.' He relaxed

visibly, but tensed up again when I put him in the spotlight. 'Freddo?'

'Huh?'

'Frédéric, what is going on?' His mother reproached, 'If there is anything we need to discuss, why hide it? You know we want the best for you.'

Fred snapped. 'How do you know what's best for me?'

I joined him behind the bar and placed a calming hand on his arm. He backtracked.

'Look, I know you want the best for me, *Maman*, but what's best for me sadly isn't what's best for the hotel.' I urged him to continue. 'I get a lot of encouragement from you and Aunt Viviane, our guest reviews are good, but I– I–' Poor Fred. He just couldn't do it. I nudged him. 'It gave me the confidence to see how far I could go and –' he exhaled and said in a whisper, 'I feel I need more training.'

'Frédéric has won an apprenticeship in a Paul Bocuse restaurant in Paris,' Arrantxa gloated.

I gave Fred a discreet pat on the back.

'How?' Muriel stared at her son and stammered. 'How– who arranged this? These apprenticeships are like gold dust.'

I cut in. 'Your sister found the position. Isn't that wonderful?'

Arrantxa opened her mouth to speak. Her husband's lip curled. She thought better of it.

The air was thick. Volleys of glances shot across the room.

Xavier crossed the bar and stood by me. It gave me the courage to go to Muriel and with his help, reassure her that I was tired of lying, that I wasn't a salad girl but a trained chef and that I could take over from Fred.

Meanwhile, the panelled dining room was filling up with guests. I remembered that we had a birthday dinner to prepare for a man who didn't deserve it.

'This brazen hussy's nothing but trouble,' the patriarch thundered. 'Get rid of her.'

'*Papa*.' Muriel confronted her father. 'She works well in the kitchen, we can't just do that –'

The old bear pushed himself from his seat. 'Why do you want to take on that foreign strumpet? She's lying!' He emphasised the words with his stick. 'I am your father, *bon sang d'bon soir* and you listen to me!'

'She's Paloma's granddaughter, Papa,' Muriel countered in a soft voice. 'She's got her gift. You might not like it, but she's a jolly good cook. Why would I throw her out when she's heaven-sent? She'll help us while Frédéric is in Paris.' She turned to me. 'Won't you, dear?' And to Xavier, 'I don't imagine your uncle Bruno will want to stay for lunch after this. You're very welcome to take his place.'

Xavier thanked her, drew me to the less crowded hall and hugged me. A huge weight fell from my shoulders. The relief was such that I didn't know whether to laugh or cry, so, safe inside his arms, I did both.

Grumbling he was hungry, the old man tottered past us to the dining room, where the suckling pig and fabulous tiered chocolate cake convinced everyone that Paris really was the only place for such a genius as Fred.

CHLOE BECOMES PART OF THE FAMILY

The birthday party was over. Downstairs, the helpers we had hired to allow Muriel and Viviane a chance to enjoy the festivities were tidying up. What was left of the party now sat upstairs in a lounge Pop might have been able to draw from memory, though the sofa had been updated in the last decade.

Large, ancient and Rembrandt-like in the chiaroscuro of a dim wall lamp, the 'birthday boy' sat on a straight chair to the right of the television. On the other side, in dull grey, was Robert, Muriel's elusive husband, an accountant. Muriel, Viviane and I perched on the modern sofa.

Xavier and Jean-Phi had gone home, but not before schmoozing my aunts and recounting the agonies of guilt I had suffered about lying to them.

'Arrantxa didn't do this to spite you, Papa. She might be brainy, but she's under Bruno's spell,' Viviane said charitably.

The old bear replied with a growl.

Robert ventured, 'We took a risk when we borrowed money from him. I said so at the time.' He quickly added to quieten the rising growl, 'we had no choice. I understand that. The interest rate at the bank would have been punishing, and Bruno was flush.'

The growl swelled into a roar. 'I run this town, I have people lining up for favours, I represent Lower Navarra in the Regional Council, I'm the *Grand Manitou!*' Fernand thumped the arm of his chair. 'And I find that in my own family –' his face reddened alarmingly '– in my own family, my daughter plots to put me out of business and my niece tries to shame me publicly!'

He had a point. I had been in the country long enough to know that for a Basque, there was no such thing as 'king and country.' Home and family were everything. *Grand Manitou,* Great Spirit, was the nickname his followers gave Fernand. Indeed, the *Grand Manitou* had grounds to be incensed, but he had got his facts wrong.

Quivering inside, too tipsy to trust my failing French grammar, I once again, prayed to Pop for help. Now was his chance to channel all the things he had been unable to say during his years of exile.

'Uncle Fernand.' I cleared my throat. 'I don't see it that way. I see you in the bar, surrounded by –' I tried to retrieve the positive word I'd once hit upon to replace arse-lickers, '– well-wishers, people who come all the way to this mountain to meet with you.' Unmollified, the patriarch pouted. Undeterred, I soldiered on. 'You couldn't wish for more devoted daughters than Muriel and Viviane.'

I had learned that poor Aunt Viviane, the teacher, had once turned down a suitor who had been promoted to Paris, so she could remain at her father's side. One day, someone should tell Fernand that Jesus had not always been his daughter's boyfriend of choice.

'They work tirelessly, day and night, to keep the Bear going, as for Arrantxa –'

'Bruno's got another woman, Papa,' Muriel butted in.

Wrinkles deepened on the *Grand Manitou's* brow.

'A divorce is bad, I know, but it is the best thing that could happen to this family,' Viviane added. 'Once we're rid of Bruno, everything will be alright again. Papa.' She added with fervour, 'don't upset yourself. Your heart bypass is in two weeks' time and you know what the doctor said.'

'That doctor doesn't know what a nest of vipers I live in! And now I'm weakened, my long-lost brother Lazarro conveniently chooses to rise from the dead and sends his granddaughter sniffing around for the spoils!'

'Stop!' I shot from the sofa. Tears spurted from my eyes. All the expletives I had drudged from Biarritz beach surged to the fore. I sifted through them as best I could and cried out, '*Tu es égoïste, despotique et cruel*! Pop never came back because of the threats you made.'

'Bah, he didn't believe them, did he?' Fernand said, baffled.

'He did, Uncle Fernand, he did. He would never have put his son's life or mine at risk. He kept a low profile.'

'He has a son?'

That man didn't have a compassionate bone in his body. No wonder Amatxi left him.

'Yes, he had a son. My father, Matteo.' I sat down again and muttered, 'Talking about sons, perhaps this would be a good time to tell your daughters.'

'Tell us what, Papa?'

He hissed, 'Witch!' but his heart wasn't in it. I could see from the clouds passing over his face that Fernand realised he could have played it differently. He could have had a son, Vicente, and a brother to help him, while Fred and I, an efficient team of cousins could be running his kitchen.

Resigned, he took a long breath. 'When I lived in Chile,' he exhaled loudly, 'there was a woman.'

'Her name was Flora Flores,' I said.

He threw me a gaze filled with vitriol. 'She had a son, Vicente Flores.' He crumpled on his seat. 'He wants to meet us.'

'Oh, but that's wonderful!' Muriel and Viviane gasped in unison. 'When is he coming over? Does he speak French? We'd love to meet him! Ah, he probably speaks Spanish.' Viviane glowed with excitement.

'We speak Spanish, we'll be all right.' Muriel clapped her hands. 'Let's send him a gateau basque!'

'Some of our lovely Ossau Iraty cheese.'

'Stop chattering like magpies!'

'Uncle Fernand, there's something else you should know.' I waited for the sharp pain to pass. My chin wobbled as I croaked, 'Lazzaro won't be rising from the dead. He died last year, heartbroken. Amatxi… Paloma died five years ago, in England.'

'W–what?'

'My dad, Matteo, lives in Australia now. My mum's Australian. I'm sorry, Uncle Fernand, but what you did was inexcusable. You never searched him out.' I was too choked to say any more. Aunt Viviane grabbed my hand and squeezed it. 'I've missed having a family. I could have known all of you, learned from you, been one of you. Instead, I grew up in some dumb *banlieue.*' I collapsed on Viviane's shoulder and sobbed.

'I did look for him.' Uncle Fernand hung his head. 'I tried to find his friends, but they'd all gone. Anyway, you know how it is with the *cuadrilla*. They closed ranks. Serves me right, I suppose.'

'But Fernand, how about Vicente?' Robert said.

'His mother was a village woman, a Quechua.' In an involuntary movement, his hand went to his head, in memory of the hat she wore, and slowly caressed imaginary tresses. 'I was young. I didn't know any better.'

There was a long silence.

I blew my nose and spoke again. 'After Pop's death, I spent ages looking for you. When I arrived, the first person I met was Arrantxa, who did everything she could to send me home. I'd heard about witches and curses and I thought I was hexed. Ridiculous, I know. Then I found this place and, I couldn't believe how wonderful it was.' I met the old man's eyes. 'People come for miles just to spend time here. It's a magical place. I just want to be part of it,' my voice trailed, 'if you'll have me.'

Aunt Muriel put her arm around me.

'All I want is a C.D.D., a temporary contract until I prove myself. I'm not after anything else. I just wanted to – to –' I never finished my sentence.

Viviane wiped a tear. Muriel hugged me so tight, I could hardly breathe.

'Where's Lazarro buried?' Fernand's face was frozen, assailed with feelings he'd never learned to deal with.

'He isn't. I've got him with me, in a tin. I'm to scatter his ashes, ahem, around here. It's the only way he could ever come back, you see.'

Fernand pushed himself from his chair. 'It's been a long day for me.' He hesitated. 'Girls, you've outdone yourselves. The meal was – very good.' He stretched to his full height and wrenched out the missing word. 'Thank you.' It cost him a great deal of effort. He turned to me. 'You're going back to England?'

'I'm off to Australia to see my parents.

'I see. When you come back, we'll have your contract ready.'

THE FUNERAL

Fred left for Paris laden with hams, wheels of cheese, *gâteaux basques* and Sargano cider, because Muriel didn't trust the Breton cider sold in supermarkets 'up there.' Stuck for a present, I gave him my Wallabies sweatshirt. He'd had his eye on it for ages. We all drove him to the station.

Fred held it together till the end but he was struggling, I could tell from the way his Adam's apple was bobbing up and down.

Urko, with a bit of luck, was lying in a shallow grave, a stake through his heart and his eyes pecked out by crows. More likely but just as humiliating, he was queuing in some *Agence Pôle Emploi* trying to find a job. It would be a long wait, though he wouldn't need money any time soon. According to the terms of his CDD, his short-term contract, we had to pay him regardless of whether he was there, and not only pay him, but contribute to his social security, his pension and his holidays. French employment law was ferociously on the side of the employee. Any socialist leanings I may have had melted away when Muriel explained that to me. I believed in a fairer world, and this was definitely not fair. Now that I was in charge of the kitchen, I saw things differently.

While Fred toiled in the bowels of the capital, I was walking my first mile in his shoes. Without Urko it was heaven. I'd convinced my parents to change my ticket and move my departure to the end of October, when the restaurant closed for winter. It had seemed a long way away at the time.

Muriel had offered me a room upstairs to save me the trip from Saint Jean, now that the weather was wet, but I'd declined and remained in my attic, our love nest.

It was to be the most intense period of my life. After the ten months of gestation in the damp and dreary King's Arms kitchen, I was reborn. I loved what I did. As long as the dish was Basque-based, I was allowed to unleash my creativity. Muriel was very accommodating.

High on adrenaline, all my senses heightened by the knowledge that I had to leave, for those last weeks, I tasted, breathed and felt every last particle of my new life. Xavier and I cooked, made love, fell asleep entwined, woke to the birds' first twitter and made love again.

I wanted to etch everything onto my mind. Xavier's body crushing mine, the smell of fresh bread and coffee, his calloused hand grazing my skin, our laughter and, as the end drew near, our tears.

'Five months, Klo-é. How can I live five months without you?' He would gaze at me soulfully. 'I cannot do it.'

We cried a lot. We cried because we were sad. We cried because the pleasure was too much. The soulful Basque choir tore me apart.

The autumn rains that fell incessantly made riding the moped a nightmare, especially at night after work, but I didn't care. I rode through the countryside, memorising its every contour, aware that I would be returning to it again and again during my lonely Warrnambool nights. I was often cold, but I did not care. The way I felt, pneumonia and a long spate in the local *clinique* were an appealing option.

It was my last Wednesday. I was piling together peppers and onions for a *piperade,* white red and green, the colours of the Basque flag. We served it as a starter with tiny rounds of spicy chorizo sausage and small slices of lightly sautéed Bayonne ham, when Maia skipped in, a huge smile on her face.

'High five Chloe!' She slapped my right hand.

'*Bonjour* Maia.' Muriel followed her in. 'You look happy.'

Maia's eyes shone with excitement. 'Did you see our latest reviews? The ones the cyclists from Paris left yesterday?'

I shook my head. I had better things to do than read reviews, like stock up on love to last me for the next few months.

Maia fiddled about with her phone and read out, '*Though the Bear Inn has no Michelin star, Chloe Etchegaray's food is so good, you see stars when you leave.*'

'Oh, this is wonderful!' Muriel rushed to share the good news with Viviane.

Maia and I had just finished chopping the peppers when the church bell tolled. I looked out of the window and noticed several cars parked below the cemetery wall.

'Strange,' Muriel said, 'I asked Dad about this funeral, but he said he had no idea who they were burying.'

'Papa?' Muriel went to the bar. 'Are you not going to the funeral?'

This was unusual. Fernand never missed a funeral. Outliving his contemporaries gave him a great boost. As Xavier said, they were tough in this part of the world.

I pushed the peppers to one side and thought of "sending Maia to know for whom the bell tolled." But whoever had written that poem was right. It tolled for me. I heaved a long wretched sigh. This time next week, smothered in factor fifty I would be flipping burgers, in my Kukuxumusu T-shirt, missing this place like crazy.

I went over to the veranda and watched the mourners file into the church. In an hour or so, they would file out again, into our little bar. Or would they? We hadn't been asked to provide the traditional post funeral drinks. It was all very odd.

I wished the bell would stop. My heart was about to shatter.

'Uncle Fernand?' I popped my head around the door to the bar. 'Anyone you know?'

'Ez.' He shook his head and growled an order to 'mind my onions.' Of course, he knew who had died. Deaths were registered at the *mairie* and he was the mayor. Such palpable indifference could only mean one thing.

My suspicions were confirmed when amongst the mourners who came into the bar for a comfort break after the service, was a man I thought I recognised. I'd seen those glasses and that mop of curly hair very recently.

I fetched my backpack and pulled out the photos Bernard had given me. The glasses were smaller now and the curly hair white, but there was no mistaking the fourth musketeer of Pop's *cuadrilla,* the one who lived in Paris. What was his name? Serge, yes that was it. Serge.

The man headed for the lavatory situated at the end of the old dining room. He had been here before, I could tell. If he really was Serge, I was keen to meet him and when I did, he would surely need sustenance of the alcoholic kind.

'Excuse me,' I said to Aunt Muriel who was tending the bar. 'May I have two coffees and a measure of Patxaran? They're on me, okay?'

'But, it's only eleven.'

'I know.'

I squirted a shot of Patxaran into a liqueur glass, added ice cubes and went to the dining room. Breakfast had been cleared but the scent of coffee still hung in the air.

'Serge?' I ventured as the man came out.

'*Pardon*?'

'You don't know me but, if you have a moment –' I made for the veranda and indicated he should follow me to a table in the corner. In the bar, conversations buzzed. The mourners had come here after all.

'Sorry, you are?'

'My name is Chloe, Chloe Etchegaray.'

'*Enchanté*.' Guarded, Serge added, 'You have a Basque name, but you don't sound local.'

I smiled, asked him to sit down, set our coffees on the table and placed the glass of liqueur between us. 'I work as a chef here. I've got a few minutes and there is something I'd like to discuss with you.'

Standing, he glanced around, confused. 'With me?'

'Sorry, did you come with someone, do you need to –'

'No. No, I came alone.'

'From Paris, right?'

He sat down. 'Yes, from Paris. How did you know?'

'Bernard told me.'

'Bernard? But he – we –' He glanced over at the churchyard. His face fell. His whole body crumpled. 'I hadn't seen him in over forty years.'

'I know. I should introduce myself properly. I am Lazarro's Etchegaray's granddaughter.'

Emotions passed like clouds over his face as the pieces of the puzzle fell together.

'Lazarro's granddaughter? This is a surprise. It explains why you sound English.'

'You knew he lived in England?'

'Yes, but he never gave me his address. How is he?'

I pushed the glass of Patxaran towards him.

He shook his head and lifted a hand. 'Sorry, it's too early.'

I left the glass where it was and told him about Pop. Shaken, Serge picked up the Patxaran and downed it in one go. Today, he had not lost one friend, but two. There are times when only Patx will do, and this was one of them.

'I'm sorry,' I said. 'You must feel as if you've lost a bit of yourself.'

'Yes.' Behind the glasses, his eyes shone with tears. He said nothing, unwrapped a sugar cube, dropped it into his coffee and stirred it for a long time.

'I wanted to speak to you because my grandfather never told me what had caused his exile. So far, I only have Bernard's version of what happened. I saw him a couple of weeks ago.' I took a sip of my own coffee and carried on. 'I'm not sure he told me the whole story. I was hoping you could.' I leaned over the table. 'Serge, what really happened that day?'

He stared into his empty glass. 'We'd been friends since primary school. After our *baccalauréat*, we all left school. Lazarro and I were conscripted. We went away for a year. Bernard was asthmatic. He was exempted.'

I sat very still, lest anything should interrupt the flow of memories. Nineteen seventy-one was a very long time ago.

'When we came back from the military, we just didn't realise how Fabien and Bernard had changed. We found them pumped up, full of talk of liberation, of independence for the Basque Country. We were so happy to be together again, we didn't take them seriously.' Serge's voice was so low, I had trouble hearing him.

He shook his head and sighed. 'I've no idea what Fabien was trying to achieve with that bomb – thank God he didn't cause more carnage than he did.' He ran a hand over his face.

'He didn't only kill himself that day. He took our lives with him, and annihilated his family's future.' His eyes met mine. There was no life in them. 'We felt dirty, compromised, and above all, guilty that we hadn't been able to stop him. We were his best friends, his *cuadrilla*. We should have known.'

'But if you were innocent, why didn't you argue your case?'

'We were confused. To tell you the truth –' Serge pulled off his glasses and polished them on a napkin '– at the time, Lazarro and I wondered where Bernard's loyalties really lay.'

'What do you mean?'

He shrugged. 'Bernard was there when it happened. It was the middle of the night. He's the one who called us. He was in a terrible state. He said Fabien had been wounded. When we got there, it was too late, Fabien was dead and the police were on their way. We panicked.'

'But –'

'We had blood on our hands.' Serge's face tightened. 'We were friends, how could we convince anyone that we weren't involved? It would have taken years of legal wrangling and money our parents didn't have. Anyway, when Lazarro heard from Fernand that thugs –'

'I know about them. Bernard told us.'

'Lazarro grabbed a suitcase and ran. He went to Paris, to my place, with Paloma. They stayed with me for a week and then we decided it would be best if we didn't contact each other again. We couldn't trust anyone.' Serge shook his head sadly. 'I can't tell you how much I've missed Lazarro. I've missed his wisdom, his deep love of nature, the things he noticed that most of us walked right past, the way the glass was always half-full.'

I could have kissed the man. That was exactly how I would have described Pop. I grappled about for a napkin and dabbed at my eyes.

He gave a little grin. 'As for your grandmother, she was a fantastic cook. I still remember her beef with anchovies, you know.'

The sound of steps interrupted us. I looked up. Fernand stood between the dining room and the veranda. 'I remember you,' he said. 'Serge, isn't it?'

Serge nodded.

The old man hovered by the door, keen to bridge the gap, but so used was he to conflict, he didn't know how to go about it. His whole life had been an endless attempt to divide and conquer, prove his worth, dull the hurt incurred in childhood when his brother stole his mother's love, to show the world what he could do, not trusting himself to love, marred as he had been by Paloma's betrayal. In spite of the armour he had built around him, Arrantxa, his own daughter had put the life of his hotel, his childhood home, his seat of power on the line. It had shaken him to the core.

I had explained to him that I didn't want to steal his hotel from him, that I was grateful for the privilege of just working there, but aware of how badly he had hurt Pop, he didn't yet trust me. I was ready to forgive him, but would he ever forgive himself?

Fernand's gaze hovered from Serge to me, wondering what had passed between us. 'I heard you got a good position in the ministry of environment.'

'That's right.' Serge smiled. 'When I retired, I was chief executive of the wildlife department.'

Fernand nodded. 'You were always the studious one.' Wistful he limped back to the bar.

'I think he's buried the hatchet,' I said.

'Aren't people strange,' Serge watched Fernand's retreating back. 'You see, in his head, Fernand still lives in the times when elders sat under the Guernica Oak and wrote our laws, when the eldest son inherited the house and the youngest went away. He's the archetypal patriarch. The one people should look up to. The problem is that we don't function like that anymore.'

'He has made progress. A least he is trying.'

'Ah our Basque utopia... While rebels like Fabien tried to keep 'progress' at bay, Fernand tried to recreate his own version of that intangible Basque paradise here in his bar.'

I lifted an eyebrow. 'How do you know all that?'

'I've kept myself informed.' Serge's shoulders slumped. 'Though I never knew that Lazarro had died.' He gazed at the valley, the backdrop to his childhood, the *fronton* where the boys had posed at the threshold of their life, the churchyard where Bernard was buried.

'I didn't see Lazarro's name on your family grave.'

'No. Not yet. I'm working on it.'

'*Bon Dieu*.' He gazed sadly at the pink fronton. 'Why did I leave it so late?' He sat back with a sigh. 'How I wish I'd done more for him.'

'Actually,' I said, 'you still can.'

CHLOE GOES TO LAKE IRRABIA

I held the Banania tin to my chest, nerves taut to breaking point. I had been waiting a year for this moment, but I still wasn't ready. I never would be.

Xavier selected the smallest key from the bunch he always carried and pushed it into the padlock that secured the gates to the lake.

The click of the padlock, clunk of the chain and squeak of the gates sent a volley of emotions through me, a volley of such magnitude, I had to steady myself on the side of the Ministry of Environment van.

Two wildlife rangers in camouflage ran in, stun guns at the ready.

Teeth chattering, I closed my eyes. Memories came flooding back, Cosmo and I laughing by the gates, running around, looking for a way in. The flash of lightning, his lifeless body bobbing over Xavier's shoulder.

I clutched the tin tighter, reluctant to part with its contents. 'This is it, Pop.' I murmured in a wobbly voice.

'The bears are still in there, are they?' Xavier said to Serge.

'Only the male is left. His name is Balou, as in Baloo the Bear. We've transferred the female and the cubs already. They're way up east of here, as far away from sheep as possible.'

Serge turned to me. 'The boys will attract Balou with corn, dart him, put him in the van and drive him to the high peaks. Once we've gone, you'll be free to scatter Laz –' the name caught in his throat. He exhaled and stammered, '– the ashes on the lake.'

It all went very fast. In the undergrowth something moved, something that looked remarkably like the Basajaun. There was a kerfuffle at the edge of the lake and brief orders. Moments later, the huge brown bear was wheeled past us, his smell strong and feral.

I buried my fingers deep into his fur. 'Good luck Balou. I hope the Pyrenees are kind to you, and you have lots of babies.'

'*Zorte on*.' Xavier wished him good luck too. He took out his phone and snapped the unconscious beast.

'We must hurry now. I really would like to see you again, Chloe.' Serge held out his hand. 'The day after tomorrow, right? Don't worry, I live on the right side of Paris for the airport.' And to Xavier, 'you two can stay here as long as you need to. Just lock up when you go.' They shook hands. '*Agur*.'

'*Agur*, not *adios*.'

The sound of the van faded away. Heart in my mouth, I handed Xavier the tin. Immune to the solemnity of the moment, L'ami Yabon thought it was all a hoot. For him, there was always cause for rejoicing.

Holding back the tears, I took off my shoes and socks, removed my trousers and took the tin. Xavier hugged me briefly and remained on the bank. This was something I had to do alone.

I licked my index finger to test the direction of the

breeze, relieved to feel it blow towards the centre of the lake. I waded in till the water reached my thighs, opened the tin and froze. It was too final. I just couldn't do it. I'd become used to L'ami Yabon. For nearly a year the Senegalese sharpshooter had been my constant companion. Though I regularly conversed with Pop, I'd sort of forgotten that his earthly body really was inside the tin.

It had been so long, the grisly contents surprised me. Fragments of bone had risen to the surface. Fragments of Pop, the real Pop, not the ethereal Pop who fluttered around and kept me safe. Grief rose from my stomach to my throat, crushed my lungs and I folded over, stunned with grief.

I felt Xavier's hand on my shoulder. I buried my face against his chest. He stroked my hair until the storm had passed.

Again, inside my mind the mournful choir erupted and tore my heart to shreds. I saw Pop and Amatxi entwined on the bank, before it all went wrong, lost in each other, trapped in their illicit love. She had promised to marry Fernand. Hitza hitz. A promise was a promise. Could she go back on her word? I cried their tears. Their parting was ours. My plane would leave Paris in two days' time.

'I can't do this.' I sobbed. 'Oh God, poor Pop, why did all these bad things happen to him?'

'He's happy now, Chloe. He's so proud of you. Look at all you've done for him. You brought him home. He's back with his family now. You've cleared his name. You talk about him, don't you? It's fantastic and *you* did it.'

Knee-deep in the lake, in our tops and underpants, we clutched at each other.

Submerged by a new tide of grief, I broke down. 'I can't bear to let him go. I can't bear to let you go.' I was gripping Xavier so tight, the tin dug into our ribs.

'Listen,' Xavier gently pushed damp hair from my face.

'Why don't I come over and see you at Christmas, huh? It won't be long, you'll see.'

'Really?' I lifted my tear-filled eyes to him. 'You'd really come and see me?'

'I love you, Chloe.' He tilted my chin. 'You know that, don't you?'

'No.' A smile crept over my face. 'I mean, y-es.'

I let him kiss away my tears.

Finally able to stand, I waded further into the water and took in the majesty of the place Pop had chosen for eternity, the lake set inside a bowl topped with vivid russet forests and, in the late afternoon the setting sun spilling across the water like a dash of blood.

It came to me that Pop had lived a life filled with love. Though exile was the price he had paid to live with Paloma, he had never complained.

Slowly the pain dissolved. I filled my lungs with fragrant autumn air, held out the tin and in a strong arc movement, cast Pop's ashes over the water where they hovered in a dull film.

'*Adios* Pop. *Maite zaitut*. I love you. Thank you for dragging me here. I wasn't sure at first but I should have trusted you.'

I hugged the empty tin to my heart. L'ami Yabon's duties were not over yet. There was another pound of ashes in storage back in Bletchley. One day I would fetch them and with Amatxi's urn, place both where they belonged inside our family vault behind the *fronton*. Their names would be written in gold letters on the headstone where I would eventually join them.

I waded back to the bank, stripped off my clothes, pinned up my hair and stood at the edge of the water.

'Chloe, what are you doing? You're crazy, it's cold.'

'I'm off in two days' time. It's spring in Australia. Soon I will be so hot I won't know what to do with myself. I want to remember this.'

One last time, my damp eyes took in the forest turning to gold.

'I want to own this lake, drink it, feel it on my skin, I want to remember everything about it.' I lowered myself into the water.

Moments later, Xavier joined me and together, we swam into the long crimson spill of the sun where the last traces of Pop were gently dissolving.

EPILOGUE

Place de la Liberté was white with crowds. Clustered around the Town Hall, the white-clad mob held up red scarves that undulated like poppies in the evening breeze.

'Baiona, Baiona!' shouted the good people of Bayonne, clamouring for Léon, their carnival king. Together we chanted, *'Oh Léon, Oh Léon'* until at last, on the brightly lit town hall balcony, stage curtains opened. A nine-foot cardboard effigy was rolled out and waved a stiff little wave that shot straight to my heart. Next to Léon, the famous rugby player Imanol Harinordoquy, affectionately known as 'the Jumping Basque' held out a large polystyrene key.

I lifted my face to my baby son, snug on Xavier's shoulders.

'Watch, Balou. As soon as the man drops the key, we'll all put our scarf around our neck. It means it's time for the party to start. Ready?'

'Bat... bi... hiru!'

As we yelled out *'hiru!'* Xavier squatted down. I reached

over and knotted the little scarf around Balou's neck. Our son grinned in delight and pointed upwards to a clump of balloons floating up, up and away into the night, over the port, towards the ocean.

We headed for the café. Patxi waved, relieved to see us. This year, whales would be safe in the Bay of Biscay. Our balloons were eco-friendly.

'It was murder keeping your seats, I tell you,' Patix said. 'I haven't ordered the pintxos. I didn't trust myself not to eat them. I'm starving.'

'I say, you do look trim.' I greeted him with a kiss and held out my arms to Balou. Poor little mite, it was way past his bedtime. 'Anyone special?'

Patxi was saved from answering by the arrival of Imanol and Charlène. I hardly recognised them, Imanol sported a short beard and Charlène had chopped her blonde mane.

'Hi, Charlène,' I said. 'Love the new style.'

She ran a hand through her cropped brown hair. 'Nun's hair to fit in with my withdrawal from the world. I feel like I've taken holy orders. I've been on the plateau for four months now. Four months without a hairdresser. I can't believe I've been allowed down for the week-end.'

'I'm sorry about your grandmother.'

'Yes, poor Amatxi. My grandad isn't coping that well. Imanol and one of my cousins are helping him out.' She sighed. 'It's time we moved in with him.'

Overhead, the fireworks were in full swing and music filled the streets.

Xavier called out to the waiter. 'A bottle of champagne and a large plate of pintxos.'

'Champagne? You're crazy,' Imanol protested, 'it'll cost a bomb if we buy it here. We can have some later.'

'Hey, live a little.'

'Hold on...' Charlène checked the busy streets. 'Where's Jean-Phi?'

'He called this morning. A bunch of angry farmers in Brittany have spilled a load of artichokes on the road. He's not sure he can make it.'

I smiled at this. Only in France.

'Who's going to the cow races tomorrow?' Charlène lifted an eyebrow in my direction.

'Chloe?' Patxi sniggered. 'I hear you're a crack matador.'

That old joke again. 'I have family responsibilities. I'm done with making a fool of myself.'

'I didn't think so at the time.' Xavier rested his brown eyes on me. 'That's when I knew you were The One.' The look he gave me made me fizz right down to my toes. 'I thought, wow she's plucky. With a girl like that, I'll never be bored.' He kissed my cheek. 'And I was right.' He put an arm around me and plonked a *musu* on top of Balou's sleepy head.

'So, what are we celebrating?' Imanol twirled his empty glass.

'Hold on a minute!' Charlène's phone pinged. 'I've just received a text from Jean-Phi. He's on his way.'

In a *gendarmerie* tracksuit, Jean-Phi jogged in as the pintxos were served.

'What are we drinking to?' He asked out of breath as Charlène handed him a glass of bubbles.

Xavier lifted his flute. 'We're drinking to you, mate, to your surviving the artichoke wars.'

We clinked our glasses in a toast. *'Topa!'*

Over the port, the fireworks reached their crescendo. The last of the crowds spilled onto the quays. Below us, fresh from the mountains, the Nive flowed with new gravitas, preparing to join the Adour and, together reach the sea in a stately march.

I hugged Balou and cast a loving glance at my husband,

my family, our friends, basking in their warmth. I had found my tribe. My quest was over.

The last of the fireworks lit up the night sky and ignited my soul. I raised my glass to the heavens and whispered a prayer of thanks, '*Eskerrik asko,* Pop, for… everything.'

AFTERWORD

Thank you for reading *The Bear and the Basque.* I hope you enjoyed this novel.

It will be followed by more stories set in other regions of France. If you want to stay updated with news about my books:

*Join my mailing list:
MichèleCallard.com/MailingList
*Like me on Facebook:
Facebook.com/MichèleCallard
*Follow me on Instagram:
Instagram.com/MichèleCallard
* Find my blog on michelecallard.com
* Join my ARC team and review my next book before it comes out.

And if you have a moment, please review *The Bear and the Basque* on Amazon and Goodreads. *Merci!*

ACKNOWLEDGMENTS

For years I toiled, hidden inside in my creative bubble, wondering how other authors came to meet the team of angels listed at the end of their books. By and by, the angels did appear. I owe my first impulse to Mario Reading, who asked, 'Have you ever thought of writing, Michèle?' Mario has passed away and is now my chief muse. In the beginning there was Ling, in Malaysia, who taught me everything I know. Then came Renate-of-the-constant-faith, in Germany, Celia-down-the-road for whom I can never write fast enough, and Geneviève and Hector Poullet in Guadeloupe. They were soon followed by Alison Ravenkilde in Norfolk, Dawn in Brunei, Susan in Dublin, Noëlle in Switzerland and, closer to home, the Wrecked Writers without whom I would be nothing. The wonderful Carol appeared and sprinkled her magic just when I needed it. The Band of Brothers unlocked the mysteries of IT, and for everything else I thank my valet, Passepartout.

This book is dedicated to all the research students who, over the years, have brought the world to our home. Especially Susana who landed on our doorstep as I was writing this story. Susana and Coro, thank you for the immersive Basque experience, the txoko, the mountain treks, the jamon iberico and all the Patxaran.

Cover design by MiblArt

ISBN: 978-1-7396956-0-6

Printed in Great Britain
by Amazon

78231629R00161